The Forever House

Lisa Stone lives in England, has three children, and has several books published under the pseudonym Cathy Glass, many of which have become best-sellers. This is her seventh Lisa Stone thriller.

Website: lisastonebooks.co.uk

Email: lisa@lisastonebooks.co.uk

/lisastonebooks.co.uk

@lisastonebooks

Books by Lisa Stone

The Darkness Within
Stalker
The Doctor
Taken
The Cottage
The Gathering
The Murder Room

Books by Cathy Glass

True stories

Cut
The Silent Cry
Daddy's Little Princess
Nobody's Son
Cruel to Be Kind
The Night the Angels Came
A Long Way from Home
A Baby's Cry
The Saddest Girl in the World
Please Don't Take My Baby
Will You Love Me?
I Miss Mummy
Saving Danny
Girl Alone
Where Has Mummy Gone?
Damaged
Hidden
Mummy Told Me Not to Tell
Another Forgotten Child
The Child Bride
Can I Let You Go?
Finding Stevie
Innocent
Too Scared to Tell
A Terrible Secret
A Life Lost
An Innocent Baby
Neglected
A Family Torn Apart
Unwanted
Unsafe

Novels based on true stories

The Girl in the Mirror
My Dad's a Policeman
Run Mummy Run

Self-help guides

About Writing
Happy Kids
Happy Adults
Happy Mealtimes for Kids
Happy Kids & Happy Mealtimes

THE FOREVER HOUSE

LISA STONE

HarperCollins *Publishers*

HarperCollins*Publishers* Ltd
1 London Bridge Street,
London SE1 9GF

www.harpercollins.co.uk

HarperCollins*Publishers*
Macken House, 39/40 Mayor Street Upper
Dublin 1, D01 C9W8, Ireland

First published by HarperCollins*Publishers* Ltd 2025
2

A catalogue record for this book is available from the British Library.

ISBN: 978-0-00-872525-9

Set in Sabon LT Std by HarperCollins*Publishers* India

Printed and bound in the United States of America

ONE

The temperature dropped as they walked into the sparsely furnished living room. Jasmine felt it fall and looked around, then at her host. The woman appeared not to notice and continued with the tour of the house.

'This is the living room,' she said. 'Through here is the study.'

Jasmine followed her into the compact room. The cold immediately lifted.

'It's lovely,' she said, and meant it. It was perfect for what they needed.

She followed her host – whose name she had immediately forgotten, having viewed so many houses – into the living room again. She gave an involuntary shiver, and her host looked at her. 'Are you OK?' she asked, concerned.

'Yes, thank you,' she said. 'Someone just walked over my grave.' She laughed but was pleased when they started heading upstairs.

Jasmine led the way as they crossed the small landing and went into the main bedroom.

'It's delightful,' she said, savouring the made-to-measure light-oak wardrobes and the view from the window.

'I'm glad you like it.' Her host smiled.

They then went in and out of the bathroom and the other two bedrooms. Jasmine was very impressed. The advantage of using an online estate agent was that you made the appointment to view the property directly with the seller.

'I'd like to bring my husband and children this evening,' she said. 'Around seven o'clock? Is that all right with you?'

'Yes, fine. We have another viewing later this afternoon, but that's all for today.'

'I'll bring him as soon as he returns home from work,' Jasmine said, and they headed downstairs.

Before she left, Jasmine asked to do another tour of the downstairs. The cold in the living room hit her again, and for some reason she turned to look at the empty sofa.

'Is everything all right?' her host asked.

'Yes, fine,' Jasmine said. She pulled herself together and followed her host to the front door.

'You have my mobile number?' her host checked.

'Yes. Of course,' Jasmine replied.

'I'm Freya Morgan.'

'Jasmine Simmons. See you later then,' she said, and stepped out of the house.

Jasmine returned to her car and sat looking up at the outside of the house, then at the houses on the left and right. As she did so, she thought she saw a figure at the upstairs window of the house she'd just left – not Freya; she wasn't dressed the same. Then the figure vanished. Strange, Jasmine thought, I had assumed we were alone in the house. She started the engine and drove home.

TWO

'We're going to see a new house this evening,' Jasmine told her children as they ate their dinner later that day, once they'd come home from school.

'Fine,' Leah, aged ten, said.

'Again?' Isabel replied.

'Yes, again,' Jasmine said. Isabel, who was eight, could be a bit contentious when she wanted to be.

Jasmine had already texted Mark, her husband, and told him she'd seen a property that was ideal, and that he'd be going to view it with her and the girls as soon as he got in. There was another couple going this afternoon. He knew as well as she did that they needed to find somewhere quickly. They now had just a month to go before they had to be out of their flat.

'Come on, eat up, both of you,' Jasmine encouraged the girls. They both sighed again.

* * *

Mark arrived home as arranged. Jasmine and the girls were ready and ran straight to his car.

'Hello, love, how are you?' Jasmine said, kissing his cheek. 'This house is perfect. I can't wait for you to see it.'

'It'd better be,' he joked. 'I'm starving.'

'We won't be long,' she assured him.

They all fastened their seat belts.

'It's just like that first house we saw, only it's closer. It's on the other side of town, about fifteen minutes away.'

Mark put the address into the sat nav of the car and began to drive, talking about work as he went. He was a manager for a string of grocery stores and had recently been promoted. He often came home with tales that he had to talk about before asking Jasmine about her day. Jasmine had got used to it. It was something she put up with. She was a PA for a firm of accountants and worked part-time from home, going into the office one day a week.

Having talked the whole journey, Mark suddenly pulled up outside 13 Ravens Lane.

'What do you think of it?' Jasmine asked, excitement in her voice.

'We've only just arrived,' Mark said with smile as he switched off the engine. He looked at the property through his side window. 'It looks nice from the outside.'

'Have we got to go in?' Leah asked, looking up from her Switch.

'I like it. It's got a garden,' Isabel said.

'Good girl,' Jasmine replied and, encouraging Leah, she opened the car doors.

They walked up the short path and Mark pressed the bell. As they waited for it to be answered he looked up at the front of the house, surveying it. Freya answered the door.

'Hello, come in,' she said with a smile. 'Good to see you again.'

'This is my husband, Mark,' Jasmine said. 'And my children, Isabel and Leah.'

'Hi. There's just me and my daughter in right now.'

Freya led the way into the kitchen-diner. Jasmine had to stop herself from rushing ahead and showing Mark around, reminding herself that this was still Freya's house. In the kitchen-diner she waited for Mark's reaction.

'Nice,' he said after a few moments. 'Very nice indeed.'

'Yes, it is,' Jasmine agreed enthusiastically, taking in again the immaculate cream cabinets and central granite island.

'Are we going to live here?' Isabel asked.

'I hope so,' Jasmine said, throwing Freya a nervous glance.

'The living room is this way,' Freya said, and she showed them into it.

Freya's daughter was watching television and looked up as they entered.

'Hi,' Jasmine said. 'Sorry to disturb you.' The daughter must have been aged about fourteen.

'I'm used to it,' she replied, without taking her eyes from the television.

As Mark looked around the living room, Jasmine stood

by the window and felt the temperature slowly drop. It was very unsettling. This is ridiculous, she thought. She needed to get a grip on herself. She looked at the radiator on the wall and the south-facing patio doors, which stretched across the entire width of the room. It was still sunny outside. It was late April and the sun hadn't set yet. This minimally furnished room should be boiling hot by now, but it wasn't. It was very chilly.

'Have you lived here long?' Mark was asking Freya.

'Only about eighteen months,' she said. 'My partner's job.' She glanced at her daughter, who continued watching television.

They left the living room, and Jasmine showed them the study, which Mark agreed was ideal. Then Freya took them upstairs and showed them the bedrooms. Mark was as elated as Jasmine had been earlier about the house, but now she wasn't so sure.

'I'll leave you two up here to have another look around,' Freya said. 'Come down when you're ready.'

'Thank you,' Mark said.

They were now in the smallest bedroom.

'Is this going to be where I sleep?' Isabel asked.

'We haven't decided yet,' Jasmine replied.

Mark looked out of the window and then wandered into the main bedroom again.

'It's nice,' he said. 'Very nice indeed.'

It was. Jasmine couldn't reasonably fault it. She followed him in and out of the other rooms as he made positive comments, then he looked at her.

'I agree. It's perfect for us.'

'You don't think we should wait and look at some others?' she asked.

'No. Not at all,' he said and went downstairs.

He walked into the living room. Jasmine took a step in and stopped. It felt fine, safe, in there now.

'Thank you. We've finished,' Mark said to Freya. 'We'll leave you to it and we'll phone the agent first thing in the morning.'

'OK,' she said. 'The couple who came this afternoon were looking for something bigger.'

'Great,' Mark said. 'We'll be in touch first thing tomorrow.'

Jasmine offered a weak smile, then stood aside to let Freya open the front door.

Walking down the path Mark said, 'We'll offer just below the asking price and, if necessary, come up.'

'I don't like that house,' Isabel said.

'You'll get used to it,' Mark said. 'We've got to move.'

Jasmine looked at her daughter, who gave a small nod.

'Good girl,' Mark said, and they got into the car.

Jasmine was very quiet on the drive home, so much so that Mark said, 'Are you all right?'

'Yes, I'm fine. It's been a very busy day. I just wondered if we shouldn't wait for a bit and think about the house. We don't want to rush into it.'

'Whatever for?' he asked incredulously. 'It's so us.'

'Yes, it is,' she said, for what else could she possibly say? She'd been delighted with the house when she'd visited earlier, and they either needed to leave their rented flat or move into a short-term tenancy agreement and then move again, which would be expensive. The other alternative was to say she'd felt something strange in that living room, which would sound utterly ridiculous. 'Yes, I like it,' she said again. 'I guess it's just that we've been living in that flat for so long it feels like home.'

'And this house will feel like home too in time,' Mark said.

Jasmine hoped that was true.

THREE

'I don't know why you're not honest with them, Mum,' Madison, Freya's daughter, said angrily as her mother came into the kitchen. 'It's not right. You're sending them on a wild goose chase.'

The moment Jasmine and Mark had gone, Madison had left the sitting room, closed the door and come into the kitchen to be with her mother.

'They seem very keen,' Freya said absently.

'Just like the others!'

'But they're desperate to move. You heard what Mark said – they have to be out of their flat within a month.'

'You know what will happen. They'll ask to come back to measure for blinds just before the exchange of contracts and then experience what we do, and withdraw their offer. That's what happened before. Then you'll have to start all over again.'

'Mark didn't feel it,' Freya said. 'It was just Jasmine and the younger one of her girls. I could tell from the look on that child's face. She couldn't wait to get out of this house.'

'Neither can I,' Madison retaliated. 'That's two out of four feeling it. How long before the other two experience it as well?'

'So what do you suggest we do?' Freya demanded, turning to her daughter. She was at her wits' end. 'Put a sign outside saying "Haunted House for Sale"? No one told us about it when we moved in. The previous owners knew, all right. I wish I could get to the bottom of it.'

'Don't ask me. I don't know,' Madison said. 'I'm going to my bedroom. It's safer up there.'

'I didn't ever want this to happen!' Freya yelled after her daughter.

But Madison continued upstairs and slammed the door to her bedroom.

Freya stood in the kitchen and looked at the clock. It would be at least an hour before her partner, James, returned home from work. She took an open bottle of wine from the fridge, sat at the table in the dining room and poured herself a large glass. The door to the living room was shut tight and she sat there staring at it. They only went in there when someone was coming to view the property, then they shut it up until the next time. She drank some more wine and thought of Mark. She prayed he would do what he said and phone the estate agent first thing in the morning and make them an offer. It didn't matter what it was. They'd take it. As long as they could leave this place quickly.

As she sat there thinking and sipping the wine, she felt the faintest tremble. It came from the living room and grew in intensity for a few seconds, then suddenly stopped. She sat at the table and finished the glass. Please make an offer, Mark, she thought, that's all I ask.

FOUR

'Are you all right?' Mark asked Jasmine that evening.

The girls were asleep in bed and they were in the living room. Jasmine had her laptop open and was checking to see if any new properties had been added within their search parameters, but they hadn't. Mark was still assuming he was going to phone the estate agent in the morning and offer just below the asking price. He had the television on low.

'Yes,' she said and closed her laptop. There was nothing out there they could consider with their budget. 'Yes, I'm fine.' She managed a small smile.

'Come and give me a hug,' he said. 'You don't seem yourself tonight.' He patted the sofa beside him.

Jasmine slowly stood and, putting her laptop to one side, went over. Mark put his arm around her and she snuggled in close.

'I know things haven't been so good for us recently,' he said. 'But I have a feeling this house is just what we need to get us back on track.'

She nodded and enjoyed his closeness, which had been lacking of late. He'd had so much on at work.

'I'll put the offer in as soon as the estate agent opens,' he said. 'Then I'll phone you once it's been accepted.'

He gave her a small squeeze. She wanted to tell him about her concerns, but what could she possibly say? That she had a feeling they wouldn't be happy there? That the temperature dropped in the living room, and she felt sure Madison didn't usually spend her time in there? That she suspected it was all done for their benefit? It would make her sound ridiculous, paranoid. So she said nothing, as she often had done in the past when she hadn't agreed with something Mark was keen on. It was difficult to voice your opinion, and then have to explain your reasons logically and rationally. It was better to remain silent. And besides, they had to move.

Mark moved his hand over her blouse and gently kissed her mouth. She kissed him back. This was the Mark she'd loved and cared for all these years. She gave herself to him willingly, on the sofa in their living room. It was just like old times.

The following morning Mark left the house at 8 a.m. Jasmine followed with the girls at 8.15, taking them to school.

'I had a funny dream last night,' Isabel quietly confided as they walked.

'Do you want to tell me about it?' Jasmine asked.

Leah smirked, which made Isabel shake her head.

'That's enough,' Jasmine told her eldest daughter, then, addressing Isabel, she said, 'You know you can tell me anything, love.'

Isabel nodded, but refused to say anything further. Jasmine took her hand. Isabel often had 'funny' or strange dreams, and Jasmine put it down to her age. She'd been the same when she was younger. An 'overactive imagination', her mother had called it. Sometimes she told her about the dreams and at other times she didn't. It was no good pressing Isabel, so Jasmine left it to her.

'Come on, you'll have forgotten all about it by tonight,' she said, and they continued to school.

Jasmine said goodbye to the girls at the school gates, gave them both a kiss on the cheek and came away. At least they would be able to stay at the same school if they moved to that house, she thought.

Outside the school gates Jasmine bumped into another mother whom she hadn't seen for some time. They stood to one side and chatted for a while, then arranged to meet for a coffee before saying goodbye. It was 9.15 as she walked home. Mark was phoning the estate agent now. After a good night's sleep, she was starting to feel a bit better about the house. If their offer was accepted, once all their belongings were there it wouldn't look like the same place. The living room would become their hub, as it was now, and in time the house would become their home. It would all work out, she was sure of it. If necessary, they could even redecorate the entire house to make it feel like theirs.

She'd just got in when Mark phoned, elated. She knew even before he'd told her that he had good news.

'They've accepted our offer,' he said, delighted. 'Freya said we can go back and visit any time. Just to give her a ring.'

'That's great,' Jasmine said, and she meant it. If Freya was offering a return at any time, that must mean there was nothing for Jasmine to worry about, that Freya couldn't be hiding anything and her fears were ungrounded.

'How about next Saturday?' she asked.

'For what?' Mark said.

'To go for another visit.'

'Oh, I see, yes, if you want to. I need to get back to work now. I just wanted you to know.'

Jasmine decided not to tell the girls about the house until they'd exchanged contracts, when it would become legally theirs and they had a firm moving date. Experience had taught her that things could and did go wrong when it came to house buying. When Mark arrived home from work that night the girls had eaten and were in the living room watching television. He kissed Jasmine as he came in and they sat down to dinner undisturbed. He opened a bottle of wine.

'To our new home,' he said, raising a glass.

'To our new home,' Jasmine repeated, and drank the wine.

'I made it clear that our offer is subject to us being in within two months – I'll ask our landlord for a month's extension,' Mark said. 'It's doable. They just need to pull their finger out and get everything sorted.'

'OK. What about another viewing?'

'I phoned Freya and asked her about going this Saturday,' Mark said. 'She said eleven o'clock would suit her, so I said I thought that would be fine for us. I emphasized that we weren't changing our minds – we just couldn't take it all in at the first viewing. Freya understood completely.'

Jasmine knew she'd feel much happier once they'd visited the house again. What Mark said was true – you didn't take it all in on your first couple of visits. You gave the property a cursory glance and decided it was somewhere you wanted to live, came away and thought about it. Next time she'd be more thorough and would lay any lingering doubts to rest.

She ate her meal and sipped her wine as Mark talked about his job. She didn't really have much to say about her own work, as she'd been doing it for so long. Once he'd finished he went into the living room to spend some time with the girls, then saw them up to bed. Jasmine cleared away the dinner things, then went up to say goodnight.

The rest of the week passed very quickly and on Saturday morning Jasmine told the girls they were going to view the house again.

'Which house?' Leah asked as she ate her breakfast. 'We've seen so many.'

'The one we saw on Wednesday in Ravens Lane,' Jasmine said.

'If we're good, can we go to the park after?' Isabel asked.

'Yes, of course.' It had become something of a routine – to view a property, then go to the park if they were well behaved during the viewing. Their landlord had given them notice – he wasn't going to rent his flat any more, as he wanted it for his daughter – so Jasmine and Mark were now trying to buy their first home. 'With a bit of luck this will be the last house we ever view,' Jasmine added.

'Forever?' Leah checked.

'Yes.'

'Yippee!' Leah shouted.

'Yippee!' Isabel agreed.

Because it was Saturday, the traffic was heavy-going through the town, and they arrived at Ravens Lane ten minutes late. A man answered the door.

'Hi, I'm James,' he said, and offered his hand for shaking.

'Mark, and this is Jasmine, Leah and Isabel.'

They smiled as they went into the hall.

'I'm afraid Freya and Madison are not here at the moment. They had to go out,' he said.

'Oh dear, that's a pity,' Jasmine said, disappointed. She knew she would have got into conversation with Freya had she been there.

'No worries,' Mark said. 'We'll just have a quick look around, then we'll leave you in peace.'

'Yes, sure,' James said amicably, and he led the way into the kitchen-diner, which Jasmine took in afresh.

They continued into the living room, which was as immaculate as before. Nothing was out of place. It was quiet and hospitable. Jasmine lingered for a moment to check, but there was no indication of the temperature dropping. James continued through to the study and they all followed, then they went back through the living room and upstairs.

'Stop me if there's anything you want to know,' James said. 'I'm not very good at this. Freya usually takes care of house viewings.'

'This is fine,' Mark said. 'I can appreciate how difficult it must be, showing people around.'

'Tell me about it,' James said, and the guys laughed.

They went into the master bedroom, which Jasmine was starting to view as her own, then the bathroom, and finally the two smaller bedrooms where the girls immediately resumed their debate on who would have which bedroom. Leah wanted what was currently Madison's room, the larger of the two. Isabel objected and said that Leah always got her own way. Mark stopped the argument. 'That's enough now,' he said brusquely. 'Behave!'

James laughed. 'Kids!' he said. 'Who would have them?'

Jasmine threw him a weak smile and they all returned downstairs. The tour was even quicker than her previous two visits.

'We've found somewhere to go,' James said. 'So everything should all go through in a couple of months. Our solicitor's instruction letter arrived yesterday and I've responded.'

'Yes, we've had ours through too,' Mark said.

'Excellent.'

'Do you want to look at anything else?' James offered.

'No, we'll leave you to it,' Mark said. 'Thank you for your time.'

'You're very welcome.'

They shook hands and James saw them out of the front door.

'I wonder where Freya was,' Jasmine said as they got into the car.

'She knew we were coming,' Mark said. 'Never mind. Are you happy with the house?'

Jasmine nodded and then turned to the girls.

'Do you like the house?' she asked them.

Leah nodded, as Isabel said, 'Are we going to the park now?'

'Yes, of course.'

Mark began to drive in the direction of the park as Jasmine gazed out of her side window, deep in thought.

'I suppose she forgot,' she said after some moments.

'Who?' Mark asked.

'Freya. She forgot our visit.'

He looked at her oddly. 'Let it go, will you? I expect the two of them had an appointment they'd forgotten about or needed to go out in a hurry.'

'Yes, you're probably right,' Jasmine said thoughtfully. 'It just seems a bit odd.'

She could never give up on something once she'd got going.

Mark drove to the park, where they stayed for nearly an hour, the girls playing nicely on the equipment while Jasmine and Mark talked. Then Mark drove them all home. Jasmine was now thinking about all the things she'd have to do if they were going to move in two months' time.

'I suppose I'd better start sorting and packing,' she said with a small smile.

'Yes,' Mark agreed. 'We don't want to leave it until the last minute, especially with both of us working.'

FIVE

Freya and Madison had returned home ten minutes after Jasmine and her family had left. They knew they'd gone because James had phoned them to let them know.

'They're not coming back?' Madison asked as she walked in the front door.

'No,' James said. 'Not until they move in, with a bit of luck.'

James checked the living room for any stray items that belonged to them, and then closed and locked that door. They wouldn't sit in there today; they never did now. It was too unstable. They put out enough items to make it look lived in just before the viewers arrived and then packed them away after they'd gone.

'I'm going to my bedroom,' Madison said, and made her way upstairs.

Freya and James went into their kitchen-diner, which was gleaming from lack of use. The cupboards were mostly empty and the white goods had hardly been used. They'd had it all refurbished prior to moving in, then stuck it out for as long as they could – eighteen months. Now Freya and Madison had admitted defeat and just wanted to leave as soon as possible. James wasn't so sure, but he went along with what his wife and daughter wanted.

He opened the fridge and took out a bottle of wine.

'Do you want a drink?' he asked Freya.

'Yes, why not,' she said, and went to the table and sat on one of the dining chairs. 'It's early, I know, but all this is really getting me down,' she sighed.

'Hopefully it will go through this time,' James said. 'They're desperate to move in a hurry.'

He poured them a glass of wine each and they drank some of it in silence. Every so often Freya would glance towards the living room. It was still quiet in there, for now.

'On a good day, when we haven't had any viewings and the house is silent, I think, why should we go? We spent so much on this place and now we're leaving it for someone else to enjoy. Then something happens again, and I'm petrified. I know Madison is too. That's why she hides in her bedroom.'

James put his hand over hers and held it. 'I know, love, but I can't think what else we can do. You and Madison can't live here, that's for sure.'

'There isn't anything else we can do, apart from move,' Freya said despondently. 'It's just such a waste of our time and effort. And I never know when it's going to happen, not for sure. We were all right today, from the sounds of it, but the last time they came we weren't; Jasmine and her daughter felt it.'

James nodded. 'It's not long now. We just need to hang in there.'

He stood and put the television on. Freya glanced towards the locked door of the living room and then returned her gaze to the screen, staring unseeing at the moving pictures, deep in thought. Three estate agents had the property now, as well as the online one, and they'd reduced the price twice. Jasmine and Mark were buying it for less than the reduced price, which meant she and James had lost money.

'I've had another viewing request for tomorrow,' James said, looking at his phone. 'What do I tell them?'

'We might as well let them come. Just in case this doesn't go through.'

'I'll reply. What time?'

'The afternoon is usually good. Between two and four,' Freya said. 'It's silent then.'

James picked up his phone to email but before he began to type, the faintest shudder came from the living room. A second later, the living room began to shake.

'Time to leave,' he said, standing and going into the hall. Madison was on her way down.

'This is ridiculous,' she said, opening the front door.

'I know, pet,' Freya said. 'It's because Jasmine and her family were here.'

They left the house to sit in their car on the front drive. The disturbance could be anything from a few minutes to a quarter of an hour, then it gradually subsided and normality returned. Tonight, the house was angry, and the living room shuddered and shook on and off for about ten minutes as they sat in their car and waited. All that could be heard from outside was a distant rumble. They stayed where they were for another five minutes to make sure it had definitely stopped, then went back indoors. The living-room door was still locked, which was a blessing. Freya would leave it locked until the next viewing when they would go in and scatter their possessions around as usual, hoping and praying that was the last time they ever had to do that.

SIX

It was raining hard on moving day, 10 June. It was a Saturday and Jasmine and Mark were up very early to finish packing the last of their belongings. Their removal firm said they'd arrive at 8.30 sharp and they expected the family to be ready to go by then. Jasmine had booked it all online and had given them the addresses – of where they were leaving and going to. They knew there'd then be a wait until the keys were released, but that shouldn't take too long. They weren't in a chain and Freya and James had agreed to move into rented accommodation while they looked around for something permanent. They wanted their next house to be just right, which Jasmine appreciated. She couldn't believe the day of moving had finally arrived.

'What can go wrong?' Jasmine asked, more to herself than anyone.

'Absolutely nothing,' Mark said. 'We are going to move to our new house today. That's it.'

It was just eight weeks since they'd viewed the house and

made their offer. The solicitors had done their jobs faster than usual, recognizing their clients' rush. Even so, when a month had passed and the searches weren't back yet, Mark had phoned his solicitor, Mr Glover, and told him off. The solicitor said he'd chase up what he could at his end. Mark had phoned him back that afternoon to be told Mr Glover was on the phone at that very moment to the Land Registry, which Mark knew to be a lie as it was all done online now. But it did the trick and later that day he received an email from Mr Glover with the land searches attached.

Jasmine gave them all breakfast, washed the dishes, dried them and tucked them into a box. They collected together the last of their items and put them into the boxes as well.

'I shall be sorry to leave here,' Jasmine said. 'It was our first home as a family.'

'I know,' Mark said. 'At least being here for so long has given us the chance to save for a decent deposit. We've got the home of our dreams now. I can't see us ever moving again.'

'No,' Jasmine said wistfully, and thought of their new home with affection.

After they'd exchanged contracts, she'd returned to view the house again, ostensibly to measure for blinds, and had taken the opportunity to spend some time in the living room. There'd been no drop in temperature at all. Jasmine had decided she'd imagined it the first couple of times and, with renewed vigour, she'd thanked Freya for all she'd done, come home, and set about sorting and packing.

At 8.30 a.m. exactly, two large men knocked on their door and Mark opened it.

'Ah, the removal men,' he exclaimed, delighted. 'Bright and early.'

'All packed up?' the lead man asked.

'Yes. Come in.'

They showed them around the flat. There were boxes as well as furniture in every room. They said it all looked good and began carrying the boxes down the flight of stairs and outside, through the pouring rain. They seemed not to mind. They continued loading the boxes and furniture into their van so that by 10.30 a.m. they'd finished. They then insisted the family went back inside their flat to check it was completely empty. Mark left the keys in the kitchen as instructed. They were going to be collected by the letting agency when they came to complete their check-out inventory.

'Can't we ever come back now?' Isabel asked, as they left for the last time.

'No, love,' Jasmine said. 'We are going to our new home now.'

With a final nostalgic glance around, they came out and shut the front door for the last time. They went down the flight of stairs and got into their car. The removal van began to drive to their new home with Jasmine, Mark, and the children following in a fully laden car.

Jasmine kept checking her phone en route, waiting for the email from the estate agent to say they could release the keys to their new home when their money came through.

There was nothing yet. The van arrived at Ravens Lane first. They parked behind it and looked at the empty house. Jasmine phoned the agent again and was told that the money had arrived and a member of staff was on his way to meet them personally at the property.

'Thank you so much,' Jasmine said, and relayed the message to Mark.

'Why are we waiting, Mummy?' Isabel asked.

'The estate agent is on the way with our keys. He won't be long now.'

Five minutes later a car pulled up and a smartly dressed young man got out, carrying a bouquet of flowers.

'That'll be him,' Mark said.

They all got out as he came over and presented Jasmine with the flowers and gave the keys to Mark.

'Welcome to your new home,' he said. 'I hope you will be very happy here.'

'Thank you,' Jasmine said, smiling.

They went to the front door, which Mark opened, and they all went in, followed by the removal men. The house looked very different without its furniture – much larger. They went in and out of all the rooms as the estate agent checked that the vendors had left the items they'd said they were going to. They went upstairs, in and out of the bedrooms, then went back down again. The agent seemed satisfied.

'I'll leave you to it,' he said, and shook Mark's hand. 'Give me a ring if you need anything.'

Mark thanked him and the agent left as the first of their boxes was brought in.

Jasmine had marked the boxes with the name of the room they were destined for – kitchen, living room, bedroom one – so the men knew where they were to go. She pointed out the three bedrooms upstairs and left them to it.

They were surprisingly quick at unloading the van and after half an hour stopped for a short break. Jasmine had put the kettle and tea-making equipment in a separate bag, which she'd kept by her feet in the car. There was also milk and sugar. She made them all a cup of tea and handed out cakes.

The removal men didn't hang around, and after another hour they wished the family goodbye. Mark tipped them handsomely. They'd done a good job and he was pleased.

The first thing the family did after they'd closed the front door was to sit at their table in their new dining room and eat the sandwiches Jasmine had made, gazing down the empty garden.

'It feels strange,' Leah said.

'I know,' Jasmine laughed. 'It will take us a while to get used to it. You've never moved home before.'

She gave another smile. She felt very happy. After all the months of planning and hoping, they were finally in their new home. It was perfect. The rain had even stopped and the sun was out.

'Once you two have finished your lunch, you can go in the garden with your bikes,' she suggested to the girls.

'Yes,' they agreed, and gobbled down their sandwiches.

Mark left his meal to find the bikes and wheeled them out the side door into the garden. While he was out there he took the opportunity to have a look around the garden.

There was secure fencing on all three sides and the gate was locked in the sideway where the bins were. That was good. He strolled down the garden as the girls came out and got on their bikes. It was about fifty feet long, he guessed. He looked back at their new home and glowed with pride. Satisfied there was nothing out here that could harm the girls, he left them to play in the now-glorious sunshine.

'We'll need to get a shed,' he said to Jasmine on returning indoors. 'It can sit at the bottom of the garden to the left. It will contain all the gardening equipment we are going to buy and the girls' bikes.'

'Sounds perfect,' Jasmine said. 'I'll plant flowerbeds running down both sides with some sort of feature in the middle of the lawn. I can picture it now.'

He kissed her cheek and then they finished their lunch. He stood and, with a final cursory glance at the girls playing in the garden, asked what he could do.

'You could make up the beds, love,' Jasmine said, 'while I see to the kitchen.'

Mark kissed her again and went upstairs. Jasmine got busy. She'd already put the items from their old fridge, which had been rented with their flat, in the new American-style fridge-freezer the vendors had left. She now added some other things that needed to be kept cool. The fridge was huge inside – too big for them, really – but she guessed they'd get used to it. Now she set about unpacking the china. There was a lot of unpacking to do, but thankfully they had the weekend to do most of it before they both returned to work on Monday. She vaguely wondered where Freya and her family were living now and what they were doing as she unwrapped the dinner plates one at a time. She carefully put them on a shelf in one of the wall cupboards. She'd wrapped each plate separately in a sheet of newspaper to prevent chips and cracks. Once this task was complete, she began on the matching bowls and stacked those next to the plates. As she worked she could hear Mark moving around upstairs in the girls' bedrooms.

Suddenly she stopped. Her attention went to the patio doors in the dining area of the kitchen-diner. Isabel was howling, really screaming, and running towards the glass. Jasmine ran to the patio doors, then realized she couldn't open them because they were still locked. She rushed to the side door that Mark had used and Isabel ran into her arms.

'What is it, love? What is it?' The poor child was delirious, crying and screaming.

'I saw her,' she blurted out. 'I saw her at the window.'

'Saw who?' Jasmine asked.

'The witch!' she screamed, petrified.

'No, you didn't, sweetheart,' Jasmine said, hiding a smile.

'I did, I did. It was just like in my dream. She was dressed in a grey jumper and green trousers, and she was standing there staring at me.'

Jasmine knew that Isabel had flights of fancy, and this was one of them.

'Has she gone now?' she asked her gently.

'I think so. Can you make sure?'

'Of course.'

Jasmine took hold of Isabel's hand and went with her

into the rear garden where Leah was still riding up and down on her bike.

'She thinks she saw a witch,' Leah called over with a touch of disparagement.

'I know, and I seem to remember that you used to believe our toilet had a wizard living in it,' she returned with a smile.

'It seemed so real at the time,' Leah said. 'I think it was the noise the flush made.'

'So where did you see the witch, love?' Jasmine now asked Isabel, looking around the garden.

'Up there.' She pointed to the upstairs window on the left, next to the double bedroom that would be hers and Mark's. It was the room they had decided would be Leah's.

'That's my room,' Leah said. 'And there's nothing there.'

'I know, love. She's gone now, hasn't she, Isabel?'

Isabel nodded.

'It's because our house is new to us,' Jasmine said. 'It's a bit unsettling, isn't it?'

She nodded.

'Now go and play on your bike while Daddy and I sort out all our belongings. Then it will feel more like home.'

Jasmine watched her daughter cycle off down the garden, then she returned indoors. A witch in a grey jumper with green trousers. Whatever next? she thought.

SEVEN

There was a thick fog outside, the likes of which Jasmine had never seen before. She was in the heart of it, running through the trees in Coleshaw Woods. She recognized the woods from her childhood. She was running flat out, as fast as she could. She could feel her heart beating hard and furiously. Her daughters were running by her side, trying to keep up with her. How did they manage it? They were much smaller than she was. It was pitch dark. She could barely see them. It must be the middle of the night. No one else was here. It was just her and her daughters. The picnickers had long gone.

Suddenly they came to a clearing in the woods where the trees ran out. They stopped and stared straight ahead at the house. They were alone in this godforsaken place. The house was an exact replica of their new home, only with the ones on either side gone. But why was the house out here in the woods? Her daughters stood close by, also watching; she could feel them at her side without looking at them. She stood there for some moments in the night, surrounded by trees and the sounds of creatures scurrying in the undergrowth. As she stared at the house, a figure slid slightly into view. Jasmine's pulse quickened and her heart missed a beat.

'It can't be,' she gasped, and grabbed her daughters' hands. 'It simply can't be.'

She could feel their soft hands in hers, holding onto her for dear life. They were as petrified as she was but said nothing. They stood there just looking at the upstairs bedroom, but this time it was the view from the front of the house. As they looked, the woman drifted into view properly. She stood there looking at them from the upstairs bedroom window. Jasmine gasped. Her hand shot to her mouth. The woman was wearing a grey jumper and green trousers. They all stared at her. Then Jasmine suddenly realized – this was the woman she'd seen as she'd sat in the car after her first viewing of the property. Finally, Isabel spoke.

'There, I told you,' she said slowly. 'She's real.'

'No,' Jasmine said. 'She's a figment of your imagination.'

'No, she's not. I can see her, so can you,' Isabel said, upset.

Fear gripped Jasmine, because what Isabel said was true. She could see this woman at the window of the house and Jasmine knew she was evil.

'We need to go,' she said, panic-stricken, and gave the girls' hands a tug.

At that moment the fog suddenly lifted and the house vanished. All that remained was that woman, a wicked witch, grinning at them malevolently. Then she too disappeared.

‘It was a figment of your imagination,’ she heard herself say over and over again as they walked home.

‘It was a figment of your imagination . . . a figment of your imagination . . . a figment . . .’

‘Jasmine! Wake up, for Christ’s sake. Come on, wake up. You’re having a bad dream. Come on, wake up, love.’

Jasmine’s eyes opened and for a while she didn’t know where she was. Walking through trees? she thought.

‘Mark?’ she asked after a moment.

‘Yes, it’s me. Thank goodness you’re awake.’ He flopped back, exhausted, onto his pillow. ‘You haven’t had a dream like that in years.’

‘Am I in my bed at home?’ she asked, looking around.

‘Yes. In your new home. It’s seven o’clock on Sunday morning. We slept here last night. Do you remember?’ he asked, looking at her.

Gradually it all came back to her. The move, the endless unpacking late into the night. It had been 1 a.m. when they’d eventually gone to bed.

‘Yes. I remember,’ she said. ‘But my dream was so real. The girls and I were running through Coleshaw Woods. Do you remember those woods?’

‘We haven’t got time for that,’ Mark said. ‘The girls will be in here soon. I just heard Leah get up.’

As Jasmine lay there trying to get back to reality, Leah knocked on their bedroom door. On Sunday mornings the girls always came into their bed.

‘Come in,’ Mark called.

The door burst open and Leah came in, grinning. She clambered into their king-size bed and snuggled down next to Mark.

'Hi, cherub, how are you? Did you sleep well in your new home?' Mark asked, putting an arm around her.

'I did. Can we have the television on?'

They'd set it up before they'd come to bed. Mark reached for the remote and found a children's television programme.

'Where is Isabel?' Jasmine asked, pulling herself up on the pillow.

'In her room, I guess,' Leah said, snuggling closer to Mark.

When Isabel appeared she would come round and join Jasmine on her side of the bed. That's what usually happened. After a couple of minutes Isabel's door could be heard opening and then she appeared.

'Hi, sweet,' Jasmine called.

She came in and went straight round to Jasmine's side and clambered into the bed. Jasmine made room for her. Isabel rubbed her eyes as she snuggled down.

'This is just like old times,' Mark said as they all watched television.

'Mummy, I've got something to tell you,' Isabel whispered so Mark and Leah couldn't hear her.

'What is it, love?'

'I wet my bed last night. I've changed my clothes.'

'Oh, love, you haven't done that in a long while.'

'I know.' She seemed very embarrassed.

'Don't worry. I expect it was because you were unsettled by the move. We all were. I had a really strange dream last night.'

'Shush,' Leah said. 'Daddy and me are trying to watch television.'

'So did I,' Isabel whispered after a moment. 'It was very scary. I think that's when I wet myself. I was so frightened.'

'Don't worry. It was just a dream. You're awake now. You'll be fine tonight.'

'Shush,' Leah said again.

'I saw that witch,' Isabel whispered. 'The one I saw from the back garden. It was at Leah's bedroom window again. Only she was at the front of the house. And the house was in the woods.'

Jasmine felt the air go from her lungs. She didn't know what to say. The same dream? Was it possible for mother and daughter to share the same dream? She had no idea.

'I'm sure you won't have it again,' she soothed.

She looped her arm around her daughter and Isabel snuggled close.

No more was said of the dream by either of them, and their morning continued as usual. Mark rose and made breakfast, then called Jasmine and the girls downstairs. They slipped on their dressing gowns and ran down. It was very strange in their new kitchen – no one knew where anything was; the bowls, cutlery, sauces and so on all had to be hunted for. There was a completely different perspective on everything. No one knew where to sit at the table any more.

'I need to go shopping today,' Jasmine said, taking an empty seat.

'I'll finish the unpacking while you've gone,' Mark suggested.

'Can I stay with you, Daddy?' Leah asked.

'Sure.'

'I'll go with Mummy,' Isabel said. This quite often happened in their household – Leah was with Daddy and Isabel with Mummy.

As they ate breakfast, Jasmine checked her phone and then quickly googled: *Can a mother and daughter share a dream?*

The answer was yes: *It's called shared dreaming and can happen when two people are very close, for example, mother and daughter. The reason is because the people are dealing with similar issues. Their subconscious responds in a similar way.*

So there it was. Now she knew. Satisfied that it was possible, Jasmine put her phone down. It was obvious, really, when you thought about it. She and Isabel were dealing with the same issue – moving house – and had a similar dream. Although it was strange that it had never happened before.

Once they'd finished breakfast, they put their bowls, plates and cutlery into the dishwasher – it had been included in the inventory of items that Freya had left – and then they dressed. Jasmine and Isabel headed for the supermarket – different to the one they had been using before. This one was closer. Their trolley was soon filled to overflowing. There'd been no point in moving a load of food and household items. The car park was filling, and on their way out Jasmine thought she saw Freya, James and Madison from her car window. She tooted but they couldn't have heard her because they drove in the opposite direction. She had no idea where they'd moved to. Perhaps it was somewhere local. She continued home.

'I think I saw Freya and her family leaving the supermarket,' she told Mark as soon as she got in. 'They didn't see me.'

'Well, we know they've gone into rented so I guess they stayed around here.'

They all helped unpack the food shopping, discussing, and sometimes arguing over, where an item would be stored. Once it was all put away, none of them could find any of the items first time and kept opening and closing cupboard doors.

'It will take us time to get used to everything,' Jasmine said, and laughed.

There was still some unpacking to do, but with everyone helping – Isabel and Leah sorted out their bedrooms – by early evening they were more or less done. Mark suggested they had a takeaway; there was an Indian not far away. He ordered it online.

It was nearly 9 p.m. before the girls went to bed. Jasmine had put out their school uniforms ready for tomorrow.

'I'll take you both in the car to begin with,' she said, which she could do, as she mainly worked from home. 'You can go on the bus when you feel confident. We'll see how it goes.'

She kissed Leah, then went through to Isabel's room to say goodnight. She'd just got to the top of the stairs when Isabel called her back.

'I won't have that dream again, will I?' she asked, worried. She was snuggled in bed, her long fair hair spread out on the pillow like an angel.

'No, darling. It's gone now. Forget about it.'

Jasmine sat on the bed and stroked a few strands of hair away from her daughter's forehead.

'Forget all about it,' she soothed.

Isabel nodded. As her mother stroked her forehead, her eyes slowly closed and very soon she was fast asleep. It had been another exhausting day, Jasmine thought as she came out, drawing the door to. She went downstairs and sat on the sofa next to Mark. The late evening news was on the television. She sat there for about half an hour and felt her eyes start to close.

'I'm going to bed,' she said, and stood.

The sun had only just set. There were no blinds at the windows in the living room so she looked out.

'I'll be up soon,' Mark told her.

Jasmine turned from the window and went upstairs. She checked on her daughters, then went into the bathroom, and finally her bedroom. Here they had curtains, left by Freya. She went over to draw them and, before she did, spent some moments looking out into the garden. The darkness was slightly relieved by next door's garden lights. It gave enough of a glow for her to see the outline of the lawn. Next year it would all be very different, she thought, imagining how beautiful it would be. She'd always wanted a garden and now she had this land to plant up as she pleased. She'd keep some space back for vegetables that Mark wanted to grow, and the rest would be hers. She'd plant rows of peonies, cornflowers – their blooms that vibrant azure-blue – white agapanthus, multi-coloured lupines, a clematis covering the south fence and plenty, plenty of roses.

As her gaze travelled around the garden, she noticed a patch of earth in the gloom. It was to the bottom left-hand corner of the garden, next to where Mark said the shed would eventually go. It appeared to have a cross at one end. She peered into the darkness. She couldn't see properly but it looked like a grave. What a pity, she thought; the previous owners must have lost a pet recently. Her next thought was that it was odd that Mark hadn't mentioned it when he'd first gone out there yesterday.

Drawing the curtains together she made a mental note to check it out in the morning. Pleasantly tired and with the optimism that comes from a new and wanted life, she got into bed, where her eyes closed very quickly. She was soon fast asleep.

When she woke in the morning, Mark was already up. She went to the window, opened the curtains and saw that the outline of the grave had completely gone. There was nothing there that was remotely like what she'd seen last night, so she assumed her eyes had been playing tricks on her. Strange, she thought. Unlike Isabel, she wasn't normally given to flights of fancy.

EIGHT

Mark left for work early on Monday morning, at around 7 a.m. Jasmine got the girls up and took them to school in the car. They were very excited and ready to tell their friends about moving. She pulled up outside the school, dropped them off, then began the drive home. She'd nearly gone the wrong way and taken the route that would have led to their old flat. She smiled to herself and fully expected to do it again. They'd lived in that flat for over ten years. Little wonder it felt strange moving and now driving to 13 Ravens Lane.

Once back at the house – it didn't feel like home yet – she made herself a coffee and looked around the downstairs rooms again. It was all so strange, especially now she was by herself. She carried her coffee through to the study. The books had to be unpacked still – they all loved their books – but that could wait. She'd have to work at the small table they'd temporarily put up in the study. Eventually they'd buy a desk. The table was a bit rickety, but it would do for now. She pulled it into position, then set up her laptop and printer. The room could be used for many things, she thought: a family room, children's playroom, cinema room or a study. She and Mark would use it as a joint study.

She sat at the desk and gazed down the garden. Next weekend they'd go to the garden centre and buy lots of plants. June was a good time for planting, she'd read. Then she caught herself. This wouldn't do, sitting here all day, dreaming. She had too much on. One of the problems with working from home part-time was that you received less money but still somehow ended up working a full week, and she'd taken Friday off to finish packing as well, so she had a lot to do. She stood up, turned the table around and pushed it up against the far wall so she was sitting with her back to the window. Now she couldn't see the garden. She would put the girls' photographs on the wall opposite when she had a moment. She began typing. It felt so strange, but nice, to be here.

At 11 a.m. she made another coffee, walked around the downstairs of the house again, then returned to the study and continued to work. About half an hour later, she jumped as the doorbell rang. That sounded much louder than their old one had. She went to answer it.

'Hi, I'm Poppy,' the woman said. 'I live next door. I wanted to welcome you to the neighbourhood.' She presented her with a cake tin.

'That's very kind of you. I'm Jasmine. Will you come in?' Jasmine asked, hoping she'd say no. 'I work from home.'

'I won't stay long,' Poppy said.

She came in and followed Jasmine into their kitchen-diner. 'You've done well,' she said, gazing around. 'You only moved in on Saturday.'

'Thank you,' Jasmine said. 'Would you like a tea or a coffee?'

'Tea, please, and a slice of my delicious cake.' She gave a small laugh.

As Jasmine made the drinks and sliced the cake – a Victoria sandwich – she saw Poppy looking around the kitchen-diner. They made light conversation, asking each other about work, children and so forth. Poppy was one of her new neighbours and Jasmine needed to make her feel welcome. She could always catch up on work later in the day. After she'd collected the girls from school if necessary.

'We'll sit in the living room,' she said, and led the way in.

She thought she saw Poppy look around nervously as she placed the sliced cake on the coffee table. Poppy helped herself.

'Are you planning on staying long?' she asked Jasmine, which seemed a strange question.

'Yes, for life.' She laughed.

'I just wondered as Freya was thinking of renting the property if it didn't sell.'

'Oh, I see. No, we've bought it,' Jasmine confirmed. 'They were only here for eighteen months or so, I believe.'

'Yes, that's right. I hope you don't mind me saying, but I think you're very brave.' She took a bite from her cake and looked at Jasmine.

'Brave?' Jasmine queried.

'After everything that happened to Freya and the family, I mean.'

'What happened to them?' Jasmine asked. A cold chill ran down her spine.

'Didn't they tell you?' Poppy asked.

'No. About what?'

Poppy hesitated. 'I'm not supposed to say anything to prospective buyers, but you've bought the place now, haven't you?'

Jasmine nodded.

Poppy took a moment before she began, staring first at the cake on her plate, then up at Jasmine. 'They had been here about a month when it began,' she said. 'They were sitting in here, in the living room, one evening, and their house began to shake. I don't mean their whole house, just the sofa in this room. There was also a massive drop in temperature. I felt it once too. Freya called me in here and I couldn't believe it. There was a strange feeling as well that I couldn't put my finger on. By the time they put the property up for sale, other things had started to happen. But you haven't experienced anything like that?' She was looking at Jasmine, waiting for a reply.

'No,' Jasmine said, shaking her head. 'We haven't.'

'I guess that's it then,' she said, relieved, and took a sip of her tea.

Jasmine was still staring at her, wondering if she should admit to experiencing something similar when she'd first looked around the house, but she decided against it. It would raise more questions than it answered, and Jasmine had largely put the drop in temperature out of her head now.

'Freya asked if we'd ever experienced anything like it in our house,' Poppy said. 'We hadn't, and as far as I knew the house on the other side of you hadn't either.'

'We've only been here for a few days,' Jasmine said, without thinking.

'Yes, of course. You must think me barmy, coming in here and talking about all of this. I expect it was just the Morgans imagining things, and that will be the end of it now. This cake is rather delicious, even though I say so myself.'

'Have another slice,' Jasmine said, offering the plate.

'No, that would be greedy. I'll let you get on with your work.' She hesitated, then said, 'I also wanted to invite you all to dinner on Saturday night.'

'That's very kind of you,' Jasmine said.

'You've got two girls and I've got two boys, so they can all play together. We won't make it too late. Say, six o'clock?'

'Yes, thank you. That would be lovely.'

'Great,' she said, standing up and placing her empty cup and plate on the table.

Jasmine saw her to the door.

'See you on Saturday then,' Poppy said. 'Forget what I said. I'm sure it's all done with now.'

'Yes, of course.' Jasmine raised a smile and closed the door.

Her heart was racing. She had no idea what to think. The drop in temperature had happened to her before they'd moved in, but not since then. There hadn't been any other incidents. Should she tell Mark what Poppy had said? No, she decided not to. He'd be in a bad mood at having to go next door to eat anyway. He hated that sort of socializing with neighbours. As she cleared away the plates, cups and saucers, she wondered why she'd agreed to go in the first place. She was being neighbourly, she supposed. But then she'd be expected to ask them back to dinner in return, sooner or later.

NINE

Jasmine and the family had a good week. By Friday she and Mark had unpacked all the boxes apart from the one with the pictures in it. They had yet to decide where those would hang. It would take them both some time to decide, so they put that box to one side for now.

Jasmine had Saturday earmarked for the garden centre, and on Saturday evening they were all traipsing next door for dinner. Jasmine hadn't seen Poppy since she'd come round on Monday, bringing with her that delicious cake, although she'd caught sight of their cars coming and going. She wondered if the dinner was still on. Mark would be hoping not. At 10 a.m. on Saturday morning, before they went to the garden centre, she went round and knocked on their door. A man she assumed to be Poppy's husband answered, although he seemed to be quite a bit younger than Poppy.

'I'm Jasmine. I live next door,' she said to introduce herself.

'Oh, yes. Harry. I'm afraid Poppy has gone shopping – for tonight. You are still coming?'

'Yes. I just wanted to make sure dinner was still on.'

'Very much so,' he confirmed. 'We're looking forward to seeing you.'

'Great,' she said, and stood there not knowing what else to say. 'See you later then.'

Jasmine thanked him and came away wondering if Poppy had talked to Harry about the disturbances in their house. But it didn't matter now. They'd been living there a full week and nothing more had happened. It was just one of those things, she'd decided.

By 10.30 they were all in the car on the way to the garden centre, where they spent two hours choosing plants, seeds and vegetable seedlings. It was a bit late in the year for some of them to be planted, but they bought them anyway and would take a chance. Jasmine was delighted. There were trays of plants everywhere. They filled the boot of the car and the girls had some on their laps. She even had some on her lap and at her feet in the front passenger seat.

Once home, they unloaded the car, had a sandwich lunch, and then Jasmine and Mark got to work in the garden as the girls played on their bikes. It was a glorious day, really warm and sunny. Mark prepared his piece of ground for sowing and planting the vegetables and added suitable manure and compost. They worked all afternoon and by 4.30 p.m. they'd more or less finished. Jasmine stood back and admired their work, then she began watering the plants, using the hosepipe that was still connected to the tap on the outside of their house.

The girls then went indoors with Mark and she had the garden to herself. It was marvellous out here, very quiet indeed. No sound of children playing in neighbouring gardens and no birds singing in the trees . . . She stopped watering for a moment and listened. It was deadly silent – a bit strange for June, she thought. She looked around the garden but there was nothing to see, just the strangest feeling that she was being watched. She looked up at their neighbours' windows, first one side and then the other. There was no one watching from there. She looked back towards her own house and then she heard it. A noise, a whisper. Someone was calling her name.

'Jasmine.'

Turning off the hose, she looked around, scanning the garden. It must have been her imagination. She was about to turn the hose back on when she heard it again.

'Jasmine,' the voice said softly.

She turned to look. Nothing, no one. It wasn't Mark calling her – it wasn't his voice – nor was it the girls or Poppy's. She stayed where she was and listened but the sound didn't come again. Perhaps it was her imagination?

After a few moments, she started the hose again and continued watering the plants, all the while looking around her, vigilant. But there was just the sound of water falling on leaves. She finished watering and switched off the hose. With a final glance around the garden, she went indoors.

'You didn't call me while I was out there?' she asked Mark. He was in the living room.

'No, why?'

'It's nothing. I thought I heard someone call my name.'

'Not me. Was it the girls?'

'No.'

She went to the open patio doors of the living room and stood, looking out, admiring the plants they'd put in. The air outside was alive now with birdsong, just as it should be in June. She stood there for a few minutes, then went to get showered and changed, ready for going next door that evening.

'Two flowers,' Harry said as he opened the door.

Jasmine pulled a face, suggesting she had no idea what he was talking about.

'Two flowers – Jasmine and Poppy,' he said.

'Oh, I see.' She gave a polite smile. 'This is Mark, my husband, and Leah and Isabel, our daughters.'

'Lovely to meet you all,' Harry said. 'Come through to the kitchen where Poppy is enslaved.'

They went into the kitchen-diner where Poppy was busy preparing the food. She said hi and continued with what she was doing. The house was a replica of their own, just in mirror image, although they'd decorated it and arranged it very differently.

'We've brought a box of chocolates for you,' Jasmine said, putting it on the centre island.

'Oh, lovely. Thank you so much,' Poppy replied.

Their boys came charging in.

'This is Hudson and Liam,' Harry said.

The two boys stopped and stared at Leah and Isabel. 'Hi,' they said sheepishly. They didn't attend the same school as the girls.

'Is that all you've got to say for yourselves?' Harry asked them, and they shrank back, embarrassed.

'Leave them alone,' Poppy said. 'I've made a pasta and vegetable bake for dinner.' She opened the oven door and put it in. 'I guessed the children would like it. In fact, I've made two, so there's plenty for everyone, followed by trifle – my speciality.'

'That sounds wonderful,' Jasmine said, and Mark agreed.

'Harry, would you like to take everyone through to the living room and pour them a drink while I finish up in here?' Poppy said. Jasmine noticed a half-drunk glass of wine by her side on the kitchen work surface.

'Yes, this way,' Harry said. 'Kids, do you want to go and play?

They all went into the living room, which was exactly like Mark and Jasmine's – she supposed there wasn't much you could do differently with it being the mirror image of their own, but Jasmine saw that they were using their study as a playroom. The boys went in there.

'Go on,' Jasmine encouraged her girls.

Reluctantly, Isabel and Leah followed the boys in.

'How old are your lads?' Jasmine asked Harry as they sat down.

'Seven and eleven, I think. What can I get you to drink?'

‘I’ll just have a glass of sparkling water for now, please,’ Jasmine said.

‘A white wine for me,’ Mark said.

Harry went into the kitchen to fetch the drinks, then returned, glasses in hand. He put them on the occasional tables within their reach and began making conversation. It wasn’t long before Jasmine and Mark discovered that the boys weren’t actually his, and he had moved in just over a year ago. Poppy came in, bringing with her a large glass of wine, which had clearly been refreshed.

‘Dinner will be ready in about twenty minutes,’ she said, and sat down.

They continued talking, and Jasmine and Mark soon learnt that Poppy worked part-time at a local dress store in town and Harry was in IT. Poppy said she wanted to work as a PA like Jasmine, as she had done before she’d had the children, but the vacancies seemed to have dried up with so many people working more from home now. As the conversation continued, predictable, safe and secure, the children could be heard playing in the playroom. Dinner was soon ready, and Poppy called them to the table in their kitchen-diner, where Hudson and Liam were reminded to wash their hands. The girls followed suit. Jasmine saw Mark start to unwind and relax as they sat down, and Harry asked him about the vegetables he was growing in his garden.

‘You can come round and have a go at our garden any time,’ Poppy said, throwing Harry a meaningful look.

‘I wasn’t aware the garden was my responsibility,’ he replied curtly.

They'd both had too much to drink, it was obvious, and this was the point at which the tide changed and the bickering became more noticeable. Little things were thrown into the conversation to make the other one react. Jasmine and Mark had seen it before between couples they'd spent the evening with. Comments not openly aggressive but with a hidden agenda. About the house and what needed doing, the garden, the boys, responsibilities – about whose job was whose.

After the main course, the children were allowed to leave the table and go to the playroom again, and the sniping continued. Mark tried changing the subject a few times, but it didn't seem to do any good. Poppy and Harry were soon back on course; they didn't need her or Mark present. Mark sipped his drink and smiled politely while Jasmine gazed through their patio doors to the garden beyond. Poppy was right: it did need a lot of work.

She brought her attention back to the table. If she wasn't mistaken, Poppy was flirting with Mark. She seemed to have moved her chair closer to his and was looking at him through soppy eyes. Harry refilled the glasses and asked Jasmine if she was ready for a glass of wine now.

'No, thank you,' she said. 'I'm fine with sparkling water.'

It was now 8.30 p.m. and they hadn't had dessert yet. It would be the girls' bedtime soon, although she supposed they could stay up later tonight.

'So, what do you think about living with ghosts?' Poppy was asking Mark.

Jasmine sat up straight and looked at her. Surely not? she thought.

'Ghosts?' Mark queried with a smile.

'You've got ghosts in your living room, haven't you?'

'Poppy!' Harry admonished. 'I think that's enough. Where's the trifle?'

'In the fridge,' she said, just as bluntly. 'That's where I usually keep it.'

The room fell silent. Harry stood. 'Is anyone else ready for dessert?' he asked.

'Yes, please,' Jasmine said. Mark nodded and moved his chair further away from Poppy's.

Harry gathered together the dirty plates and called to the children to come to the table. No one came, so Jasmine stood and went to fetch them. The door to the playroom was shut. She knocked before she opened it, and then there was silence as they all looked up at her guiltily.

'Is everything all right?' she asked them.

No one replied. Leah and Hudson had their heads down.

'Trifle is ready,' Jasmine said, studying the girls.

They stood and filed out.

'Are you all right?' she asked Isabel as she passed.

She nodded and followed the others to the table.

The atmosphere was now very different. Sombre and tense. Something must have been said or a summit reached beyond which Poppy and Harry didn't go. Poppy served the trifle in silence, then drank her wine as they all ate, complimenting her on the wonderful dessert. She smiled, marginally pleased. It was a very different gathering now to the one it had been before, and Jasmine just wanted to go. At 9 p.m. she said they needed to be off. Harry protested, but Poppy didn't. Standing, Jasmine thanked Poppy and Harry for a lovely evening.

'You're welcome,' Poppy said. 'Say goodnight, boys, and then go straight to bed.'

'Night,' they both said and disappeared up to their bedrooms.

'Thanks again for a very nice evening,' Jasmine said on the way out.

'You're very welcome,' Poppy repeated.

With a heavy heart, Jasmine walked down their front path, aware that at some point they'd have to reciprocate and invite them to dinner. It was what neighbours did.

TEN

'What were those comments about ghosts?' Mark asked as they got into bed that night.

'It was just something that Poppy mentioned when she came over with the cake earlier this week,' Jasmine replied. 'It's nothing to worry about. I'm more concerned with what the girls were doing in that playroom. They looked guilty and wouldn't tell me what had happened. I'll bring it up again tomorrow. I think they were too tired tonight.'

She got into bed and Mark turned to her, ready to make love.

'So, you got on well with Poppy?' Jasmine asked, an edge to her voice.

'She's OK,' Mark said.

'You were flirting with her.'

'No, I wasn't. Well, maybe a bit. She's the type of woman guys flirt with.'

'How sexist,' Jasmine exploded.

'You know what I mean.'

'Do I?' Jasmine asked, and glared at him.

He must have seen from her expression that she was upset, but he clearly couldn't be bothered to argue now so he turned over onto his back and didn't say anything more. He was soon fast asleep, brought on by the alcohol and a day in the garden. Jasmine, who'd had no alcohol all evening, lay awake thinking about Poppy flirting with her husband and then about all the plants they'd put into the garden. They'd done a good job. Before long, she too was asleep.

'Did you have a nice time last night?' Jasmine asked the girls over breakfast the following morning. Mark had eaten his breakfast and was now upstairs getting dressed.

'Yes,' Leah said, not very enthusiastically.

'What about you, Isabel?' Jasmine asked. 'Did you have a good time?'

'It was OK,' she said with a small shrug.

'What did you do in the playroom?' You couldn't be too careful now. Hudson was eleven, after all.

'I didn't like it,' Isabel admitted after a few moments. 'But Hudson said we had to stay in there and play because we were kids. He hates his stepfather and wants to live with his dad.'

'You could have stayed at the table,' Jasmine said. 'I suppose he meant it was more fun for you playing in there rather than talking with the grown-ups.'

They didn't reply but continued eating their cereal.

'Hudson said there were ghosts in our house,' Isabel said

as she finished. 'He said they come out at night. I saw one last night. I called to you, but you didn't come.'

'I'm so sorry, love,' Jasmine said. 'I was very tired what with gardening all afternoon and then going out in the evening. I would have come if I'd heard you.' Isabel had a wonderful imagination.

'It's OK,' Isabel said. 'She went after a while. I was only a bit scared. She gave me a message to give to you and then vanished.'

'What was the message?' Jasmine asked. She took a bite of toast.

'She said she doesn't want the shed put at the bottom of the garden on the left. It's her garden.'

Jasmine looked at her daughter. 'How did you know that's where Daddy was thinking of putting the shed?'

'The ghost told me.'

'Don't be silly,' Leah said. 'There is no such thing as ghosts.'

'Yes, there is. I saw her last night and she told me to tell Mum.'

Leah was laughing now.

'All right, I think that's enough talk of ghosts. Let's get ready. We've got another busy day ahead.'

Mark came downstairs smiling. They'd made love that morning before the girls woke up, so all was well again and Poppy was forgotten. He came into the kitchen and kissed his wife on the cheek.

'We'll start on the box of pictures today,' he said. 'Have you thought about where you'd like them to go?'

'I've got an idea where some of them will hang,' Jasmine said.

Mark fetched the large box and carried it into their kitchen-diner. The bottom of the box was loose and some of the wrapped pictures were in danger of falling out. Jasmine opened the top and then unwrapped the first photograph. The glass had a large crack right across it.

'Oh dear. I guess it got broken in the move,' she said, and put it to one side.

She began unwrapping the next, carefully removing the wad of newspaper from the picture. That was broken too. Disappointed, she placed it on top of the first and very carefully opened the third. She couldn't believe it. Broken like the other two. She began on the fourth, fifth, sixth, gradually working her way through the whole box. Mark was standing beside her, as saddened as she was by the breakages. She continued. Ten, eleven, twelve – they all seemed to be broken. They were portrait photos of them all, but mainly the girls' school photos. It was very sad indeed.

'I guess the removal firm dropped the box,' Jasmine said, puzzled.

'But would they all break in the same way?' Mark asked, picking one picture up and studying it. Each of the photos had a single large crack running diagonally from the top left-hand corner to the bottom right. 'It almost looks as if someone has done it on purpose.'

'That's ridiculous,' Jasmine said.

There were sixteen photos in all, each one wrapped in newspaper to stop them from being broken. They unwrapped the last picture and that was broken too, with the same single line running across it from top to bottom.

'I don't understand,' Mark said, staring at the pile of broken photographs. 'How on earth did this happen?'

'I'm guessing the removal firm dropped the box from a height,' she said.

'But the single line running across them all? That doesn't make sense. I mean, maybe a few would get broken, but not all of them.'

He picked up one of the frames and stood there looking at it.

'I'll contact the firm in the morning and put in a claim,' Jasmine said.

'Yes, OK. Let's take out the photos to save them.'

They began carefully removing the pictures from their frames and stacked them to one side.

'We'd better keep the frames for now, until you've spoken to the firm,' Mark said. 'Evidence. I'll put them outside for safekeeping.'

He began gathering the broken frames together, a few at a time, and taking them out the back door.

'This is when we could do with that shed,' he said, returning. 'Let's get that ordered this afternoon.'

As he picked up the next frame the glass cut into his hand.

'Ouch,' he cried and stared at it.

A crimson line of blood immediately appeared in the palm of his left hand. The cut was deep and he ran to the sink to stop it dripping onto the floor. Turning on the cold tap, he held his hand under it, letting the water wash away the blood. Jasmine hunted for the first-aid kit and eventually found it in a kitchen drawer, but each time he removed his hand from the cold water the cut began to bleed again. Eventually, after about ten minutes or so, the bleeding slowed and then more or less stopped.

'Thank goodness,' Jasmine said, and she put a large sticking plaster over it.

'I still don't know how they all got broken,' Mark said.

'Neither do I,' Jasmine agreed. 'Don't worry. Perhaps the firm will be able to throw some light on it tomorrow.'

That afternoon they went shed hunting. They found a large store about five miles away called Sheds and Garden Buildings. They spent some time looking at their assembled range and then chose one. It was ten feet by six feet and had a window at the front. The girls wanted to use it as a playhouse, but Mark said it would soon be full of gardening equipment, including a lawnmower they had yet to buy. They also paid to have it delivered and erected on Friday. The company said they would phone to confirm a time. Satisfied with a positive outcome, they returned home, where Jasmine began making dinner.

They hadn't been in long when the doorbell rang. Mark answered it and, to his surprise, found Poppy carrying a bouquet of flowers.

'Sorry for our behaviour last night,' she said, and thrust the flowers into Mark's hands.

Jasmine, hearing this, stopped what she was doing and

went to the front door. 'That's very kind of you,' she said, smiling.

'It's nothing. I hope you enjoyed some of last night.'

'Yes, of course we did,' Jasmine said. 'Thank you for the flowers.'

'You're welcome.'

Poppy turned and headed down the path, obviously eager to be away.

'Thanks again!' Jasmine called after her.

Poppy waved and then disappeared into their front garden.

Mark and Jasmine closed their door, looked at each other, and began to laugh.

Jasmine found a large vase and arranged the flowers in it. There were roses and peonies, and something she didn't know the name of. She cut off some stems and arranged the flowers in a really attractive display. She carried the vase into the living room and placed it in the middle of the coffee table in the centre of the room, then stood back to admire it. Perfect, she thought.

She went through to the kitchen and continued making dinner – roast chicken, with all the trimmings. As they sat at the table eating, she thought she heard a noise, a buzzing sound, and looked up. There was nothing in this room. Mark had heard it too. There it was again. It was a buzzing coming from the living room.

'There's a bee or wasp trapped in there,' she said.

'I'll see to it when I've finished eating,' Mark said.

The adjoining door to the living room, which had a glass panel in it, was thankfully closed.

After a few minutes the bee or wasp noise suddenly escalated into a calamitous buzzing. Jasmine and Mark both put down their cutlery and locked eyes. The girls stopped eating and looked at the door.

'What's that?' Leah cried.

'It's nothing to worry about,' Jasmine said, and stood.

Mark was standing too; they both went to the adjoining door. The noise was rising in intensity. They looked through the door.

'What the hell!' Mark exclaimed.

'I don't believe it!' Jasmine cried in dismay. 'Don't open the door.'

'As if I would!'

Through the glass door they could see a massive swarm of wasps lodged around the ceiling light. There were hundreds of them; the shade on their light was black with the humming, moving swarm. More were coming from the flowers in the vase, even as they watched.

'I don't believe it,' Jasmine said again. 'It can't be.'

Mark backed away from the door. 'Keep it closed. I'll phone a company to come and remove them,' he said, panic in his voice.

With his hands trembling – he hated wasps – he took out his phone and began scrolling through local pest-control firms, but it was Sunday and none of them were open, according to their websites. The girls had now left their chairs and stood, petrified, flattened against the wall on the other side of the room.

'What are we going to do?' Jasmine cried, looking

through the glass door and into the living room. The wasps seemed to be angry; they circulated the light shade, buzzing agitatedly.

Mark thought for a moment. 'If I go outside and open the patio door to the living room, do you think they'll swarm out into the garden?' He looked at her uncertainly.

'It's worth a try, but I just don't see where they could have come from.'

'Neither do I,' he said.

Isabel was crying now. Jasmine went to her and took her hand and drew her close to her.

'I think this place is haunted,' Leah said.

'Don't be silly,' Jasmine admonished. 'Of course it's not.'

Mark opened the dining-room door that led onto the patio before he could lose his nerve, and stepped outside. As he did so, it was as if the wasps sensed what he was doing and their buzzing increased. The girls screamed and moved closer to their mother as the noise continued, a flying mass of wasps.

Mark opened the patio door to the living room and ran back into the kitchen-diner where he closed the door tightly. He and Jasmine watched through the glass in the connecting door. The wasps seemed not to notice or care about the fresh air coming into the room. They stayed in their shape around the light for some minutes.

'What will we do if it doesn't work?' Jasmine asked.

'I've no idea,' Mark admitted.

What happened next was quite uncanny, unreal almost.

A single wasp flew from the light and went straight out of the door. It was as though the others had seen it and soon another followed, then another and another. A mass of them took off and flew straight out the door. The last to go were the wasps in the flowers themselves, which left one at a time. The room was still. They'd all gone, disappearing out through the patio doors and going somewhere else to establish their colony.

Mark and Jasmine waited and watched until they were sure the room was clear, then Mark gingerly opened the door to the living room and went in.

'Give me a minute to check the room,' he said.

Jasmine shut the door again and the girls watched as Mark hunted around, removing cushions, looking under and behind sofas. He closed the door to the patio so the swarm couldn't return and finished checking the room. Once he gave the all-clear, Jasmine quickly went in and picked up the flowers.

'What are you doing with them?' Mark asked.

'Throwing them away.'

'But the swarm couldn't possibly have been concealed in their blooms,' Mark said. 'They're not big enough for hundreds of wasps. It's simply not feasible.'

'So where did they come from?' Jasmine asked.

They both looked around the room. There wasn't even an old fireplace with a chimney they could have swarmed down.

'I don't know,' Mark admitted helplessly.

Jasmine continued from the room, taking the flowers

with her. She went straight out of the back door and threw the bunch into the bin. She looked up and around to make sure the wasps hadn't swarmed to under an eave on their house, and then headed back indoors.

'I know it seems unlikely the wasps were in the flowers, but they got in somehow,' she said. 'I can't think of another way.'

'The wasps won't be waiting outside for us, will they?' Leah asked, afraid.

'No, love, they'll be long gone now.'

'I think this house is haunted like Hudson said,' Leah said again, which made Isabel cry.

'Now look at what you've done,' Jasmine cried, her nerves shot to pieces. She went to her younger daughter and took her onto her lap. 'I don't want any more talk of ghosts, do you understand me? Somehow a swarm of wasps got into the living room but now they've gone.'

But she knew, as did Mark, that there must be another explanation. Hundreds of wasps couldn't conceal themselves inside a bunch of flowers and then swarm out. It simply wasn't possible. But try as she might, she couldn't think of how else it might have happened, and it niggled away at her all evening. Mark referred to the incident a few times as they sat alone after the girls were in bed, but he couldn't think of a rational reason either. Whichever way you looked at it, it didn't make sense, and so the two of them sat in the living room, every so often looking around it for any sign of a wasp.

ELEVEN

'Yes, every single one is broken,' Jasmine said to the woman at the removal firm on Monday morning. 'Sixteen in all.'

'I don't understand how that could have happened,' she replied.

'Neither do I,' Jasmine admitted. 'But it has.'

'Did the box fall?' she asked.

'Not as far as I'm aware. But your guys will know more than me.'

'I'll need photographs, and I'll speak to our boss,' the woman said. 'You'll have to fill in an insurance form.'

'That's fine. Can you email it to me, please?'

'Of course.'

Jasmine said goodbye and put down the phone, wondering how she was going to explain that each glass in every single frame had been damaged in exactly the same way. She'd omitted to mention that to the woman. It didn't seem relevant – or was it? She sat there thinking about it and after a minute or so decided to take just three photographs of the broken frames. That should do it, and the woman needn't know about all the others.

Jasmine went to the box, opened it and removed the top three frames. She took a photo of each of them and emailed them to the firm. She then returned to her laptop, ready to begin work. Fifteen minutes later the woman from the removal company phoned her.

'I've got your frame photos, thank you,' she said. 'You're the Simmons family, aren't you?'

'Yes, that's correct,' Jasmine said.

'And am I right in saying that the family who moved out of that house were the Morgan family?'

'Yes.' There was silence from the other end. 'I'm sorry, but what's that got to do with our claim?' Jasmine asked. Time was ticking on, and what with dropping off the girls at school and taking the photographs, she'd barely done any work.

'Will you photograph all the broken frames and send the photos to me, please? I believe you're claiming for sixteen.'

'Yes, but surely a few is enough?' Jasmine asked.

There was silence again. This firm was taking the mick, Jasmine thought.

The woman cleared her throat before she spoke. 'It seems that the Morgan family emailed us with a similar breakage eighteen months ago when they moved into your address.'

'I'm sure you must have a lot of claims,' Jasmine said, slightly annoyed.

'Not really, our chaps are very experienced, which is why these two stood out. The pictures of the frames you both sent all had a singular crack running from the top left-hand corner to the bottom right. The Morgans didn't claim for anything else.'

Jasmine was shocked and didn't know what to say. But how did she know it wasn't a trick by the company in an effort not to pay out?

'Are you sure?' she asked.

'Positive.'

'Can you email me the photos the Morgans sent to you?' Jasmine asked.

There was silence again and Jasmine thought, *got you*, before the woman replied, 'Yes, I suppose I can. We paid their claim. I'll send a photo of all their breakages, and will you do the same, please?'

'Yes,' Jasmine said, and the call ended.

Jasmine sat there thinking about the Morgans' broken frames. All broken. What was the likelihood of that happening? She had no idea. She hadn't asked how many pictures of the Morgans' had been broken. She supposed it wasn't something the woman would remember. But it was definitely odd, she thought.

She finally set herself to work properly, occasionally turning to glance through the window behind her and out to the garden beyond. She was pleased with what they'd done over the weekend. It looked good, very good indeed.

An hour later an email with an attachment arrived from the removal company. Jasmine stopped what she was doing, clicked save and opened it. She looked at the picture that had accompanied the Morgans' claim: it showed a row of frames set out on the floor so they were all visible. It hadn't just been photographs that had been broken, but framed pictures of scenes too. Jasmine stared at them. There was no doubt now. Without exception, every one had a single diagonal line running from the top-left corner to the bottom, just like theirs did. But how was that possible? Had they broken like that as they fell or had another heavy box been loaded on top of them, maybe?

She turned to her computer and googled: *What are the chances of pictures being broken in the same way?* Up came pages mostly about images breaking up on websites – not relevant to her. She tried, *Pictures breaking the same during a move*, which brought up similar results. She couldn't find a single reference to what had happened to her and the Morgans, so she decided it hadn't happened to anyone else – or, if it had, it was too rare to report. Breakage cracks occurred often, but not uniformly.

Jasmine hadn't taken any more photos of her own breakages yet, expecting the woman at the removal firm not to send the Morgans' photographs. She retrieved the frames, then spent some time on her knees arranging them across the carpet so they were all visible while she took some photographs. She emailed the photographs to the woman and put the frames away. Almost straight away, she received an email acknowledging receipt of her email, but nothing more that day. She did some work and then left to collect the girls from school. As usual, Isabel had had a good day and talked about it non-stop all the way home, while Leah had had a bad day and grumbled about it consistently. By the time they were indoors they'd talked themselves out. They had a drink and a snack and watched television while Jasmine finished her work and then made dinner.

The girls had eaten and were on their way to bed by the time Mark came home. They heard the front door open and ran downstairs in their pyjamas to smother him in kisses. He gave them a perfunctory kiss each and sent them back upstairs.

'Daddy's in a bad mood,' Leah said.

'Never mind,' Jasmine said, and kissed them both goodnight.

She went downstairs. Mark was in the living room, sprawled out and staring into space.

'Are you OK?' Jasmine asked him.

'My hand is hurting,' he said.

Jasmine had to think for a minute before she remembered that Mark had cut his hand yesterday on the broken glass from the frames. From the look of it, he still had the same plaster on his palm.

'I would change the dressing if I were you,' she said, without much sympathy. She suspected he was making a fuss about nothing.

Jasmine went into the kitchen to serve dinner, which she and Mark ate in the dining part of the kitchen, looking out onto the garden. Jasmine remarked how nice it would be once all the plants had grown, but Mark wasn't up to small talk. He ate his dinner in silence.

'What's the matter?' Jasmine asked. 'Something at work?'

'I've told you. It's my hand. It bloody hurts,' he snapped.

'It shouldn't be hurting that much,' Jasmine said. 'After dinner you need to change the dressing.' Sometimes she thought he needed a mother rather than a wife, and it had been the catalyst for some of their arguments in the past.

He left some of his dinner, which wasn't like him, and stood and went over to rummage through the kitchen drawers.

'Where are the frigging plasters?' he asked her.

She got up and went and found them straight away.

'Here,' she said, thrusting them onto the work surface close to where he was standing.

She began clearing away the dinner things as he picked at the edge of the plaster. It wouldn't come away easily, and he picked and agitated it until eventually it tore off.

'Good grief,' Mark exclaimed. 'No wonder it hurts.'

He held his hand towards Jasmine and her stomach lurched as she looked at the cut.

'The wound is much bigger than it was yesterday,' she managed to say. 'It's full of pus. How did it get like that?'

'I don't know, but it bloody well hurts.'

Jasmine braced herself to take another look at the wound. It was bad, very bad indeed. You couldn't see the cut for the pus that was oozing from it.

'Wash it under the tap, then put another dressing on it,' she said. 'Have you got a temperature?'

'I don't know,' he said, disgruntled, for which she could now forgive him.

The wound wasn't only bigger than it had been yesterday, Jasmine thought; it was as though his skin had split. The vile yellow substance was oozing from it; it had congealed with the blood on the plaster, but since he'd taken the plaster off it was now seeping from the wound even more, almost as if it had been released.

Jasmine dug out their first-aid kit and opened it. She took out the antiseptic cream, a fresh dressing and a thermometer, as Mark kept his hand under the running tap. Every so often he'd stop and look at it.

'Have you changed the plaster since yesterday?' Jasmine checked.

'No, it wasn't hurting this morning, so I left the plaster on. I thought I'd be able to take it off tonight.'

The cut was now about two inches long, when yesterday it had been no more than an inch. Perhaps his skin was tearing like an old person's did? Jasmine wondered. Perhaps he had an inherited condition that hadn't shown up until now?

Mark ran his hand under the tap for some time as the mixture of blood and pus seeped out. Jasmine glanced at it occasionally. She'd never seen anything so revolting in her life.

'If it's no better tomorrow, I think you need to go to the hospital,' Jasmine said.

'It'll have to be after work. I've got too much on,' he said glumly, and continued to hold his hand under the water.

'Up to you, but if it was my hand I'd get it seen to. These things have a habit of becoming infected.'

'I think it's already infected,' he said.

'You haven't got some glass still left in it?' she asked him.

He switched off the tap and looked closely at the wound. Jasmine refused to look as he prodded and poked, every so often crying out in pain. If it had been one of her children who'd been cut, she could have dealt with it, but not an adult.

'I can't see anything,' he said, and put it under the tap again.

Ten minutes later the oozing had slowed, and Mark held out his hand. Taking another deep breath, Jasmine smoothed on the antiseptic cream, then put on a lint dressing and finally covered it with a very large square plaster – the biggest in the box. Mark looked quite pale now and Jasmine suggested he go and relax in the living room.

'Let's take your temperature too,' she said, and fetched the thermometer.

It was only slightly raised, nothing to worry about, although she'd keep an eye on it.

'Do you want a paracetamol?' she asked.

'Yes, please.'

She went to fetch the packet from the kitchen.

'You'd better make it two,' he said, holding out his good hand.

She'd never known him to take medication before, priding himself on being very fit and healthy. It was an indication of just how much the cut hurt that he now requested two painkillers.

He swallowed the tablets with some water that Jasmine brought in. She then sat beside him on the sofa. The patio doors were still open.

'I was going to tell you about something strange that happened today,' she said at last.

'Yes?' Mark said, taking her hand in his good one.

'I phoned the removal firm this morning and put in our claim for the box of breakages. The woman I spoke to asked for a photo, which I sent. She called me fifteen minutes later.' Jasmine paused.

Mark looked at her. 'And what?'

'The Morgans who used to live here had put in the exact same claim when they moved in, for a box of broken frames, nothing else.'

'I would think it's the most likely thing to get damaged,' Mark said, slightly dismissive.

'But all their breakages had a diagonal line running from the top-left corner to the bottom right, just like ours did. I thought the firm might be trying to pull a fast one, you know, to escape paying the claim, so I asked for a photo of the Morgans' breakages. She sent it. Here it is.'

She picked up her phone and showed him the two photographs, side by side.

'Perhaps that's how framed pictures break?' he suggested.

'It's not. I googled it. No one else seems to have experienced anything like this before. I'm not sure if the company is going to honour our claim or not. But don't you think it's odd?'

Yet sitting in their living room on a pleasant June evening with the patio doors open, it didn't seem so odd at all. She was starting to think that maybe she'd overreacted, and that the breakages were accidental after all. She looked up at Mark. He had his head resting on the back of the sofa and his eyes were half closed. He looked so lost and vulnerable, childlike, when he was going to sleep. Her heart went out to him. She loved him so much. This was the move that was going to make everything all right again.

She touched his arm, and he murmured slightly but didn't open his eyes. She continued to gaze at him, then down at his hand. The plaster was clean. Before long, his breathing changed as he went into a deep sleep. His head lolled to one side. She took away her hand and reached for the remote and switched the television off. Mark didn't stir and slept on beside her, then after some time she went into the kitchen to clear up the dinner things.

Going back into the living room, she silently closed the patio door and switched on the television again. She watched a film with Mark asleep beside her the whole time, and at ten o'clock she switched off the TV and gently woke him.

'Time for bed, sleepy head,' she said.

He rubbed his eyes and, still in a stupor, stood, went upstairs and into the bathroom. Jasmine went up too, checked on the girls, then pulled the curtains in her bedroom closed and got changed into her night clothes. Mark appeared and got gratefully into bed with a sigh. By the time she'd finished in the bathroom, he was fast asleep again.

As she lay there in the still of the night she thought about the picture frames and decided that while it was an odd coincidence – the contents of both boxes breaking in exactly the same place – she supposed it wasn't impossible. Like Mark had said, maybe that was how pictures broke when dropped. It was strange that she couldn't find anything online about it, though. Very strange indeed. Most topics were talked about on the internet at length.

TWELVE

'My hand! Look at it!' Mark cried.

It was 6.30 the following morning, and although Jasmine didn't have to get up yet, Mark did. He had an early start at work. He'd come from the bathroom, where he'd taken off the plaster, and was holding his hand. Unable to believe what he was seeing, he turned to his wife.

'Look at it,' he said again, and thrust his left hand under her nose.

Jasmine opened her eyes expecting to see the worst, but as she looked, she couldn't see anything beyond a faint pink scar. The wound had completely healed during the night. She stared at it in disbelief. She'd seen it the previous evening, red and oozing. There was no way it could have healed in ten hours, it was impossible. She sat up in bed.

'It must be that antiseptic cream that came with the first-aid kit,' Mark said, still examining his hand. 'I thought I'd be going to the hospital tonight. In fact, I was sure of it.'

'So was I,' Jasmine said, as perplexed as he was.

The cream couldn't heal a wound that quickly, Jasmine thought, continuing to stare at his hand.

'It just shows what a good night's sleep can do,' Mark said happily, and he went to get dressed.

Jasmine lay back on her pillows and tried to close her eyes to think straight. Did angry wounds heal themselves in under ten hours? She had no idea, but she didn't think so. In which case, what had happened to make it heal? Was a good night's sleep really the answer, as Mark had said? She lay there thinking of the possibilities and soon her mind went to the box of broken photographs that were the same as the Morgans', the wasps concealed in the bunch of flowers, and finally Mark's cut hand. It had all happened in a little over a week, since they'd moved in.

She lay there listening to the sounds of Mark getting dressed in the bathroom, then, as he called out bye, ready to go, she got up. A fresh day, she thought. She'd take the girls to school – she would continue to do this for as long as they wanted her to, then, when they were ready, they could get the bus – and once she was home, she would need to water the plants in the garden. She opened her bedroom curtains and looked out on another glorious day. They'd watered the plants well when they'd bought them and put them in the beds, but they would need watering again today. They hadn't had any rain for some time and none was forecast. Their roots wouldn't be as established as older plants yet, she'd read. She'd spend fifteen minutes watering the plants and could still log in for work on time at 9 a.m.

She got dressed, woke the girls and put out fresh school uniforms for them.

'We've got a test today,' Isabel said mournfully, rubbing her eyes.

'I know. You did some revision last night.'

'But that's not enough,' she said, and pulled a face.

Isabel could worry about school tests, just like she worried about other things.

'Just do your best,' Jasmine told her, and kissed her cheek.

Isabel took a while to get dressed and come downstairs, then said again that she was worried about the test. Leah, who was sitting at the table eating her breakfast, teased her by saying, 'Those tests are easy-peasy.'

Isabel began to cry, so Jasmine told Leah off. Isabel couldn't be persuaded to have anything for breakfast, just a drink of juice. In the car Jasmine told her again not to worry, that she'd be fine. Once they arrived at school, she took them both to the gate where Isabel spotted a friend and dashed over. 'Have a good day,' Jasmine called after her. Leah had already gone off to join her friends.

She returned to her car thinking how they'd all become unsettled by the move and that it was going to take time to adjust. Isabel was far more tearful now than she used to be, and Leah couldn't resist digging at her. Jasmine felt pretty unsettled too, if she was honest, more so than she'd anticipated. She guessed the girls must be feeling so much worse. It was strange, not knowing where anything was. That was only part of it, though. There was something else, she thought – all the odd happenings in the house . . . there was something unsettling that seemed to be affecting them all. They hadn't moved before and she had assumed that you just packed up, arrived and got on with your lives. Was that really it? Although the Morgans had recently painted the house, she and Mark wanted to paint it again. Perhaps the girls could help? Once it had their mark on it, they'd all start to feel better. She was sure of it.

She parked on the drive and let herself in the front door. Now she needed to water the plants. She went straight inside and then out through the back door, which was on the side of the house. She went down the short passageway and into the garden, then stopped dead and cried out in dismay. It couldn't be, it wasn't possible. She looked at the garden. All the plants were dead, shrivelled up beyond recognition. How could this be? She'd looked at them a number of times before she'd gone to bed last night and then again when she'd opened her bedroom curtains this morning. They were alive then, surely? She would have noticed if they were dead. How could they have died while she'd taken the girls to school? It wasn't possible, was it?

Jasmine began walking down the garden alongside the flowerbeds. All the plants looked the same. They'd put in a mixture of flowers and vegetables, and they had all died in under an hour. She blinked. Was she dreaming? All that money they'd spent and the time they'd taken to plant them. What had they done wrong?

She continued to walk around the garden, unable to believe what she was seeing. It was almost as if someone had intentionally sprayed the plants with weed killer. Was that feasible in such a small space of time? she wondered. There was a strange smell in the garden too. Was that weed killer? She had no idea, and anyway, who would do such a thing?

She went to the side gate. It was still closed and the bolt was drawn. But, of course, the fence was only six feet high – low enough to climb over if someone was determined. Had a neighbour watched them leave this morning and, aware the house was empty, quickly climbed over the fence and sprayed all their plants with weed killer? Or maybe it had been done during the night? Weed killer wasn't instant, was it? It took some hours to work.

She stood at the bottom of the garden and looked over to her neighbours' houses. She didn't know the people on one side and Poppy lived in the other. She hadn't seen her or her family since she'd brought round the flowers. Could she or one of her sons have killed off all the plants in their garden? It was possible, although she didn't think they had the malice in them. She looked from Poppy's house to the other neighbour's. As she did so, she thought she saw the outline of someone darting behind their bedroom curtain. Was there a person up there watching her now? She couldn't be sure. She stood there looking, but there was no one there any more. Time to introduce herself, she thought.

Angry that someone had done this to their plants, Jasmine marched down the side passageway, out the front and down their neighbour's front drive. A car was parked on the drive, so she guessed someone was in. With her heart racing from anger and distrust, she rang the doorbell and waited. After a few moments a middle-aged woman answered.

'Can I help you?' she asked.

'I'm Jasmine. We've recently moved in next door.'

The woman nodded.

'I wonder if you know anything about my plants,' she said, trying but failing to keep a note of accusation out of her voice. 'They've all died overnight. Every single one.'

'Have you watered them?' the woman asked, barely able to conceal a small smile.

'I was going to, but when I got home I found them all dead.'

'I'm afraid I can't help you. I know people struggle to grow things around here. It's the soil. We persevered and now our garden is fine. I don't think the people who lived in your house before bothered with the garden.'

Jasmine looked at her. Could that be the explanation? That the soil wasn't right? Was there a rational explanation to this? She suddenly felt very foolish.

'Try composting it first,' the woman added, and began to close her door.

'Yes, I will. I'm Jasmine,' she said. 'Sorry for barging over here.'

'Sandra,' the woman replied, and the door shut.

Jasmine stood there wondering if she should ring the bell again and explain that she wasn't usually this dotty, but she'd just had a big shock. She decided against it. The woman would only ever be distantly neighbourly now, so she'd blown it. She walked away, downhearted, and returned home. Mark often said she acted impulsively, with no thought of the consequences. She'd seen the garden, had immediately jumped to the wrong conclusion and rushed round to the neighbour's house to accuse her.

She stood at the living-room window looking out over the garden. She hadn't got as far as asking the woman about weed killer, thank goodness. She'd already come across as completely mad. She needed to get a grip on her disappointment.

Jasmine made herself a coffee, took it through to the study and sat down. She logged on to her computer. It was 9.45, which didn't really matter as the office worked flexi-time. She usually logged in at 9 a.m. She tried to concentrate, but her thoughts kept returning to the garden and what Mark would say about it. There was no point in buying more plants until they'd worked out what had gone wrong first and fixed it. Was it that it had never been composted? She read about the benefits of composting online, but surely that just made for bigger and better flowers and vegetables? It didn't mean they all died without it. She glanced behind her at the garden. It looked post-apocalyptic, with rows of dead plants, the bare fence and a patch of lawn in the middle. She wanted Mark to see it. She'd tell him as soon as he came home from work.

When Jasmine collected the children from school, she listened to their news first, then told them that the plants in their garden had all died. They weren't very interested until they were home and saw them. They had wanted to play in the garden but quickly changed their minds.

'Why don't you pull them all up?' Leah asked.

'I will do once your father has seen them,' Jasmine replied.

'Why?'

'Because if he doesn't, he'll blame me. It's not something you see every day – plants that have died in the space of an hour.'

'Who killed them?' Isabel asked, looking through the patio doors.

'No one. I'm not sure. It's something I have to discuss with your daddy.'

'Did you water them?' Leah asked. 'Our teacher told us we had to water the beans we planted at school.'

'I was going to water them this morning when I got back from school, but they had died by then.'

Neither of the girls wanted to play in the garden among the dead plants.

'It's like zombie land,' Leah said a while later, which described it perfectly, Jasmine thought.

So they stayed indoors on a beautiful summer afternoon and played in their bedrooms until dinner was ready. Then they began their homework on the table downstairs so Jasmine could help them if needed.

Mark arrived home from work shortly after 6.30. He called 'hi' from the front door and went straight upstairs to change out of his office suit.

'Did you water the plants?' he asked Jasmine as he came down.

'I didn't get a chance. I came back from school to find them all dead. I'm sure they were all right first thing this morning.'

He went straight outside before he'd eaten. Jasmine went too. He walked down the path, stopping every so often to examine a plant. He looked at what was going to be his vegetable patch.

'I rushed next door and accused the woman who lives there,' Jasmine admitted sheepishly. 'She's called Sandra. I thought someone might have poisoned them.'

'I don't know why they've died,' Mark said, baffled. 'I'll give them a good drink before I eat and we'll see what they're like tomorrow. It's a pity you didn't water them this morning.'

'But they're all dead!' Jasmine exclaimed, looking incredulously at the rows of plants.

'Maybe they'll revive with a drink,' Mark said, and he went to fetch the hose pipe.

Jasmine went indoors and watched him through the patio door as he watered the plants. The ground was soaking wet by the time he'd finished, but the plants were still dead. He came in. Jasmine went to the kitchen and served dinner, leaving the girls watching television in the living room. They'd already had theirs, so she and Mark sat at the dining table alone to eat. He wanted to talk about work and Jasmine listened, although she kept looking at the plants. They're not going to revive, she thought. They're all dead.

Their evening proceeded and they checked on the plants before they went to bed – as much as they could in the dark – through the window upstairs. They didn't look much better, and Jasmine talked about replacing them that weekend.

'We'll see what they're like in the morning,' Mark said.

They made love that night, quick and to the point, and when Mark got up in the morning and opened their bedroom curtains, he was delighted with what he found. 'Excellent,' he said. 'Watering the plants has made a huge difference.'

Jasmine got up and went to the window. About half the plants had fully revived and another quarter were well on their way.

'Do you think water was all they needed?' Jasmine asked, bewildered.

'Yes, of course. I have to go to work now, but I want you to water them all when you get back from taking the girls to school. OK?'

He looked at her and Jasmine nodded. She could see the plants were recovering; it was why that bothered her. 'I'll do it now while the girls are still asleep,' she said, and got dressed.

It was 7 a.m. as she pulled on trousers and a sweater and went outside. It was so quiet at this time; only the June birds were busy. She unravelled the hose, switched it on and began watering the plants. It was going to be another hot day. As she worked, she caught sight of Mark moving around their bedroom, getting ready to leave. Her gaze drifted to their neighbours. Poppy's curtains were still closed, but Sandra's were open wide. Jasmine glanced over every so often as she watered but there was no sign of Sandra. Once she'd finished she returned indoors, said goodbye to Mark and woke the children.

'The plants are looking much better,' she told them happily as they came downstairs for breakfast.

Leah went to the window. 'Yes,' she cried. 'What made them sick?'

'I honestly don't know,' Jasmine said. 'I'm sure they were all dead yesterday – you saw them too. They looked dead for sure. But we've watered them, and they seem to be recovering.'

'So did watering make them come alive again?' Isabel asked.

'It would seem so,' Jasmine replied.

She thought about it as she made breakfast and then drove the girls to school.

THIRTEEN

Jasmine thought about the plants coming alive again as she drove home. They had certainly been dead yesterday morning and all through the day. She'd looked out of the window enough times, and she knew a dead plant when she saw one. Was it possible she could have imagined they were all dead? Maybe they had wilted from lack of water, but hadn't been dead yet? She thought about them constantly and, once home, went straight outside and watered the garden again. As she did, she glanced up at Sandra's window and saw her standing there watching her in full view. Cheeky moo. Jasmine didn't know whether to wave or not. Was Sandra just being friendly?

She looked away and concentrated on watering the plants, aware that Sandra was observing her. All the plants needed was a drink of water, she thought. Sandra had asked her yesterday, with a barely concealed smile on her face, if she had watered them. She kept the hose trained on the plants and twenty minutes later, once the earth was sopping wet, she switched it off, glancing up at Sandra, who was still standing there, and then returned indoors.

She kept glancing out of the window at the plants for most of the morning, and then at lunchtime, with the sun high in the sky, she gave them another good drink. By the time she left to fetch the girls from school they had all recovered and were standing up straight, not shrivelled and dead at all. She couldn't make it out and decided to put the matter from her mind for now. The plants were well again and that was all that mattered.

The week passed, the shed was delivered as arranged on Friday morning in large pieces, then three men arrived an hour later to erect it. Jasmine oversaw most of it, taking the men tea and biscuits and praising their good work. They finished around 2 p.m. so that by the time the girls and then Mark arrived home it was fully erect and the men had gone. Mark usually came home early on a Friday. The shed was painted duck-egg blue. The girls didn't say much about it – it was, after all, a shed – but Mark was far more garrulous.

'Excellent. I'm really pleased,' he said. 'It looks bigger in our garden than it did on their site.' He went down the garden to look at it – inside and out. 'It's a fine evening. After we've eaten, let's get all the things in there.'

He returned indoors, changed out of his suit, gobbled down his dinner, and was ready to load the shed. The girls wanted to help, and they had the weekend to do their homework, so they were allowed to. They took their bikes in there, then their other large play equipment and Mark's tools. The shed was only a fraction full. They hadn't owned a shed before. There'd been no option to, living in a rented flat.

'We'll go shopping tomorrow and buy a lawn mower now we have space to store it,' he said. 'And a large fork, spade, hoe, and whatever else we need. It will soon fill up. Perhaps we'll buy some paint to decorate the house, and we can keep that in there. Although painting is best left to winter.' He was like a child in a sweetshop, Jasmine thought. The girls were delighted too.

They went to bed that night a very happy family, planning their next day. Jasmine thought how much they'd achieved in the two weeks since they'd moved in.

On Saturday morning they were up early, and after breakfast they got into their car and went out to purchase a lawn mower and gardening equipment. They bought a lot more than they'd anticipated, including a rake, a kneeling mat and an arch that had to be assembled for growing a clematis around it. The lawn mower would be delivered on Monday.

Once home, Jasmine made lunch while the girls helped their father put what they'd bought into their shed, and assemble the arch for the clematis they had yet to purchase. The plants had all fully recovered now and Jasmine was pleased. She'd make sure it didn't happen again. Even Mark's vegetable patch seemed to be doing well, and he was delighted. He spent time out there looking at the plants to see how much they'd grown.

'We'll be eating our own produce this summer,' he said, and Jasmine smiled happily.

It rained heavily at one o'clock that night. It was the first proper rain they'd had since they'd moved in, and it woke Jasmine. She lay there listening to the sound of the rain pounding on the roof and against the window. At one point there was a flash of lightning, followed by a loud clap of thunder – a proper storm. It woke Isabel too, who cried out. Jasmine immediately got out of bed and went to her. She was lying with the duvet pulled up over her head, crying out for her mother. Jasmine gently eased it down. The poor child was petrified.

'I saw her again,' she suddenly cried, sobbing. 'She came into my room. That wicked witch in her grey jumper and green trousers.' She pulled the duvet up to her chin.

'It's OK, love,' Jasmine soothed. 'It was the flash of lightning that created the pictures when you were half asleep.'

'No, the woman was in here,' Isabel insisted. 'I saw her at the window.'

Jasmine assumed that Isabel was remembering Sandra looking down on her while she'd been playing in the garden, which they had been doing most afternoons that week on returning from school.

'It's all right,' she soothed again. 'There's nobody here.'

'She told me you mustn't put the shed at the bottom of the garden.'

What a vivid imagination the child had, Jasmine thought. She kept stroking Isabel's brow, reassuring her it was all right, and eventually her eyes closed and she returned to sleep. The storm had passed now, leaving the air still and quiet. Jasmine returned to her bed wide awake and thought about what Isabel had said. She seemed fixated on the shed; that was the second time she'd spoken of it in the same negative way. Jasmine eventually put it from her mind and fell into a fitful sleep.

On Monday morning a letter addressed to Mr and Mrs Simmons arrived. Jasmine opened it. It contained a cheque for £50. Jasmine read the letter, which was from the removal firm they'd hired.

> *Dear Mr and Mrs Simmons,*
>
> *Please find enclosed a cheque to the value of £50 to cover your box of breakages. This will be in final settlement.*
>
> *Yours faithfully*

It was signed by the manager.

It was less than they'd applied for, but Jasmine was pleased. She'd doubted they'd get anything from the company after the woman's comments about the Morgans also putting in a claim. She'd made it sound like a conspiracy. Smiling to herself, she returned the letter and cheque to the envelope and propped it up for Mark to read when he got home from work. She then got on with her own work at her computer until the doorbell rang at lunchtime. It was the lawnmower company. She showed them down the side passageway towards the shed at the bottom of their garden. They unwrapped the lawnmower and assembled it, all within twenty minutes. They started it and, once Jasmine was satisfied it was all in working order, they put it in the shed. Jasmine signed the delivery note and began to see them out. As she left the garden she glanced up at Sandra's window and saw her standing there watching her again. She must have seen the large van pull up and wondered what they were doing.

Once she'd seen the men out, Jasmine went indoors and texted Mark to say the lawnmower had arrived and was working fine. She didn't hear back from him, and it was 7.30 p.m. before he arrived home, stressed from work. He'd had a very busy day, but was pleased with the cheque for £50. He hadn't thought they'd get anything either. The girls had already eaten but they sat with him as he ate, then afterwards he went outside to cut the grass while Jasmine put the girls to bed.

'We want to help him,' Leah moaned.

'At the weekend. You've got school tomorrow,' Jasmine reminded her, and continued ushering the girls into bed.

She went downstairs, and found that Mark had returned from cutting the lawn.

'That woman next door – Sandra, is it?' he asked her. 'She's been at her upstairs window watching me the whole time I've been mowing the lawn. I waved, but she moved back and just disappeared into her room.'

'Now you know what I've been dealing with,' Jasmine said.

He nodded.

'I was thinking of buying some fast-growing shrubs for that side of the garden,' Jasmine said.

'Good idea. I guess it's because we're new here,' Mark replied. 'She'll get fed up of watching us after a while.'

Jasmine agreed.

'Do you ever see our other neighbour, Poppy?' Jasmine asked.

'Sometimes. I saw her on the way in tonight. She said hi.'

'Anything else?'

'Not really. I said they'd have to come round one evening for dinner.'

'Sure,' Jasmine said, offering no real commitment, and left it at that.

But that was a change, she thought. Mark didn't normally like that type of socialising. She had no wish to see Poppy again, though, and hopefully Mark would forget it before too long. He returned to the garden to water the plants; the sun was dropping now. Even with the rainstorm, they didn't want to take any chances by underwatering the plants. Jasmine sat in the living room and watched him through the window. She saw him glance up at Sandra's window. When he came in he said, 'She's a funny woman. She appeared again. I think we need to get some of those shrubs planted quickly.'

FOURTEEN

'I think it's time you told them,' James Morgan said to his wife. 'Or at least gave them an indication of why we left the house. They must wonder, given that we were only there eighteen months.'

'I suppose she'll know we haven't moved far away – it's going to be difficult to keep avoiding her,' Freya said.

'So tell her, rather than having to keep running to your car in the supermarket. It can't do us any harm now. We're out of there. And who knows? They might not have experienced the same thing. I think back sometimes and wonder if it really happened at all.'

'It did,' Freya said forcefully. 'You weren't in the house all day. Their daughter felt it, I'm sure of it.'

'I'm just pleased we don't have the problem now,' Madison put in. 'The whole thing was so creepy. Do you remember how that priest who came to see us thought I was the one causing the problems? A poltergeist, he said. I looked it up online.'

'What did it say?' Freya asked.

'They're a kind of spirit that manifests itself through noises, knockings and moving things. Some people think they're caused by teenagers; that's what that silly priest was thinking. But it wasn't anything to do with me. Honestly, it wasn't.'

'I know, Madison,' Freya said, and then she paused. 'We'll get over it in time. We've got a six-month lease on this place, one month has gone already. I'll need to start house-hunting again.'

'Good idea,' James said with a hint of derision. He was out at work all day. 'The sooner we move into our permanent home the better, a long way from here. This place is costing me a fortune.'

'All right!' Freya said with attitude. 'I'll start looking tomorrow. I promise you.'

It was now Wednesday, just over four weeks after they'd moved in, and Jasmine had the day off work. She only worked four days a week, so usually took Wednesdays off. She'd taken the children to school and returned home, intent on having some 'me' time. The garden was coming along and apart from Sandra, who insisted on looking out at them, they had nothing to complain about.

She made herself a coffee, sat down with it in the living room and switched on the television. She hadn't watched daytime TV since they'd moved in and she adored the cooking programmes. Fifteen minutes later the doorbell rang. She put down her coffee and went to answer it.

'Good morning, I'm Father Tim Ashridge,' the man said. He was wearing a clerical collar.

Oh, no, Jasmine thought. Poppy had warned them this might happen. That she could expect the priests from the main denominations to call on her at some point after they'd moved in with a welcoming message. Give it a month, she'd said, and they'd all laughed.

'I thought I'd pop in and make sure you're all right,' he said. A man in his forties, he had an earnest expression on his face.

'Yes. We're all fine, thank you,' Jasmine said, determined not to invite him in unless she had to.

He looked at her. 'I'm pleased. It seems the house settled down when the previous owners moved out. The Morgans asked me to pay you a visit.'

Jasmine felt the smallest frisson of fear run down her spine.

'I'm sorry, I don't understand. I thought you were from our local church?'

'Oh, no, I was called in by Mr and Mrs Morgan. I'm from the Bureau of Exorcism.'

'Exorcism?' Jasmine repeated, her stomach clenching.

'Yes. That's correct,' he said matter-of-factly. 'We're made up of a small number of priests from various denominations. We practise exorcism away from our main church calling. We don't get many cases, but the Morgans felt they needed some help.'

'Did they?' Jasmine asked. She stared at him in disbelief, hesitated, then asked him to come in. She showed him through to their living room and switched off the television.

'You've made the place nice,' he said. He looked around and sat down.

'Would you like a coffee?' Jasmine asked nervously.

'No, thank you.'

She sat down and looked at him carefully.

'You've settled in well,' he remarked again.

'Thank you,' Jasmine said and waited. He wasn't very forthcoming. 'You mentioned the Morgans asked you to come here?' she prompted.

'That's correct.'

'Can you tell me why?

'They weren't here very long, and they had previously been in touch with me about some unusual activity they couldn't explain. They thought you might have experienced something similar.'

Jasmine became increasingly uncomfortable. 'Did you find anything?' she asked.

He smiled resolutely. 'That's not how we work. I was asked to come here to make an assessment, then I had to get permission from my senior. I returned a week later and we all said some prayers.'

'And that was it?' Jasmine asked.

'Oh, no, I came back regularly. Every month. More often if they'd experienced a lot of activity. At one point I thought their daughter might be responsible for some of it, but it was never proved. I take it you haven't experienced anything unusual?' he asked.

Jasmine gave a brief shake of her head. To admit what they had experienced would give credence to the strange occurrences.

'That's good,' he said. 'I'm pleased. We must have done our job well.' Another small smile. 'I'll leave you with one of my business cards. Give me a ring if you need me.'

He took a card from his pocket and handed it to her.

'So, there's definitely nothing I can help you with today?' he asked, glancing around the living room again.

'No, thank you. We've settled in fine, as you can see.' Did she want to know more about his activities? No. She certainly didn't.

He gave a small nod. 'It's a nice area around here. Do you have children?'

'Yes, two girls.'

'Lovely,' he said.

They continued to make polite conversation for a few minutes, then he stood. Jasmine went with him to the front door and saw him out.

Her heart was racing and her cheeks burning as she returned to the living room. Yes, they'd had a few strange experiences, but nothing that merited getting a priest involved in an exorcism. She hadn't even realized priests still carried out exorcisms. But what about the Morgans? They had never mentioned that they'd had a priest visit them regularly, and Jasmine was annoyed. But if they'd told her, would it have made any difference to them buying the house? She doubted it would have. They had loved the house from first seeing it and were determined to make it their home. She forced what the priest had said from her mind. Mark would laugh at the notion, and it would worry the girls.

So much for the 'me' time, Jasmine thought, and she got on with her day. Despite her best intentions, however, her thoughts kept returning to the priest and what he'd said. Then it was time to collect the girls from school. She said nothing to them about the priest's visit.

When Mark returned home from work it was around 6 p.m., and the first thing he said was, 'You've had a priest here today?'

Jasmine nearly dropped the cooking pot she was holding.

'What made you say that?' she asked.

'Poppy. She recognized him from his visits.'

'Oh, I see. Did he ever visit her?' Jasmine asked.

'I've no idea. She just saw me coming in and called over. What did he want?'

'Just to welcome us into our new home and make sure we were all right. The Morgans asked him to visit us.'

Mark laughed. 'I guess we'll get the others visiting before long too,' he said. 'Just as Poppy said we would.'

'I guess we will,' Jasmine replied, unsure of what else to say.

It was the following Saturday. Jasmine was at the supermarket, and while walking up and down the aisles she spotted Freya Morgan a little way in front. Like her, she'd come early without her family. Jasmine kept walking, following her a few paces behind. She considered turning the trolley around and heading in the opposite direction but instead continued going in a straight line. Freya was now a shopper but one in front of her. After a few moments she stopped and began examining the tins on the shelves. Jasmine caught up.

'Freya,' she said. 'Fancy seeing you here.'

'Jasmine,' Freya exclaimed, turning. She immediately went red.

'How are you?' Jasmine asked, with feigned light-heartedness.

'We're all OK. How are you? Settling in?'

'Yes. Thank you. I've seen you in here before.'

'Really?'

There was now an awkward silence when neither of the women knew what to say. 'I'd better be getting off then,' Freya said, and she began to walk away.

'We had a priest visit us on Wednesday,' Jasmine called after her. 'It was about an exorcism.'

Freya stopped and Jasmine took the few steps forward to catch up with her.

'He thought we might need his help,' she added, watching Freya carefully.

Freya looked at her. 'And do you?' she asked, which took Jasmine by surprise.

'I don't think so,' she replied. 'Did you, when you lived at 13 Ravens Lane?'

Freya opened and closed her mouth, then said, 'That's all right then.' And continued wheeling her trolley away.

Jasmine stayed where she was, wanting to continue

the conversation, but not knowing what else to say. The supermarket was very busy with shoppers.

'Perhaps I can come and see you sometime,' she called after her, but Freya didn't answer. With a new firmness in her gait, Freya kept pushing the trolley up the aisle, then turned left into the next one. Clearly, whatever had happened in the past was just that as far as Freya was concerned. But seeing her preyed on Jasmine's mind.

FIFTEEN

'I saw Freya at the supermarket,' Jasmine told Mark as he helped her unpack the shopping. 'But she didn't want to talk.'

'No? Oh, well,' Mark said as he continued with the unpacking.

She didn't say anything further; there was nothing really to tell him, apart from the truth.

They had a pleasant day; the children played in the garden, riding their bikes and generally amusing themselves with their other toys. It was so much better not having to leave the flat to take them to a park to play every day. Isabel seemed to have forgotten her fixation on the position of the shed, together with the other nightmares she'd had, and played happily down the bottom of the garden. Mark tended his vegetable patch and watered the entire garden. By the time evening came they were all spent, and after dinner they sat and watched television together.

When it was the girls' bedtime Mark took them up to bed while Jasmine stayed on the sofa, feet up and stretched out, still watching TV. He often took them up at the weekends, and she thought it was no more than he should do as their father. She heard him go with them into the bathroom, then they went into Isabel's bedroom where he read them a story. From the rise and fall of his voice, she thought it was *The Secret Garden*, a story they all loved.

Then, as she sat there watching television, the temperature began to drop and Jasmine gave an involuntary shiver. She glanced out of the window. The sun had moved from the rear of the house to the side. Perhaps that was why? A moment later the sofa shuddered and the TV switched off. She grabbed the edge of sofa and felt it move again. It trembled for a few seconds, then stopped. Her feet were off the ground, spread along the sofa. She sat there, petrified, waiting to see if it would happen again, but it didn't. The room was still. Then the television came back on and the heat in the room rose. She looked around her, but the rest of the room was untouched.

Trembling, she slowly got off the sofa, bent down and looked beneath it. There was nothing to see there. The carpet was still in place. She felt for the feet on which the sofa rested, and they were all screwed on tightly. She stood and felt round the back and the ends of the sofa, then lifted up the cushions, but everything seemed normal. Yet it had moved for a few seconds. She was sure of it.

She went quickly upstairs to check on the girls and Mark, but they seemed all right. He was still reading to them. 'Did you feel that?' she asked him.

He shook his head.

'Feel what, Mummy?' Isabel asked.

'Nothing, love.'

Mark continued reading from *The Secret Garden* and Jasmine returned downstairs to check the living room again. Only when Mark returned from putting the girls to bed did she tell him.

'It happened just now,' she said. 'The sofa moved. I'm sure of it. The television went off and the temperature dropped. Did you really not feel anything?'

'No,' he said. 'I didn't. Are you sure?'

'Of course I'm sure. It was like a mini-earthquake,' Jasmine said, annoyed by his denial. She was still upset.

'Perhaps it was a mini-earthquake,' he said. 'I expect you're tired. Why don't you go to bed?'

She didn't like his dismissive attitude. 'I'm not that tired and I'm not hallucinating,' she said, irritated.

He went into the kitchen. 'Do you want a cup of tea?'

'No, thank you,' she said, still annoyed.

'I hope you're not filling the children's head with silly nonsense,' he called after her.

'It's not silly nonsense. It was real.' She strode up to the master bedroom and lay on the bed. She had felt the sofa move. She was sure of it.

She stayed on the bed, staring at the ceiling and thinking, for some time. Eventually Mark came up to her.

'I'm sorry, darling,' he said. 'Are you all right?'

She nodded but didn't look at him.

'Of course I believe what you told me, but the sofa moving? I mean, how far did it go?' he asked.

'I don't know. It wasn't that type of movement. It was more like a shake. It did move, Mark, honestly. I wouldn't make up something like this.'

'I know. I was just wondering if perhaps you dozed off and imagined it?'

Which, when Jasmine thought about it, she agreed was a possibility. She turned over and moved closer to him. He climbed onto the bed and put his arm around her.

'I want us to be happy here,' he said.

'I know. I'm sure we will be. I must have fallen asleep,' she said, for lying there in the crook of his arm, safe and secure, it seemed the only rational explanation.

She turned to him and offered her lips up, ready to be kissed and to make up, but at that moment they stopped dead. A distant rumble was coming from the room below – the living room!

'What was that?' Mark cried, and jumped off the bed.

Jasmine leapt off too and followed him downstairs as the rumbling continued. It was going on longer than when she'd experienced it earlier. As they approached the living room it stopped. The room was exactly as she'd left it, quiet and still. But there was a strange feeling in there, which Jasmine couldn't identify. She glanced at Mark, who had gone white. He was looking around, trying to work out where the noise had come from. They both stood there, looking at the sofa, and suddenly it moved again and stopped.

'What the hell!' Mark said, and he went over.

Jasmine followed him.

'It must be something in our sofa,' he said.

He moved it away from the patio doors and turned it over. He prodded and poked but couldn't find anything. He turned it back over again, so it was the right way up. His face was ashen. He went in and out of the study, but that was all as it should be. He then went outside. Jasmine followed him into the garden and they looked up at the back of the house for any sign of cracking or other instability. They couldn't see anything; it all seemed fine.

They returned indoors to the living room. Mark was clearly thrown by what he'd seen and, white-faced, went back to the sofa. He knelt down and saw the dents in the carpet where the feet had rested were not exactly lined up to where they had been. They were a few centimetres forward. He wasn't sure if he'd done that when he'd upturned the sofa, and tried to think. At that point Isabel cried out in terror from upstairs. 'Mummy! Daddy! Come quickly. She's here.'

Jasmine and Mark shot upstairs into Isabel's room. She was sitting up in bed, her eyes screwed shut, crying out loudly.

'I saw her again, I did, I did. She was in here,' she screamed, pointing at the corner of the room.

'Open your eyes,' Jasmine said. 'There's nothing for you to worry about now.'

'She was here. I saw her. I felt her. She touched me on my arm.' The child was hysterical and refused to open her eyes.

Mark came over and spoke to her more harshly. 'Isabel,

open your eyes now. Stop this. Do you hear me?' Jasmine thought he was still stressed from seeing the sofa move, but it did the job. Isabel slowly opened her eyes and looked around the room, then at her parents.

'She was here. I saw her,' she said again. 'She was wearing that same grey jumper and green trousers. I felt her touch my arm. She was very cold.'

'Enough!' Mark said. 'Whatever you think you saw has gone now.'

Isabel looked around the room as if half expecting to see something again.

'How do I know she isn't hiding somewhere?' Isabel asked, fresh tears forming.

'Where love? Where could she possibly be?' Jasmine asked, holding her daughter. 'I expect you saw Sandra from next door while you were playing in the garden. I've seen her standing at her bedroom window too, and she often wears a grey jumper.'

'No, no. It was a witch. I saw her,' Isabel cried, and burst into tears again.

Jasmine held her close while Mark left the room and returned downstairs.

Gradually Isabel's tears subsided and she lay, spent, in Jasmine's arms. Jasmine asked her, very quietly so Mark couldn't hear, 'Did you hear anything tonight, love?'

She nodded. 'When the witch spoke to me I heard a noise,' she said.

'What sort of noise?'

'Like something moving downstairs.'

Jasmine didn't know what to say. 'I want you to go to sleep now,' she said. Perhaps an external noise could be incorporated into a dream? 'Can you lie down for me?'

Isabel lay down. 'Will you leave my door open?' she asked. 'And the light on?'

'Yes, of course.'

Jasmine brought the duvet up to her chin.

'Why do I keep seeing her?' Isabel asked, her brow creasing.

'I think it's because you've become unsettled by the move,' Jasmine said honestly. 'It will all be all right soon. I know it will.'

'I want to live in our old flat again. Can we?' Isabel asked.

'No. That's not possible. You'll settle here soon. Give it a few more weeks and you'll be fine. Think of the lovely big garden we have here.'

'But it's got a witch in it. I want to live in the old flat.'

'Sshh, you're OK,' Jasmine soothed. 'Now close your eyes and soon you'll be asleep. It's very late.'

Isabel eventually closed her eyes, and Jasmine stroked her forehead until she gradually drifted off to sleep. It was about half an hour after Mark had left when Jasmine went out, dimming the light and drawing the door to a little. She checked on Isabel again about half an hour later. She was fine. This time, when she went downstairs, she found that the front door had been left slightly open.

'Mark?' she called, stepping outside. It was a clear night and the street was quiet.

'Come and have a look,' he said, suddenly appearing from behind the car. 'I've found the cause of the movement in the living room.'

He went to the side of the house and there on the floor were a number of slates from the roof, which had fallen off and now lay shattered on the floor.

'That's what caused it,' he said, triumphant. 'The tiles slipping from the roof.'

Jasmine stared at them, then up at the roof. She supposed it was possible. But the other possibility was that the ground beneath the sofa had moved and caused the tiles to slip.

'Tomorrow I'll buy some more tiles and replace them,' he said. 'I'll need to buy a ladder too.'

SIXTEEN

The following morning, Sunday, after breakfast, Mark took the girls shopping with him to buy the tiles and an extending ladder. They'd need a ladder from time to time now they owned a house anyway, and Mark didn't want to keep borrowing a neighbour's – assuming they even had one, of course. The girls wanted to stay with their mother and play, but Mark insisted they went with him.

'Your mother can have a rest this morning,' he said. 'She needs it.'

Jasmine was going to object and say the girls could stay with her but then thought better of it. She didn't need a rest, but there was something she wanted to do.

'Go with Daddy,' she encouraged them. 'You won't be long.'

Ignoring their grumpy faces, she saw them off in the car, waving until they were out of sight, then returned indoors. She went directly to the kitchen and picked up a large brown envelope, which had arrived yesterday. It was addressed to them both, but Mark had opened and closed it again, putting it aside for later. It was the final letter from their solicitor and contained the deeds to the house, and it was lengthy. She slid out the wodge of papers and began to look through them. She wasn't sure what exactly she was looking for, just something. She'd know if she found it.

She looked at the original sale of land deed and noted that the house was built on agricultural land, as most of them around there were. She examined the homebuyers' report again, which she'd already seen. There was nothing more to be gained from it. The house had been sold many times before, perhaps more than she would have anticipated, but she had no idea how long people stayed in houses for as a rule. She continued to leaf through the many papers.

Sometime later she finally came to the conclusion that there was nothing to be learnt from it, nothing they weren't already aware of, and returned the paperwork to the envelope. Then she went to her laptop in the study and googled their address. She learnt that the asking price over the years had gone up and that there was a fracking ban in the area, but there wasn't much else of interest. It was pretty much what you'd expect to find on a search of any house. She switched off her computer and went into the garden, down to the bottom where the shed was. She turned and looked up at her neighbours' houses, but there was no one there. The garden was nice now, but as she'd told Isabel, it would be a while before they all felt properly settled, maybe a few months. It was a nice house and the right move, she told herself for the umpteenth time. With hindsight, they felt better now than they had when they'd first arrived. She picked up the hose and watered the garden, then returned indoors.

Mark and the girls arrived back two hours later, and they were all excited by what they'd bought. 'Look at the roof of the car!' Leah cried with delight.

Jasmine went out the front to look. She saw the long ladder strapped to the roof of the car, sticking out over the bonnet and the boot.

'I'll need your help to get it off,' Mark said to Jasmine, taking out the tiles from the boot.

She helped him take the ladder off the car, then prop it at the side of the house. He checked it to make sure it was firm, then proceeded to climb up as Jasmine and the girls watched from below.

'Are you all right?' Jasmine called after him.

They couldn't see him now. There was no reply.

'You OK?' she tried again.

Mark appeared over the rooftop, looking very shaken.

'I'll need to go up into the loft,' he said, and began to climb down the ladder.

'Why? What's the matter?' Jasmine asked.

He came down and went indoors. Jasmine followed him in. 'Crows flew into the roof last night,' he said. 'Lots of them are dead.'

'Oh,' Jasmine said, shocked. 'How did that happen?'

'I honestly don't know.'

She followed him upstairs and onto the landing, where

he lowered the loft ladder and climbed up. They'd only been up there once before, just to check it over. Jasmine followed him to the top of the ladder but didn't go into the loft space. She didn't have to; she stared at the mess before her in absolute horror.

'How many are there?' she asked as Mark found and put on the light. She gave a cry of alarm. 'This couldn't have all happened last night.'

'I guess it did,' Mark said.

The floor was covered with a mass of large black crows. Not one was still alive, but they weren't rotting. 'It must have happened very recently,' she said, and saw daylight coming through the roof where they'd crashed through the tiles.

'Get me some large bin bags, will you?' Mark said.

Jasmine descended the loft ladder and went in search of some bags.

'What's the matter?' Isabel asked, coming into the kitchen.

'It's nothing for you to worry about. Some crows flew into the roof last night. It made the house shudder.'

'I heard that noise too,' Leah said. 'Do crows usually fly into roofs?'

'I don't know,' Jasmine replied. She found the rolled-up bin bags in a kitchen drawer, together with some rubber gloves.

'You go and play,' she told the girls.

She took the bags up the ladder to Mark.

'Don't come in,' he said, reaching his hand down through the loft opening.

She passed up the bags and gloves and returned to the foot of the ladder to wait, completely shocked by what had happened. She could hear Mark moving around in the loft, putting the dead crows into a bin bag. When the first bag was full he appeared at the loft opening and left the bag there, then disappeared inside again. He filled a second bag and put that with the first, then went back inside to check he had all the crows.

'How many were there?' Jasmine asked as he brought down the bags and then closed the loft hatch.

'I counted thirty-six,' he said solemnly.

He checked the knot in the bags and put them straight out the back door and into the bin.

'Thank goodness the bins are emptied tomorrow,' she said when he returned. 'I don't want that sitting around here for too long.'

She made a late lunch, thinking about all those poor crows that had died. It had been a large flock, and she guessed they'd all followed the first one in when it had crashed through their roof. Perhaps some of the tiles had already been broken. As she worked in the kitchen, Mark worked on the roof. She hoped it didn't happen again. Were crows like pigeons and kept flying into the same window? Not as far as she knew. It had only happened once since they'd moved in.

Half an hour later Mark appeared, having replaced the broken tiles and put the ladder away in the shed.

'I checked the rest of the roof while I was up there,' he said. 'The rest of the tiles seem fine. I guess a couple of them were already broken and the crows just flew into the roof without enough time to realize what they were doing.'

Jasmine turned to him. 'The only thing is, the broken tiles were on the side of the house. Am I correct?'

'Yes,' Mark said.

'So how could the crows have worked up enough speed to crash into the roof there? I mean, the house next door blocks their route down one side. And they'd have to turn if they were flying in from the front or down the other alleyway. It doesn't make sense.'

'I've wondered that too,' Mark said. 'But what other explanation is there? That one of the crows got in through a broken tile and the others followed and couldn't get out, thereby committing mass suicide? We didn't hear them moving around last night and they definitely all died recently.'

Jasmine nodded thoughtfully and then called the girls to eat. They'd only just sat down when they heard a loud crash on the roof.

'Oh, no!' Jasmine cried. 'Not again.' She jumped up from the table.

She rushed after Mark, out through the patio doors, where he began looking around. It wasn't long before he picked up a ball. A voice from Poppy's garden called, 'Can I have my ball back, please?' It was one of their lads.

'Yes, of course,' Mark said, relieved, and threw it back.

Jasmine began to laugh. Mark did too. They went indoors, where they continued to laugh. The tension had been building and their relief was palpable. Mark took her in his arms and kissed her, to the girls' dismay.

They went to finish eating and had just sat down when they heard a similar sound, followed by a voice outside.

'Sorry, can we have our ball back, please?'

Mark went in the garden and threw the tennis ball back. 'Try to keep it on your side,' he called.

But the lads didn't. Every few minutes while they ate, and after, as they sat in the living room, a ball could be heard banging on their roof. Mark threw it back to them straight away to begin with, then after a while began to keep them waiting for longer and longer. Each time he returned it, he asked them to keep their throws low. Finally, after some time, the game ended and Mark, Jasmine and the girls spent the evening in peace. When Mark went outside to water the plants that evening there were six balls in the garden, some of them quite hard.

'Maybe it was one of these that broke the tiles in the first place,' he said. 'I'll speak to Poppy and Harry about it. I don't want any more tiles broken.'

He collected the balls up and put them into a bag, ready to give back.

SEVENTEEN

On Monday morning Jasmine was sitting at her desk in the study. It was 10.30 when the doorbell rang. A woman who Jasmine guessed to be in her eighties stood there carrying a small bunch of flowers, the stems wrapped in newspaper.

'Hi, I'm Mrs Sullivan. I live next door but one, that way.' She pointed to the other side of Sandra. 'I picked these from my garden.' She handed the flowers to Jasmine.

'That's kind of you. I'm Jasmine. Would you like to come in for a short while? I'm working from home.'

'Thank you, dear.' She stepped into the hall. 'It's nice in here, isn't it?' she said, looking around, and made her way into the living room. 'Very nice. And you've got a study through there.' She peered in.

'Would you like a tea or a coffee?' Jasmine asked with a small smile.

'A tea, please,' she said, and sat in an armchair. 'It's a nice day today.'

'Yes, it is,' Jasmine said, and went into the kitchen to make the tea.

She put the flowers in water, then made their drinks. She supposed it was good of her neighbour to visit her and extend the hand of friendship. She just hoped she didn't stay too long, poor dear. She wasn't to know it was during her working hours. She made the hot drinks and put some biscuits on a plate, then carried the tray into the living room.

'That looks lovely,' Mrs Sullivan said.

'Good.'

Jasmine passed her the tea and offered her a biscuit.

'Thank you,' she said, taking one. 'You won't know but my husband, Bert, died a year ago and I get a bit lonely now.'

'I'm so sorry,' Jasmine said, sitting on the sofa beside her.

'He had an accident in the garden,' she said, taking a sip of her tea. 'You have to be very careful out there.'

'We are,' Jasmine said. 'That's shocking, though. I expect you miss him dreadfully.'

'We were married for forty-five years,' she said. 'I miss him every day. That's why I like to come to my neighbours' and see someone. We're not sure what happened in the garden. The coroner said he fell on his electric saw. I called an ambulance, but it was too late. It was pronounced an accident, but I don't believe them.'

'What do you mean?' Jasmine asked, setting her cup in her saucer.

'The saw had a cut-off on it so it should have stopped straight away, rather than slice him in half.' Jasmine winced at the image. 'The coroner said it must have got stuck, but she couldn't say how. It was tested and found to be working all right. The assumption was that it was something Bert did wrong, but I can't figure out what that could have been.'

'How dreadful,' Jasmine said. 'I'm so sorry for your loss.'

Mrs Sullivan concentrated on drinking her tea and eating her biscuit. Jasmine's heart went out to her. She seemed so lost and alone.

'We're doing up our garden,' Jasmine said brightly. Mrs Sullivan nodded. 'We've put in flowers and Mark, my husband, has begun a vegetable patch.'

'You won't be able to eat any of it,' Mrs Sullivan said.

'Why's that?'

'It'll go rotten at some point. That's what happened to the previous owners. I don't bother much with our garden now, except to grow a few flowers. Bert saw to all that. I have someone come to cut the lawn every two weeks. He's OK but he keeps putting up his prices.' She tutted and took another biscuit.

'It's the same everywhere,' Jasmine agreed. 'Prices going up and up.'

Mrs Sullivan nodded, then continued the conversation, slowly and sporadically, about the garden, her house, her only son who lived in New Zealand. She took out some photographs of her grandchildren, which Jasmine admired.

'I won't see them again,' she stated categorically, tucking the photos into her bag.

'Whyever not?' Jasmine asked.

'I'll be following Bert soon. Perhaps I'll go into the garden and wait for him there,' she said, and suddenly stood. 'Thank you for the tea and biscuit. I'll let you get on now with your work.'

'You're very welcome,' Jasmine said. 'Perhaps I could come to you next week?' she suggested.

Mrs Sullivan paused. 'Perhaps, but I don't think so. There won't be time.'

Jasmine gave a small smile, puzzled. 'What do you mean – there won't be time?' she asked. 'Are you going away?'

Mrs Sullivan didn't answer. She shook her head and made her way out, slowly down their front path, then along the street and up to her own front door. Jasmine watched her until she'd gone into her own house, then closed her front door. Poor old dear, she thought, and made a mental note to buy her some flowers or chocolates and call on her next week.

It was now midday. The morning had virtually disappeared. This was another problem with working from home – you were at the mercy of callers. She probably shouldn't have invited Mrs Sullivan in, but what else could she have done? She wanted to be friends with her neighbours.

She made her usual sandwich lunch and took it to her desk. Her computer seemed to have automatically shut down, so with a sigh she set about rebooting it, eating her sandwich while she waited. It took some time to reboot, there was clearly something wrong with it, as a number of error messages landed on her screen – but then it settled. It seemed to be working fine. She opened the file she'd been working on and thankfully everything was still there. She continued working until it was time to collect the girls from school.

'Have you had a good day?' she asked them in the car.

'Yes,' Isabel said and began to tell her all about it. Leah said nothing. She was still processing her school day and would tell her later about it, probably after dinner, which was what she usually did.

When they pulled into the road outside their house Jasmine's heart missed a beat. There was an ambulance parked further up outside Mrs Sullivan's home.

'I wonder who's ill,' Leah said.

'I want you two to go indoors and wait for me. I need to check on her.'

'What? All alone?' Leah asked, amazed.

'Yes. I won't be a minute. Now hurry up, please.'

She bundled the girls out of the car, unlocked the front door and let them into their house.

'One minute, stay inside,' she said, and closed the door.

She walked quickly up the pavement to Mrs Sullivan's house. The front door was closed and so too were the rear doors of the ambulance. She pressed the bell and waited. One of the paramedics opened the door.

'Is everything all right?' Jasmine asked. 'Only I saw Mrs Sullivan earlier today and she was fine then.'

'I'm afraid she's dead,' he said.

Jasmine stared at him in horror. 'But how? She seemed all right earlier when she visited me.'

'It looks like a cardiopulmonary arrest – a sudden heart attack. We found her in the garden. You're not the neighbour who called us, then?'

'No. It wasn't me. What a dreadful, dreadful thing to happen,' Jasmine said, shocked to the core. 'She didn't suffer, then, if it was sudden?'

'Not at all. She would have been dead before she hit the ground.'

'That's something, I suppose. Thank you,' Jasmine said, and left.

In a state of shock, she went back along the road, down her path and in her front door. Both girls were waiting for her.

'What's the matter?' Leah asked, as tears began down their mother's cheeks.

'The lady who used to live next door but one has suddenly died. I met her for the first time this morning. It was almost as though she had a premonition,' Jasmine said. Then she stopped herself from saying any more. She'd wait until Mark was home and tell him instead.

She couldn't concentrate on anything and was snappy with the girls as she kept running through Mrs Sullivan's visit that morning in her head. She'd said, *I'll be following Bert soon. Perhaps I'll go into the garden and wait for him there.* What had happened when she'd returned home? At some point during the afternoon she'd gone into their garden and had had a massive heart attack. Did she really have a premonition or did something else happen?

Jasmine shivered at the possibilities. She hoped she hadn't suffered, whatever had happened. She hadn't thought to ask the paramedic what time she'd died but the window of opportunity was very small. She'd left here shortly before twelve and was dead by three forty-five. The ambulance must have been called just before Jasmine returned home. It wasn't there when she'd left to collect the girls from school, so there was a three-hour opportunity. It was almost as if Mrs Sullivan had done it on purpose, somehow making the trip to see her first. Jasmine wondered if she'd been having chest pains for a while and hadn't thought to mention it. It was the most likely explanation.

She made and served the girls' dinner, then called them to the table. She had no appetite herself and would wait for Mark to come home before she ate. Leah now began to tell her about her day at school. Jasmine nodded while thinking of poor Mrs Sullivan dying alone in her garden. What had made her go into the garden to die? she thought over and over again.

Once the girls had finished eating, she loaded the dishwasher with their cutlery and china, then helped them with their homework. They were ready for bed when Mark arrived home; he was later than usual. They heard him come in and ran downstairs to kiss him goodnight before returning to bed.

'Sorry I'm late,' he said to Jasmine when she went down. 'I got held up in the Coleshaw branch.'

She nodded. This was one of the drawbacks of the promotion: he never knew which store he'd end his day in.

Sometimes it was very late when he arrived home. He went upstairs to change from his office suit while Jasmine pinged their dinners in the microwave.

'Thanks, that looks good,' he said, sitting with her at the dining table.

She looked at her dinner and watched him eating ravenously for a few seconds before she began.

'I had a strange visit this morning from Mrs Sullivan, who lived next to Sandra.' She picked up her knife and fork.

'Oh, yes?' he said.

'She just popped in on the off chance that I was around, as far as I can make out. We had a chat about things in general. She didn't stay long and left here just before twelve. Then, when I came home from collecting the girls, there was an ambulance parked outside her house. A neighbour must have called it. I knocked to see what the matter was and the paramedic said that she'd been found dead in her garden this afternoon.'

'Oh dear,' Mark said, and carried on eating.

'It must have happened between twelve and three,' Jasmine said. 'The thing is, she said something very odd while she was here – that her husband had died a year ago from an accident in their garden. Then she said, "I'll be following Bert soon. Perhaps I'll go into the garden and wait for him there." It was as though she had a premonition of her death. I've been thinking about it ever since.'

Mark looked up from eating.

'It's a coincidence, nothing more,' he said. 'These things happen all the time.' He continued eating.

Now she'd told him she began to doubt her own feelings. Mrs Sullivan was very old, after all, and could easily have died at any time. She was still suffering from her husband's death, and it was only natural to sit in the garden on a fine afternoon. If she had a heart condition, she could have been taken at any time, Jasmine thought.

'Yes, I suppose you're right,' she said, and finally began to eat. 'It was nothing more than a strange coincidence, that's all.'

Having talked to Mark about it and heard his rational view, Jasmine now felt much better. Although she didn't forget Mrs Sullivan, the incident lost some of its sinister feel and she was able to put it out of her mind and continue as normal, more or less.

The following morning, Poppy caught her on the way back from school and asked her if she'd heard about Mrs Sullivan.

'Yes, I have,' Jasmine said, going to the low fence at the front that separated their gardens. 'She came to visit me yesterday morning. I was really shocked to learn of her death in the afternoon.'

'It was her heart, you know,' Poppy said. 'Everyone around here expected her to go before Bert did. Bless her, at least it was peaceful.'

'Yes, thank goodness. I've been thinking about her a lot,' Jasmine said in a rush of relief. 'You never came for dinner. How about this Saturday?'

'That sounds good,' Poppy said. 'I'll check with Harry and let you know.'

'We'll make it early so you can bring the boys if you like.'

'Oh, no, I'll get a sitter. I'd rather. I see your husband coming in quite a lot in the evenings. I guess our paths cross.'

'Yes,' Jasmine said. 'I expect they do.'

It was important to get along with your neighbours, Jasmine told herself, and she continued indoors.

EIGHTEEN

'Poppy said they can make it this Saturday,' Mark said when he returned home from work the following day. 'It's nice of you to invite them. I didn't think you liked her.'

Jasmine shrugged. 'She just takes a bit of getting used to and we need to get along with our neighbours.'

'I agree,' Mark said. He kissed his wife, then went to change.

He was early this evening and was able to spend time with the girls, playing with them and then overseeing their schoolwork, before taking them upstairs to bed. When he came down again, Jasmine said, 'You were right about Mrs Sullivan. Her dying was a coincidence. Poppy said she had a heart condition.'

'I can see why it played on your mind, though,' Mark said. 'It must have been a big shock for you, having just seen her. If dinner isn't ready, I'll water the plants first.'

'It'll be about fifteen minutes,' Jasmine replied.

Mark disappeared out the back door and into the

garden. He returned almost immediately, looking very shaken.

'My vegetables are all dead,' he said. 'Come and see.'

Jasmine quickly turned off the hob and followed him into the garden. She saw the vegetable patch the moment she stepped outside; it was hidden from the house, a small patch of land to the left. The plants were now all shrivelled and brown. Immediately, her thoughts went to Mrs Sullivan, who said that this had happened before. Jasmine looked in dismay on what was left of the vegetables, then turned to her own flowers, which seemed fine.

'But I watered them all this morning,' she said, perplexed.

Mark was shaking his head and examining the plants.

'It's not a lack of water that's killed them all. The soil is still damp, and we haven't had much sunshine today. Something else has killed them, and very quickly.'

He pulled up a few of the vegetables and examined the roots. The lettuces, radishes and carrots were all the same – shrivelled to oblivion.

'I don't understand it,' he said. 'They've been growing fine until now – look at the roots. Not only have they stopped growing but they've all shrivelled up.'

Jasmine stared at them, bewildered. 'Shall we try watering them again?' she suggested.

'We can, but I don't think it will do any good, somehow. I'm no gardener but I know a dead plant when I see one. It's really strange.'

He fetched the hose pipe and gave all the vegetables a

good drenching. Jasmine stood by, watching him, hoping she wasn't to blame, although she didn't know what she could have done wrong. It was a dry day but there'd been very little sun. She'd watered them this morning and had thought how well they were doing. What could have killed them so quickly? She was no gardener either, but those plants were well established and shouldn't have died so quickly.

She watched Mark as he continued to water, then glanced up at their neighbours' houses. Sandra was standing at her upstairs window, watching them.

'I'm really getting fed up with seeing her there,' Jasmine said, looking away. 'How did she know we were out here?'

'She probably heard the water running. It's a fine evening and the windows are open.'

'Shall I wave?' Jasmine asked.

'If you want to.'

Jasmine looked up and gave a smile and a wave. Sandra immediately stepped back from the window and disappeared into the room.

'She's gone,' Jasmine said.

She glanced up every so often as Mark finished watering what was left of the vegetables, then he moved on to her plants. The vegetables didn't look much better, Jasmine thought. Her plants seemed to be doing all right, though. Every so often Jasmine glanced up towards Sandra's window, but she didn't reappear. Mark finished watering and they both went indoors.

'We'll see what the vegetables are like in the morning,' he said. 'But I'm not very hopeful, not at all.'

Jasmine finished cooking the meal and they ate. Later that night, shortly after it was dark, they went into the garden and checked on the vegetables. There was no difference. Sandra's bedroom curtains were drawn so Jasmine assumed she was in bed.

'Perhaps I should invite her to dinner?' she suggested as they returned indoors.

'Really?' Mark asked.

'Why not? I expect she's very lonely.'

'Up to you,' he said.

The following morning when they looked out of their bedroom window it was obvious all the vegetables were definitely dead.

'I'll get rid of them tonight,' Mark said.

Jasmine nodded solemnly.

It was eleven o'clock the next day before Jasmine took a break from work, during which time she summoned the courage to go next door to Sandra's and invite her to dinner on Saturday. No one answered. She knew she was in because she'd just seen her looking out of her upstairs window. She pressed the bell again and waited some more, but there was no reply. She came away. She'd try again later and then not bother again. Clearly, if the woman didn't answer, she didn't want to be friends.

Jasmine worked for an hour and a half more, then had a quick sandwich lunch and went to Sandra's again. She rang the bell and waited. All the windows at the back of the house were now open so she knew she was still in. Jasmine rang again, waited some more, then reluctantly walked away. As she did so, she glanced at the living-room window and saw Sandra standing a little way back, presumably thinking she couldn't be seen. She was wearing a grey top. Jasmine stopped on the pavement and stared at her. Should she go up to the window? And do what? If she didn't want to be contacted, it could be embarrassing, so she continued home. They were friends with Poppy and her family, so that would have to do.

The week flew by and early on Saturday morning Jasmine went to the supermarket without the girls to do a big shop. As it would only be adults tonight, she would cook adult food and had decided on chicken and potato gratin with a homemade parsnip soup to start. They could have individual cheesecakes for dessert. Perfect, she thought. They would arrive at 7.30 p.m., by which time the girls would be ready for bed, so they could say hi and go up. Poppy had suggested the time so she could get her boys ready before their sitter arrived.

Mark cleaned the house that afternoon as Jasmine worked in the kitchen. It was the first time they'd entertained since they'd moved in, and Jasmine wanted it to be as near perfect as possible. They were using their best Royal Doulton china and Arthur Price cutlery, only brought out for special occasions and Christmas. She spent most of Saturday cooking. The girls had to amuse themselves and were mainly in the garden. Mark had pulled up all the dead vegetables and planted some more carrot and sweetcorn seedlings he'd bought. 'A tester,' he said stoically. 'To see if they survive.'

By 7.30 they were ready for their guests. Jasmine had changed into a Lipsy floral dress and Mark had changed into clean jeans and an open-neck shirt. The girls were in their pyjamas. The bell went exactly on time and they all trooped to answer it. Jasmine's heart sank as she looked at the family with their two boys in tow.

'Sorry, my sitter let me down,' Poppy said, not appearing apologetic at all. 'The boys can play with your two in your playroom.'

'We haven't got a playroom,' Jasmine said.

They all came in and Poppy gave Jasmine a box of chocolates. The boys saw that the girls were dressed ready for bed and laughed.

'They've got their PJs on!' Liam cried.

'That's enough,' Poppy chastised. 'Where do they go to play, then?'

Jasmine looked at Mark. 'I supposed they could go up to one of the girls' bedrooms,' he said.

'Cool,' Liam said and shot upstairs.

'I'll go up and make sure the room is tidy,' Mark said.

'I wouldn't bother, mate. It won't be for long,' Harry said, and Poppy laughed.

Jasmine would have preferred it if Poppy had cancelled rather than bring her sons, but there was nothing they could do about it now. As Mark went upstairs with the children, Jasmine ushered Poppy and Harry into their living room and offered them a drink.

'A beer, please,' Harry said, taking in the living room.

'A glass of white wine for me, please.'

Jasmine left them admiring the room and went into the kitchen. She put the box of chocolates to one side and poured their drinks, still a little disgruntled that they'd brought the boys with them. Mark came downstairs.

'I've left them all in Leah's bedroom with the door wide open. I've told them to come down if they're bored or have finished playing.'

'What are they doing?' Jasmine asked.

'Just playing. I know it's not ideal, but they'll be all right.'

Jasmine thought it was far from ideal. 'I'll serve dinner straight away,' she said.

Mark took the drinks into the living room, leaving Jasmine to heat the soup. Poppy was laughing very loudly, but Jasmine couldn't hear what she was saying, just her high-pitched laugh. She'd only laid the table for four, although there was plenty of soup. She went through to the living room.

'I've made extra soup. Do you think the boys will want some? It's parsnip.'

'No. They've already eaten,' Poppy said, and continued talking to Mark.

Once the soup was fully heated, Jasmine asked them to come through to the table. It was obvious Mark had been telling them about their dead vegetables.

'We've never tried growing anything in our garden,' Poppy said. 'The boys would trample it down. Maybe when they're older, but we probably wouldn't try vegetables in any case.'

They sat at the table and Mark refilled Poppy's glass and asked Harry if he wanted another beer or a glass of wine.

'Another beer,' he said. Mark fetched it from the fridge. It was the same brand they'd drunk while at their place.

As they ate their soup and broke the rolls, they began to hear footsteps running across the landing, going from room to room.

'It sounds as though the kids are having fun,' Poppy remarked.

'I'll go and check on them,' Mark offered, meeting Jasmine's eyes, and he left the table.

As he neared the landing, the children must have heard him because there was a stampede of feet back to Leah's room. Jasmine glanced up at the ceiling. He was up there for a few minutes, then came down.

'I sent them out of our bedroom,' he said, returning to the table.

Jasmine wasn't pleased that the girls had gone into their bedroom. They knew they weren't allowed in there by themselves. Egged on by the boys, she thought. They'd just finished their soup when the footsteps started running about again. Jasmine looked pointedly at Mark.

'I'll go,' he said and went upstairs.

'That was delicious,' Poppy said, putting down her spoon.

'Yes, it was,' Harry agreed.

'Thank you,' Jasmine said. 'I've made chicken and potato gratin with fresh vegetables for the main course.'

'Not the vegetables from your garden, I hope,' Harry quipped. Poppy laughed loudly. She was tipsy, Jasmine thought, as she collected together the soup bowls and took them to the kitchen.

'You know you said Mrs Sullivan had passed away?' Poppy called over to her.

'Yes. On Monday.'

'Well, you must have misheard. I saw her yesterday. She'd just come out of hospital. She was in there for a few days. She had a funny heart. I nearly had a fit, seeing her.'

Jasmine stood very still, the colour draining from her face. She turned and looked at Poppy.

'But that's impossible. I couldn't have misheard,' she said. 'The paramedic told me she was dead before she hit the ground. He said they called it a cardiopulmonary arrest. He asked me if I was the neighbour who'd called them.'

'Well, she's definitely alive,' Poppy said with a small laugh. 'Perhaps it was someone else?'

Jasmine stood there staring. It wasn't, she thought. Poppy must be the one who'd misunderstood. She ran through in her mind what the paramedic had told her: *a cardiopulmonary arrest – a sudden heart attack. We found her in the garden. She was dead before she hit the ground. You're not the neighbour who called?* they'd said.

Mark reappeared. 'The children are back in Leah's bedroom. I've given them Monopoly to play with.'

'Mrs Sullivan isn't dead,' Jasmine told Mark. 'Poppy saw her.'

'She's definitely alive. I saw her yesterday,' Poppy confirmed.

'I suppose I must have misheard,' Jasmine muttered, and began putting the food into the serving dishes. Preoccupied, she nearly dropped one. She carried them to the table, gave everyone a dinner plate and told them to help themselves from the servers.

She was dead before she hit the ground, Jasmine thought, as she too sat at the table. Did paramedics ever make a mistake? she wondered. Had they just arrived at the property? Is that why they weren't sure? No, they'd called it a cardiopulmonary arrest so they must have examined her. It didn't sound as though they'd just arrived.

'I wonder who called the paramedics,' Jasmine said out loud, and stared at the untouched food on her plate.

'I've no idea,' Poppy said. 'This looks delicious.'

NINETEEN

By 9 p.m. Mark had had enough of resettling the children and brought them all down into the living room. He and Jasmine were clearly both hoping their guests would go soon – they could hardly put the girls to bed while the boys were there. Isabel and Leah were very excited to be downstairs so late. They were all hungry, so Jasmine went into the kitchen and made toasted cheese sandwiches, which Poppy said would give them nightmares. Jasmine didn't really care. The evening had been ruined by having the boys there and by what Poppy had told her about Mrs Sullivan. She was still thinking about it when, half an hour later, Poppy and Harry decided to leave. Poppy was very drunk and kept thanking her and Mark for a truly lovely evening.

'We've had a great time,' she said, kissing Mark for a second time.

He had to unhook her from his shirt while Jasmine and Harry gave each other a more neighbourly hug and said goodbye.

'Come on up to bed,' Mark said to the girls as he closed the front door. The boys could be heard shouting in the street outside, together with Poppy yelling at them to be quiet.

'We'll leave the clearing up until tomorrow,' Mark said, and began taking the girls upstairs.

'I'll stay down here for a bit,' Jasmine replied.

She'd hardly eaten a thing and hadn't really enjoyed the evening. She walked through the kitchen-diner to the patio doors and, opening them, went outside. It was a cool evening for July, but the air was still. She stood on the patio and looked up at the crescent moon high in the sky. What was the matter with her? Could she have misheard the paramedics? She thought about what they'd said again and then quickly returned indoors. She walked through the house, picking up her front door keys as she went. She let herself out and went past Sandra's house to Mrs Sullivan's. The curtains were all closed. They hadn't been before, she was sure of it. And there was a light on in the bedroom. Mrs Sullivan was in her room.

Returning home, Jasmine ran through again what she'd been told. A cardiopulmonary arrest – a sudden heart attack. We found her in the garden. She was dead before she hit the ground. She really didn't see how she could have misheard. But she must have done, for dead people didn't resurrect.

On Sunday morning, Mark and Jasmine cleared up the dinner dishes while the girls got up. They were later than usual this morning, but the girls said they'd enjoyed the dinner party and wanted to know when they could play with Hudson and Liam again. Leah's room was an absolute mess and Jasmine told them that after breakfast they were to tidy it. Leah moaned, then went off to do something else. Jasmine told her again, more loudly, and she and Isabel went upstairs and began tidying the bedroom. While they were up there, Jasmine baked a small Victoria sandwich cake for Mrs Sullivan. The woman was clearly alive, and a cake seemed the best way to visit her. She couldn't just call in and say, *Hi, I see you're still alive*.

Once the cake had cooled, she put it into a tin and, telling everyone she wouldn't be long, went down the street. In truth, part of her wanted to see Mrs Sullivan just to make sure she *was* still alive. The curtains were open again and Jasmine pressed the bell.

'Oh, it's you,' she said, opening the door with a smile.

Jasmine was delighted to see her looking so well.

'I've brought you a cake I made,' Jasmine said, and offered the tin to her.

'That's very kind of you, dear. Do come in.'

'I won't stay long,' Jasmine said. 'I've got everyone at home.'

She followed her down the hall. The house was similar to their own, but hadn't been updated. They went into the kitchen.

'Can you put it on the side, please?' she said. 'I'll take it out of your tin and let you have it back.'

'There's no need. We have plenty of tins,' Jasmine said,

and she put the cake where Mrs Sullivan indicated. 'I have to admit, it's a bit strange seeing you, though.'

'Why's that?' Mrs Sullivan asked.

'Well,' Jasmine said, not quite sure how to say it. 'I thought you'd passed.'

'Me?' Mrs Sullivan said, shocked. 'No, dear. Whatever gave you that idea?'

'On Monday when I arrived home from collecting the girls from school there were paramedics here. I came down to see what the matter was and one of them told me you'd been found dead in your garden. At least, I thought that's what he said.'

Mrs Sullivan laughed, then said, 'It's true, I had a funny turn on Monday afternoon. Sandra saw me in my garden and called an ambulance. The paramedics took me to A&E. I stayed there until Wednesday. But I'm not dead, as you can see.'

Jasmine smiled warmly. 'I'm very glad to see it. I'd better be getting back, then.'

'Yes, dear. I'll pop in and see you from time to time. If that's all right?'

'Yes, I'd like that,' Jasmine said, and she meant it.

Before she left, she gave the older woman a big hug and a kiss.

There was nothing else to do but put it from her mind. Mrs Sullivan was obviously alive, and Jasmine was very pleased. She must simply have misheard.

* * *

The schools were breaking up for the long summer holidays at the end of the week, and Jasmine had booked two weeks off from work to take the children out. Mark hadn't booked any time off as he'd only recently started his new role. The girls understood that Jasmine would be working four days for most of the holidays, but at least they'd have her home and didn't have to attend an activity camp like some of their friends did. Jasmine thought that by September they'd feel confident enough to go by bus to school.

On Monday afternoon, when Jasmine collected the girls from school, Miss Mason, Isabel's teacher, came up to her as she waited in the playground. She asked if she could have a quick word. Leah wasn't out yet, so she followed the teacher into the classroom, where Isabel was sitting at a table, looking very sullen.

'Hi, Isabel, everything OK?' Jasmine asked her.

She nodded quietly.

Miss Mason closed the classroom door and came over to her. Jasmine wondered what she wanted to say.

'I've been meaning to have a chat with you for a few weeks now,' she began.

Jasmine's senses immediately went to high alert; she didn't like the sound of this. What had Isabel done?

'I understand you moved house just over a month ago?'

'Yes, that's correct,' Jasmine replied. 'I've told the school of our new address.'

Miss Mason nodded. 'During the last few weeks, Isabel has begun talking to her fellow classmates about a ghost that lives in your house. She's made one of the girls in her class very fearful, so much so that she won't go into her bedroom at home by herself any more. Her mother came in to see me this morning.'

Jasmine stifled a smile. 'I'm so sorry. Isabel can be a bit fanciful at times. I'll speak to her.'

'If you wouldn't mind, I'd appreciate that,' Miss Mason said. 'I've talked to her about it in school.'

Jasmine nodded and glanced at Isabel, who was looking down, staring at the floor. 'Is that everything?' Jasmine asked.

'Yes, she's doing very well in all aspects of her work.'

'Good. Thank you for letting me know,' Jasmine said. 'I'll definitely have a chat with her.'

'Thank you,' Miss Mason said, and opened the classroom door for Jasmine and Isabel to leave.

'Am I in trouble?' Isabel asked as they headed across to the far side of the playground, where Leah was waiting with her teacher.

'No, not really. But you mustn't keep talking to other children about ghosts.'

'I tell them what I see,' Isabel said.

'Well, don't. Some parents don't like it. OK?'

She nodded.

Jasmine collected Leah from her teacher. 'Sorry I'm late. I had to see Miss Mason,' she explained.

The girls fell into step beside her as they left the playground and crossed the road. Isabel was very quiet. Jasmine thought it wouldn't do her any harm to think about some of the things she'd said. They got into the car and she drove home. Once indoors, Isabel went straight up to her bedroom, refusing a drink. Jasmine gave her ten minutes, then went up after her. Her bedroom door was closed. Jasmine paused outside. She could hear a small voice coming from inside. It didn't sound like Isabel, but it couldn't be anyone else. Puzzled, she gave a brief knock and went in. Isabel was sitting on her bed.

'Everything all right?' Jasmine asked, looking around the room.

She nodded. 'I was telling her that she wasn't to come here any more, like Miss Mason said.'

'Telling who?' Jasmine asked.

'The ghost. The woman dressed in a grey top and green trousers.'

'So she's gone now?'

'Yes, but she wasn't happy. She said she'd get her own back tonight. Mum, I'm not sure what she meant. I'm very frightened.'

TWENTY

Jasmine sat beside her daughter on the bed and put her arm around her shoulders. Isabel had burst into tears after she'd said she was frightened and now Jasmine soothed her, talking to her gently.

'Come on, it's all right. Nothing can harm you here. Try to think of something else.'

'Do you think she's angry with me?' Isabel asked through tears. 'It wasn't my fault. It was Miss Mason's.'

'No, love. She's not angry with you, but you need to stop pretending she's here. I know lots of children have imaginary friends, but you need to let her go now.'

'She's not imaginary,' Isabel persisted. 'She's real, and she's not my friend. I see her in the garden and in the house and now she's angry with me.'

'No, she's not,' Jasmine said. 'She's not angry with you. She's not real.'

At that moment Leah came upstairs to find them. They

heard her come slowly along the landing and then she appeared at Isabel's bedroom door.

'You've been up here for ages,' she said.

'I can't have my ghost any more,' Isabel responded tearfully.

Leah rolled her eyes. 'Come and play with me,' she said. 'I don't like it downstairs all alone. We could go in the garden before dinner.'

'That's a good idea,' Jasmine encouraged. 'Come on, let's all go downstairs now.' She wiped her daughter's eyes and drew her from the bed.

Isabel got changed out of her school uniform first and went with Leah into the garden. Once they were playing nicely, Jasmine went into the kitchen and began to make their dinner. Every so often she glanced through the patio doors. It was nice seeing them playing together, just as sisters should do. Once school had finished for the summer, Jasmine hoped they would play together while she worked. It had been different at the flat where they were all cooped up. This house was much better.

Once dinner was ready, she called the girls in. They washed their hands, then took their places at the table, both smiling, happy and talking about the game they'd played.

'Good girls,' Jasmine said. 'It's lovely when you play nicely together.'

There wasn't much homework with the end of the school year approaching, so once they'd finished dinner Jasmine suggested they play outside again. They went out eagerly, chatting and laughing. She checked on them every so often but left them outside until 7.30 p.m. Mark had come home just before and had gone straight to the study to take a Zoom call for work.

'You've had a great time,' Jasmine told the girls when she called them indoors.

They nodded and were still chatting brightly. She took them upstairs and into the bathroom to get ready for bed. Isabel was exhausted and, after a quick wash, she collapsed into bed and closed her eyes. Jasmine said goodnight and then went into Leah's room, telling her again it was good of her to play with Isabel, and well done.

'I like playing with her when she's in a good mood,' she said, and snuggled down for sleep.

Jasmine kissed her goodnight, came out and went downstairs. Mark had finished his Zoom call and was now outside watering what was left of the plants. She could see him through the patio windows. As she'd come into the living room, she noticed a strange smell. She now opened the patio door wider and waved to Mark. He waved back.

She watched him for a few moments, then sat on the sofa and picked up the TV remote. At that moment, before she switched it on, the temperature suddenly dropped and the sofa began to tremble. Jasmine screamed and gripped the armrest. It lasted for a few seconds and, just as abruptly, stopped again. Shaking, and with her heart racing, she got off and stared at the sofa, not sure what to do. She tentatively peered beneath it. There was nothing there. She checked the wheels, while thinking it wasn't that type of movement. It was a shudder similar to the one she'd experienced before.

She bent and felt each wheel separately, but they were all screwed on tightly. She reached under the sofa and ran her hand over the carpet, but that was all smooth.

She stared again at the sofa. The temperature was coming up again; that cold chill had gone, and it was growing warmer by the second. Mark was still watering the garden, apparently unaware of anything wrong. As she stood there and looked out at Mark, she became aware of something behind her. She turned to see Isabel. She'd come silently downstairs and was now standing at the living-room door, her face blank and her eyes staring.

'What's the matter?' Jasmine asked.

Isabel continued to stare, expressionless and not speaking.

'What's the matter?' Jasmine tried again. There was no reply. It was as though she hadn't heard her. Her face was blank.

'Isabel,' Jasmine said, more loudly, and went over to her.

The child silently turned and, leaving the living room, began slowly upstairs. It was as though she was in a trance, Jasmine thought, as she followed her up the stairs and into her bedroom.

'Are you all right?' Jasmine asked her.

There was no reply.

Jasmine watched Isabel as she climbed into bed, lay on her back and pulled the duvet up to her chin. Her eyes were open and she was staring straight ahead. Was she sleepwalking? If so, she'd never done it before. Jasmine looked at her daughter, unsure of what to make of it. Gradually, her eyes closed and, still without speaking, she went back to sleep. Jasmine went to check on Leah. She was fast asleep. She returned to Isabel's room. She appeared to be sleeping peacefully now.

'Isabel,' she whispered.

There was no reply, so drawing her door to, Jasmine returned downstairs, brimming with apprehension about what had just happened. The strange smell in the living room had gone now. She looked around for its source, but couldn't see anything obvious. The sofa was where it always stood and was motionless now too. She looked out through the patio doors to where Mark was still watering the garden. He looked up at her.

'Everything OK?' he called.

'Yes. Are you all right?' she replied.

He nodded.

Jasmine sat on a chair in the living room and thought. The room was now as it should be, but what was wrong with their house? There was something strange going on here. There'd been too many incidents since they'd moved in, and the Morgans had only been here eighteen months. That wasn't right. As she sat there thinking, wondering what they could do, there came an ear-piercing scream from Isabel upstairs. Jasmine jumped up. Mark had heard it too and rushed in.

Upstairs in the bedroom, Isabel was sitting up in bed, eyes open, pointing to a corner of the room.

'She's there!' she screamed. 'Over there.'

Mark and Jasmine looked towards the corner of Isabel's bedroom, and just for a second, before she vanished, they saw the misty outline of a woman wearing a grey top and green trousers.

'What the hell?' Mark exclaimed.

'It's because you made me tell her to go away,' Isabel cried.

'I knew there was something wrong here,' Jasmine said, picking up her child. She carried her through to their bedroom, where she held her close and soothed her. 'It's all right. It's OK,' she said. 'You're safe now.'

Mark followed them in, his face white.

'Have you seen that woman before?' he asked Isabel.

'Lots of times,' she said. 'But she's angry tonight.'

'Why?' he asked, looking like he couldn't believe the conversation they were having.

'Because Mummy made me tell her to go away after Miss Mason said so.'

Jasmine looked at her daughter in utter desperation.

'Did you hear the sofa shake a short while ago?' she asked Mark.

'No.'

'It did, like before, just for a few seconds. And there was a strange smell in the living room and the temperature dropped again. And now we've both seen something that we really can't explain away. What are we going to do? Move like the Morgans did?'

'No. We're not moving,' Mark stated categorically. 'No way. This is our house now. Perhaps there's a rational explanation for what we saw, like a reflection of something outside. Has Leah seen her?' he asked Isabel.

'I don't know. She never says anything about her. If I

try talking about her, she tells me to be quiet. The ghost is angry because you told me to pretend she wasn't here. I expect she moved the sofa too. She exists. I've seen her and now so have you.'

'Well, we certainly saw something. I'm sorry I doubted you,' Jasmine said.

'So can I tell my friend at school that she's real?' Isabel asked.

Jasmine glanced helplessly at Mark.

'It's probably better if you don't,' he said.

'Your friend will tell her mother, and she won't be pleased,' Jasmine pointed out. 'So best not talk about it at school.' Then to Mark she explained, 'Miss Mason asked to see me at the end of school today. She told me that since we've moved Isabel has been talking about a ghost in our home. I thought it was a load of nonsense, and I dealt with it accordingly, but maybe I was wrong. Where else have you seen the woman?' Jasmine then asked Isabel.

'Mainly in the garden and my bedroom, but sometimes in the living room,' she said.

'Not at school?' Mark said.

Isabel shook her head.

'What does she talk to you about?' he asked.

'She doesn't really speak to me. She appears and watches us play. But tonight she was angry because of what Mummy and Miss Mason said about her not being real.'

'I understand,' Jasmine said.

'She's nothing to worry about except when she's angry,' Isabel said in a matter-of-fact tone.

Jasmine gave a small nod.

'Do you think you could go back to sleep while Daddy and I have a chat?' she asked.

Isabel nodded.

'Good girl. Now snuggle down.'

She shuffled beneath the duvet in their bed.

'Don't worry, Mummy,' Isabel said. 'She's not angry any more now she knows you won't be going, and she's staying here for good.'

Jasmine stroked a few strands of hair away from her daughter's forehead. She seemed to be taking it very well, but then children often did take the strange and unexplained in their stride. They didn't try to rationalize or justify. They just accepted it – good and bad.

'When did you first see her?' Jasmine thought to ask, before Isabel dropped off to sleep.

'The first time we visited the house. I saw her then,' she said. 'She was standing in the living room and the temperature dropped. I thought you felt her too.'

TWENTY-ONE

Jasmine and Mark went downstairs once they'd settled Isabel, where Mark poured two large glasses of wine and handed one to Jasmine. Mark had gone into Isabel's room to check it before coming down, but there was nothing in there apart from the usual toys and books.

'Is it true what Isabel said – that you felt it when you first came to view the house?' Mark now asked Jasmine, walking into the living room with his drink.

'I felt something, but I had no idea what,' she said, following him in. 'I didn't bother to tell you at the time. I thought it was my imagination.'

'Well, it clearly was something,' he said, sitting down and taking a large sip of wine.

Jasmine drank hers too. She needed it like nothing else.

'What are we going to do?' she asked after a moment. 'Call a priest? Father Tim Ashridge was here before. He helped the Morgans in the past.'

Mark gave a snort of derision. 'No. There must be a

rational explanation for what we've just seen. It's just about deciding what it is. I personally don't believe in ghosts, as you know, but there was certainly a glimpse of something tonight that we all saw.'

Jasmine took another large sip of wine and waited. Mark was clearly thinking, deliberating in silence, as he did sometimes. Shortly he'd say something meaningful and put an end to the conversation, but what could he possibly say that would give a satisfactory explanation to what they'd all witnessed tonight?

After some moments he looked at her. 'I think it was a reflection in the mirror in Isabel's room,' he said, and drank some more of his wine.

Jasmine stared at him. 'The mirror is on the wall by the window,' she said.

'It's angled so that it catches the light. It could have captured something outside. Isabel has mentioned a woman in a grey jumper and green trousers before, so it would have been on our minds. It was our imagination. We only caught a glimpse of whatever it was, after all.'

Jasmine was going to dismiss this, but took another sip from her glass, stood and said, 'Come and show me.'

They set their glasses on the coffee table and Jasmine followed Mark upstairs. She hadn't been in Isabel's bedroom again since they'd moved her and was a little hesitant about going in. Mark went in first and Jasmine waited by the door. He was silent for some time as he looked around, then he called, 'Come in. I think I've got it.'

She took the few steps into the bedroom and stood

close against the wall by the door. They both looked at the mirror on the far wall over by the window where they'd seen the reflection. It wasn't showing them at all but a different part of the room. Mark took a step into its line of vision, and his image followed. He moved again, slightly forward, until he could see his full reflection.

'I want you to do the same,' he told Jasmine.

She took a step into the room, closer to the bed, and looked at the mirror. She couldn't see her reflection at all.

'We were here by Isabel's bed. I'm sure of it,' she said.

'Perhaps the mirror got moved,' he said, and adjusted it until their images were in it.

This was ridiculous. The mirror would need to have moved quite some distance. She was about to say something, but then looked down at Isabel's bed.

'Who made the bed?' she asked.

Mark looked at it. 'You?'

'I carried Isabel into our bedroom,' Jasmine said. 'This is the first time I've been back in here. What about you?'

'I came in here again, but I didn't touch the bed. I expect you did it automatically, without thinking,' he said.

'No, I didn't,' Jasmine said. 'I would remember.'

'Then it must have been me,' Mark said, and he left the room.

Jasmine left too, then checked on Isabel, who was sleeping peacefully in their bed, and went downstairs. She sat in the living room, sipping her wine, and waited for Mark to come in.

'What are we going to do?' she asked. 'Where is Isabel going to sleep until we get this mess sorted out?'

'I'm going to finish my glass of wine, then I'm going to rearrange all the furniture in her bedroom,' Mark said. 'Once it's all changed, it will look like a completely different room.'

He was up there for nearly an hour. She could hear him moving Isabel's furniture into different positions in the room. She supposed the nice thing would have been to have gone up and offered to help him, but she didn't want to go in there again, not yet. She sat in an armchair and drank her wine, then refilled her glass. By the time he called her to come up, most of the bottle had gone.

She went upstairs and into Isabel's bedroom. It looked totally different. All the furniture had been moved around. The bed was on the other wall and the bookshelves were where the bed had been. Mark had taken down the mirror and it was on the landing, ready to be put away. He said a girl of eight didn't need a mirror, anyway. Jasmine looked around the room.

'Do you think Isabel will sleep in here?' she asked.

'I don't see why not,' Mark replied.

At that moment they both heard a noise coming from their bedroom. Then Isabel slowly walked in, still seemingly fast asleep. She walked to where her bed was now positioned, climbed in and pulled up the covers. 'It's much better,' she muttered, then turned over and started breathing deeply.

'Isabel?' Jasmine asked her, touching her forehead.

There was no reply. She was definitely asleep.

Jasmine and Mark stood there for a few seconds looking at their daughter, then silently left the room.

'How did she know her bed was ready?' Jasmine asked, closing the door.

'She heard us, of course. Don't read anything into that. Now, let's finish that bottle of wine.'

Downstairs, Mark drained the last of the first bottle, opened a second and refilled their glasses. He was ready to talk about something else, but Jasmine certainly wasn't. She kept asking if he thought the new arrangement of furniture in Isabel's room would work and if Isabel would be happy in that room long-term.

'She'll have to be,' Mark said, obviously growing tired from the cross-examination, his tongue loosened from the wine. 'There's no alternative. We can hardly ask Leah to swap bedrooms with her, can we?'

'Of course we can't,' Jasmine said with more force than was necessary. It was the wine talking for her too.

'Tomorrow she will have forgotten all about it,' Mark said, picking up his phone as a means of deflection.

'Supposing she hasn't?' Jasmine persisted. 'I wouldn't want to sleep in that room again, if I were her.'

'Isabel is not you,' Mark said bluntly.

'Aren't you worried about your daughter?' Jasmine asked.

'Not especially. What we saw tonight was an optical illusion brought on by the position of the mirror. Of course there isn't a ghost in that room.'

The wine, and hearing Mark so easily justify what they'd both seen, finally caused Jasmine to lose her temper.

'What about the sofa, then?' she demanded. 'Everything that's happened here can be reasoned away by you, but that can't.'

'I didn't see the sofa move this time,' he said obstinately. 'But I'm sure there's a rational explanation.'

'So that's it? Everything can be explained away.'

'Yes, of course it can. What do you want me to say? That our house is haunted? Of course it's not. It's just taking us a while to settle in, that's all. You said yourself it would take us time and you were right. After the long summer holidays, when you've spent lots of time here with the girls, it will be fine.'

She stared at him, annoyed. He was so calm and convincing she could almost have believed him.

'I'm going to bed,' she said and, drinking down the last of her glass of wine, she went upstairs.

She was angered by Mark's attitude and went into Leah's room first. She was sleeping soundly. Then she went into Isabel's room. It really did look like a new room with the furniture in different places. She turned to her right towards the bed. Isabel was fast asleep. She bent and kissed her forehead. Hopefully she would stay asleep until morning.

She turned and began to leave the room.

'She's still here.'

Jasmine stopped and looked at her daughter. She thought she'd heard Isabel's voice, but she was still fast asleep.

‘Isabel?’ she asked. There was no reply. ‘Isabel?’ she tried again.

Had she really heard her daughter or was it her imagination? She waited for a few moments longer, still looking at her daughter, then came out, leaving the door open. What were they going to do? Could Mark be right and the six weeks’ summer holiday would solve their problems? She wasn’t sure.

She continued into their bedroom and sat on the edge of the bed, dog tired from all the wine. It was only Monday. Mark could justify anything if he wanted to, even when there was no justification to be found. Jasmine knew what she had to do. First thing in the morning, on returning home from school, she’d call the priest.

TWENTY-TWO

'Oh, no!' Mark exclaimed as he opened the bedroom curtains the following morning. 'Not my vegetables! Not again.'

He grabbed his dressing gown, pushed his feet into his slippers and ran downstairs. Jasmine went to the window. She looked out and saw all the dead vegetables. They'd been growing well last night when Mark had watered them. What had gone wrong overnight? As she looked down, she saw Mark appear in the garden, and watched him pull up some of the dead plants, examine them, and throw them to one side. As far as she could see, they were all dead, rows and rows of dead carrots and sweetcorn. Yet the other plants – her plants – seemed to be still growing. It didn't make any sense.

'That's it, I'm finished with trying to grow vegetables,' Mark said when he returned. 'That's the second lot that have all died overnight. It's too late to plant any more this year.'

Jasmine could see how disappointed he was. It was as though the plants had won some unspoken battle. But after last night, when they'd both gone to bed in a mood, she didn't feel like saying anything to cheer him up. It was strange that his part of the garden seemed to let the plants grow for a while, then suddenly stopped supporting them, while the rest of the ground seemed fine. The lawn was thriving. She would have thought that beside the shed, with the partial sunlight, was the ideal location for vegetables, but then again, what did she know about gardening?

'It's useless. They're all dead,' he said.

He took his clothes into the bathroom to shower and dress. Jasmine got ready in the bedroom, then went to wake the girls. Leah was still fast asleep and took some shaking to wake up properly. Jasmine went into Isabel's room and found she was already awake. She was looking around and seemed to be worried.

'Are you OK, love?' Jasmine asked, going to the bed in its new position. It would take a bit of getting used to.

'Why has all my furniture been moved?' she asked, frowning.

'Don't you remember, we moved it late last night?' Jasmine said.

'I don't remember.'

Jasmine was about to tell her what had happened, but then thought it might upset her, so instead she said, 'You were upset and Daddy thought it would help if we changed around your bedroom. Do you like it?'

'Yes, I think so. Where's the mirror gone?'

'It's been put away until you're older.'

Isabel looked sad.

'I liked that mirror. I used to see her in it.'

Jasmine was taken aback. 'Isabel, I want you to forget all about that now. No more talking about the woman in the mirror, especially at school, all right? It's the summer holidays soon, so lots to look forward to.'

She nodded. 'Only four more days to go,' she said excitedly.

'That's right. Then you'll have six weeks off to play all you wish.'

Isabel jumped up, threw her arms around her mother and kissed her. Jasmine hugged her daughter, then left her to get dressed.

'Do you want me to get rid of the vegetables?' she asked Mark as she went downstairs. He was in the hall about to leave for work.

'No. I'll water them again when I get home, like I did before, though I'm not holding my breath.'

He was going to be late for work, Jasmine thought. He didn't kiss her and let himself out the front door. She heard his car start and pull away. She then took the girls to school and saw them in. On her return, she went straight to her phone and pulled a business card from her wallet. She then sat toying with the card, unsure of whether to phone the priest and what to say. After a few minutes, she steeled herself and dialled Father Tim Ashridge's number. It went through to answer machine and she breathed a sigh of relief. She left a message.

'Good morning. It's Jasmine Simmons. You called at my house on Ravens Lane when we first moved in. Could you give me a ring back, please, on this number?' She finished and hung up.

Would he remember her? Should she have said more? She turned and looked out of the window. The vegetables were still dead. Perhaps the soil in Mark's part of the garden was less fertile than the rest? Was that possible? Would that cause all the plants there to die overnight, not once but twice?

The phone rang and she answered it.

'It's Father Tim Ashridge here,' he said. 'You phoned me just now.'

'Yes, that's right,' Jasmine said, and stopped. What could she possibly say?

'How can I help you?' he asked after a moment.

'I think there is something in this house,' she blurted. 'My husband would disagree, but he's not here right now. Can you come and do what you did before?'

'With Mr and Mrs Morgan?'

'Yes, please.'

There was a small pause. 'Yes, I can certainly visit you. Just a minute.' She presumed he was checking his diary. 'Would twelve o'clock today be all right for you? I've had a cancellation. Otherwise, it will be Friday.'

'Yes, today is fine. Thank you.'

She put down the phone and immediately regretted phoning him. She nearly called him back to say he should forget the whole thing. It was ridiculous to call a priest and claim their house was haunted. Mark would be furious if he found out. She'd already decided she wouldn't tell him. She sat for a while and decided to leave the call. Tim Ashridge could come and do his job and that would be the end of it. Just one visit, that was all that was required.

She switched on her computer but couldn't settle to work. It was now nearly 10.30 a.m. Her thoughts kept returning to what she was going to say and do when the priest came. She knew very little about how this type of priest worked, and wondered what he'd done with the Morgans. She supposed she'd have to tell him about all their strange experiences in the house. Make a list, she thought – there were so many. She stopped work again and began to type on a separate page everything that had happened since they'd moved in. The sofa moving, the temperature dropping – that had happened before they'd moved in as well – on her first visit. The sightings of the woman in a grey jumper and green trousers, Mark's cut hand, the broken picture frames, the wasps in the flowers, those crows in the roof, the plants in the garden. She glanced out of the window again, then crossed the plants off the list. That was a silly thing to include. Anybody's plants could die, she thought, and then she printed out the sheet.

She wasn't sure which rooms he would want to go in, so, having printed out the list, she began tidying the house. It was a mess after the weekend, with the girls' toys scattered all over the place. She gathered them together, carried them upstairs and put them into Isabel's bedroom. The moment she stepped into the room it became instantly colder. She looked towards the window and saw that the sun was up. Don't be silly, she told herself, and came out of the room, leaving the bed unmade. By 11.30 she'd done virtually no work, but the house was very tidy, at least.

She sat down at her computer again and tried to work, then looked at the list she'd made. It was a long list when she saw it printed out like that. She thought back to their old flat. There hadn't been any need for a list like this; no sinister or unexplained event had occurred there in all the years they'd lived there.

The doorbell rang, making her start, and she went to answer it.

'Hello, Father Ashridge,' she said.

'Mrs Simmons.' He smiled and came in.

'Please, call me Jasmine. Would you like a drink?' she asked the priest nervously.

'Yes, please, a coffee would be lovely.' He followed her into the kitchen and looked around the room as she made his drink.

Once it was ready, Jasmine suggested they sit in the living room.

'Wherever you feel most comfortable,' he replied.

She wasn't sure where she felt comfortable in this house but led the way into the living room. It was where they *should* feel very comfortable and able to relax, but they couldn't, not really. She watched him sit and take a sip of his coffee.

'Very nice and much appreciated,' he said. 'I've had a busy morning. Not with this type of work, but normal church matters.' He took another few sips and set his mug down squarely on the coffee table.

'So, tell me why you find you need my services?' he said to her. 'Why do you think your house is haunted?' His voice was even and relaxed.

Jasmine took a breath and reached for the printed sheet of paper.

'I made a list of the strange things that have happened here,' she said. 'I thought you might find it useful.'

He took the sheet and read it, then looked up at her.

'All these things have happened on a regular basis?' he asked. 'Since you moved in here?'

'A couple of things were one-offs,' she said. 'The crows in the loft, the wasps in the flowers, Mark's cut, but other things have happened regularly. Can you tell me if these are the types of things that the Morgans experienced when they lived here?'

'I can't disclose what exactly took place here, as it's confidential,' he said. 'But I suppose you could say that their manifestations were similar and you're not alone in this. The need for exorcism has grown tremendously in recent years. I am telephoned half a dozen times a week from those asking for help.'

'Really?' Jasmine said, surprised. 'I thought it would have been the opposite in this day and age.'

He shook his head. 'Far from it. But I don't see everyone who contacts me; some of them I refer for psychological help.' He paused. 'I need to ask, have you ever sought help for psychological problems yourself?'

Jasmine knew why he was asking. A number of people who contacted him were presumably severely mentally ill.

'No, never,' she said.

'I have a few other questions before we think about your manifestations,' he said.

She nodded and he took out a pen and paper.

'Have you any alcohol or drug addictions?' he asked.

Jasmine thought about the wine they seemed to be drinking more of since they'd moved in and decided it didn't matter.

'No,' she said.

'Have you ever engaged in the occult before, or tried to connect with spirits?' he asked.

Was that what she was doing now? she wondered. Surely not?

'No,' she said again. He made a note.

'Do you really want this house to be cleansed of the demons you believe inhabit it?' he asked, and looked at her in earnest.

At that moment Jasmine suddenly felt someone, or something, standing behind her and she instinctively turned. The space was empty. There was no one there. But the priest's gaze followed her to the empty space, and then he seemed to be tracking something across the room.

'You're seeing something?' Jasmine asked, her breath catching in her throat.

He crossed himself as he said something in Latin, which she didn't understand. Then he stood and, raising his hand at her, he made the sign of the cross. 'I claim you for Christ our Saviour by the sign of the Cross.'

Jasmine remained sitting and stared at the priest as he slowly sat down again.

'Did you see something?' she asked again.

He'd gone quite pale and had started perspiring heavily.

He was about to answer when she felt a tap on her right shoulder. She turned and screamed. There was no one there. She rubbed her shoulder and stared at the priest.

'There's someone there, isn't there?'

'I promise you I will seek permission straight away and return before the end of the week,' he said. 'I daren't do this without it. It's not allowed. Can you tell me again in your own words why you want my help?'

Jasmine opened her mouth to speak but nothing came out. She tried to form the words, but nothing happened. It was as though she was being stopped – as if there were a gag over her mouth.

'I . . .' she began. 'We . . .' The rest was blank. She tried again 'I . . .'

In desperation, she picked up the piece of paper the priest had left on the table and pushed it towards him.

'This is what has been going on,' she said, thankful the words came out. 'Ever since we moved in. I've had enough of it. I want you to come back as soon as you can and make it stop.'

Tears were forming in her eyes.

'I understand,' he said nervously. 'Can I suggest you put up a cross in this room and in Isabel's bedroom? It will help.'

'No. I'm sorry. My husband would never agree to that. He doesn't even know you're here now.'

'We'll say a prayer together, then I'll leave you and come back as soon as I can. I may bring someone else with me.'

He lowered his head, closed his eyes and clasped his hands together. He began praying. Jasmine lowered her head out of respect, even though she didn't think she truly believed in good or evil or God.

'Soul of Christ,' he began. 'Body of Christ, save me, Blood of Christ, inebriate me. Water from the side of Christ, wash me. Passion of Christ, strengthen me . . .'

Once he was done, the priest stood. 'I'll be back soon,' he said, and headed out of the room.

Jasmine followed him to the front door, where he left, saying a quick goodbye.

TWENTY-THREE

Jasmine's legs wobbled as she walked away from the front door and went into the kitchen for a glass of water. She looked out of the window and saw the priest's car pull away, then took the glass of water into the living room. He'd been there for over an hour. She was about to sit, but then saw his coffee mug on the table. It had red teeth marks around the rim. With a small cry of alarm, she put down her glass, picked up the mug and carried it at arm's length through to the kitchen. She dropped it into the washing-up bowl and turned on the hot tap. The mark was as vivid as ever. It didn't come off with running water even when she scrubbed it hard. What the hell was it? Not lipstick, for sure. It looked like blood. Maybe he'd bitten his lip, she tried to tell herself. She put on her rubber gloves and scrubbed some more and eventually the mark began to come off.

It was now 1.30 p.m. and Jasmine didn't feel like any lunch. She wasn't at all hungry. She went through to the study, sat at her computer and googled, *Blood red mark on cup*, but couldn't find anything.

Who was he asking for permission? she wondered, and learnt from looking online that it must be from the bishop. When would he come back? He said by the end of the week. Should she tell Mark? That was the most important question of all. She sat there thinking about what she should do.

Time passed. She tried to work but the priest kept coming into her mind. She suddenly had a thought and googled Father Tim Ashridge. She stopped dead. He was a very well-known exorcist and did his work in a number of parishes. She began to read the online articles and learnt that he'd been practising exorcisms for over ten years and had treated hundreds of people during that time. There were excerpts from the prayers he'd said, like the one he'd said to her, and short video clips of people being exorcised. One was of a teenage girl, white and snarling – she looked like an image from the film *The Exorcist*. She stopped and looked away.

But it wasn't a person she had asked for help with, it was this house. She found a webpage containing information on house exorcism. This appeared to be a much shorter job and needed fewer visits: 'Those seeking exorcism of their home should contact their local parish priest,' the article read, which she had done. She sat at her desk googling and reading for most of the afternoon, until she suddenly realized it was time to collect the girls from school. She'd done virtually no work again, and with her head full of priests and exorcisms, she locked up the house and drove to school.

She was quiet as she walked into the playground, thinking about what she'd read. She knew she'd be counting the days until Father Tim Ashridge returned.

The girls came out of school very excited – with the end of term on Friday, they were going on an outing tomorrow. They talked about it non-stop on the way home. All Jasmine had to do was look as though she was listening while still thinking about the priest.

Once home, she made dinner while the girls played outside as usual. Mark arrived home at 6 p.m. The girls had had their dinner and returned to play in the garden by then. Mark came in and presented Jasmine with a bouquet of flowers. It was the first bunch he'd bought her since they'd moved in.

'That's very kind of you,' she said, and kissed him. 'What are they for?'

'I was a bit of a pig last night and this morning,' he admitted.

She nodded and noticed a large plaster on his left hand.

'Have you cut yourself?' she asked, concerned.

'No. That wound opened up again. It looks nasty.'

'What wound?' she asked, frowning.

'From when I cut my hand on the glass from our photographs when we first moved in, you remember?' he said.

'But that was ages ago,' she said. 'That cut can't have reopened. It healed up quickly. You must have cut yourself again.'

She looked at him, drained and pale, and put down the flowers. She picked up his hand and began to gently remove the plaster. She nearly passed out when she saw what lay beneath it.

'Good grief,' she said, staring at the mess. 'It's dreadful. It really is. And it's in exactly the same place as it was before. But it wasn't there this morning, was it?'

'No, I don't think so.' He shook his head and looked at the gash. 'Perhaps I cut it at work?'

'But on what, love?' she asked him. 'And in the same place?'

'I honestly don't know what happened,' he said. 'But it bloody well hurts. It just appeared as I was working.'

'Let's put on a fresh dressing,' she said and, setting down his hand, she started rummaging in the drawer for the first-aid kit.

She gently washed the cut as he grimaced. 'Sorry,' she said. Then she took the largest plaster and, peeling off the sticky cover on the back, carefully stuck it over the wound.

'If it doesn't look any better tomorrow, I think you should go to the doctor,' she said, concerned.

'Yes, I'll have to,' he agreed, and kissed her again. 'I'll go and get changed now.'

While Mark was gone, Jasmine arranged the flowers in a vase of water, then put them on the coffee table in the living room. It briefly crossed her mind that this was where she'd put the flowers Poppy had brought over, which had been full of wasps. She quickly dismissed the thought. They looked beautiful. She decided on the spur of the moment to tell Mark about Father Tim Ashridge. When he came downstairs, she set their meals on the table.

'How's your hand?' she asked.

'Not too bad,' he said. 'I'll take a paracetamol later if it keeps throbbing. How was your day, anyway?'

'I called a priest,' she said bluntly. 'The same one who came here before. Father Tim Ashridge.'

'Why?' Mark asked.

'I thought we needed some help.'

'Because of what?' Mark asked.

'Because of all the strange goings-on. We talked and then he said a prayer. He's going to get permission, then come back again.'

'Permission to do what?' Mark asked.

'To do an exorcism.'

'You what?' Mark said, his face setting.

'It's no good pretending. Things are happening in this house over which we have no control. Look at your vegetable patch. All the plants are dead again. Then last night we both saw something in Isabel's bedroom. It's no good pretending we didn't. There have been a lot of strange happenings since we moved in and the Morgans were only here for eighteen months, so maybe something drove them out too. I wrote a list of things that have happened to us to show the priest. It was long. We didn't have anything like that happen to us at the flat and we were there for ten years.'

Jasmine was going to tell him more about the priest's visit when a scream erupted from the garden, ear-piercing and intense. They immediately both stood and looked down the garden. Isabel had fallen from her bicycle. Jasmine went out to help her. She checked her knee and brought her indoors.

'Hello, Daddy,' Isabel said tearfully. 'I fell off my bike.'

'I know, pet. Mummy will make you better,' he said.

Mark resumed eating as Jasmine took Isabel to the counter in the kitchen and bathed and dressed the hurt knee. It was more a graze than a cut. Once suitably bandaged, Isabel wanted to play outside again. Jasmine told her to be careful and sent her off, then sat down at the table and picked up her knife and fork. The moment had passed to continue talking about the priest; it didn't feel right. Perhaps there would be another opportunity after he had visited again. Mark changed the subject and began talking about work. Jasmine ate a little of her dinner and then cleared the table.

That night, she lay awake for some time thinking about Father Tim Ashridge and what he would do at the exorcism, before she finally fell asleep. She awoke some time later, lying flat on her back and aware that something was badly wrong. Mark was on his side, asleep, his breathing regular and heavy.

The room was dark – there was no moon tonight – and the house seemed as quiet as it should be. After a few moments Jasmine reached out and touched the sheet. It was wet – not damp with the light moisture that comes from water, but heavy with something sticky and cloying. She drew her hand over the sheet, then brought it up to her eyes. She couldn't see anything in the dark. She turned over, switched on her bedside light and screamed. Her hand was covered in blood. Thick, dark blood.

She threw back the duvet and stared at the sheet. It was covered in blood. It was coming from Mark's side of the bed. He was still fast asleep. What was the matter? Then she saw where the blood was coming from and instinctively moved away. The plaster she'd put on his hand last night was now dripping with blood, running down onto the bed. There was so much of it seeping out, he would surely be drained of life very quickly.

'Mark! Wake up,' she shouted and began pummelling his shoulder. 'Wake up!' she yelled. 'You're bleeding to death! Wake up!'

The front of her nightwear was covered in blood and as she looked at his boxer shorts, they were too. It was everywhere. 'Mark, wake up!' she tried again. 'You'll be dead soon if you don't.'

Fear gripped her. The bed was awash with blood, dripping from Mark's hand and pooling between them. As she beat his chest to wake him, he gradually surfaced and sat up. He looked at her as blood dripped from his wrist onto the bed. Dear God, he couldn't have long to live now, the bed was full of it, full of Mark's blood.

'Jasmine.' She heard her name being called. 'Jasmine, it's Mark.'

She looked at him – his lips were moving but nothing was coming out. The blood was still everywhere, forming in pools on the bed.

'Jasmine, wake up!' Mark cried, and she felt a hard shake. 'Wake up now. You'll disturb the girls. Wake up!'

She gradually opened her eyes and looked around, then immediately went to turn on the bedside lamp. All the blood had gone. She picked up Mark's hand and stared at it in disbelief, then she looked at her own nightwear. It was completely clear of blood, as was the bed. The sheet was off-white as it should be – no blood there. She checked the rest of the bed and flopped back onto the pillow, exhausted.

'I had a bad dream where you were bleeding to death,' she said, and picked up his hand to double check it was just a dream. There was no sign of blood, only the plaster she'd put on the cut last night.

Still half asleep, Mark vaguely looked at his hand. 'It's all good,' he mumbled. 'Put your light off and go back to sleep.'

Hot and sweating, she turned towards the clock. It was nearly 2.30 a.m. She was reluctant to switch off the lamp and try to go back to sleep – the dream still felt so real. Mark would be asleep soon and the girls hadn't woken, but her heart was racing. She'd been convinced she'd woken up in a pool of blood and that Mark was bleeding to death. She patted the bed again and then looked at the sheet. It was nothing more than a dream, a very realistic one, she thought, and turned over. She left her light on so she could watch as Mark went back to sleep quite quickly. She dared not close her eyes again for fear of the dream returning – all that blood. It had been so realistic. The last time she looked at the clock it was 5.05 a.m. and then the next thing she heard was Mark's voice again.

'Wake up, sleepyhead. I'm going to work. You've over-slept. It's 7.30 a.m.'

She opened her eyes and the first thing she did was to check the bed again. It was clear.

'How's your hand?' she asked him.

'Healing nicely. I'll see you tonight,' he said.

He kissed her cheek and left the room. They were going to be late for school. She hurried into the girls' bedrooms to find that they were already dressed.

'We're going on an outing today,' they exclaimed excitedly.

'Yes. Of course,' she said.

TWENTY-FOUR

The following afternoon, as Jasmine was driving to school to collect the girls, Father Tim Ashridge called her mobile. He asked how they all were and she said they were OK over the hands-free.

'I can come and see you on Friday morning,' he said. 'I'll bring a colleague with me.'

'Do you know what time?' she asked him.

'Ten o'clock, if that's all right with you. My colleague has another appointment later in the day.'

'Yes, that's fine with me. I'll see you on Friday,' she said, and ended the call.

She wondered why he needed a colleague with him, but hadn't liked to ask, since she'd been concentrating on the road and wanted to finish the call quickly. Once at the school, she stood in the playground and waited for the girls to appear, then listened as they told her about their outing.

The rest of the week passed without incident, so much so that Jasmine even considered cancelling Father Tim's appointment on Friday, for there was nothing to see or experience in their house. The vegetables were definitely dead, but apart from that it could have been any three-bedroom semi they were living in. Mark was late home every evening that week and then wanted to talk about work. He didn't ask when the priest was coming. In fact, he didn't mention him at all, and Jasmine didn't bring him up either. It was better that way.

On Friday, the day of Father Tim's visit, the girls were very excited, as it was their last day at school for six weeks. Jasmine dropped them off and wished them a pleasant day, then turned around and drove home.

It was 9.15 by the time she pulled into the drive, so she had a little while before Father Tim was due to arrive. She got out of the car. Almost immediately, she sensed something was wrong. She looked at the house and walked slowly to the front door. She couldn't see anything. She looked at the window on her right. There was a slight movement. Something was crawling on the inside of the net curtains. She looked closer and saw a large fly, a bluebottle, crawling across the window. As she looked, she saw another one join it, then another. Before long they were gathering in small groups. She stared at the windowpane as it quickly filled with flies. There must have been a hundred of them moving across the inside of the window, trying to get out. She stood there, horrified and fascinated, not knowing what to do. If she went in, who was to say they wouldn't swarm all over her? There must be over a hundred now – how on earth could they have got in?

She could wait outside, she thought, but for how long? She stood there mesmerized, watching the flies moving over the window. There were hundreds of them now and many more were still arriving. It was like the wasps that had come from Poppy's flowers, she suddenly thought. Had these flies been hiding in the flowers Mark had bought earlier in the week? But that was impossible. There were too many of them. They must have got in from somewhere else, but where?

Not knowing what to do, she returned to her car and wound the window down a little. The day was hot. Father Tim was due shortly – perhaps he'd know what to do? She sat there in the car, watching the flies crawl in mass over the window, aware that this wasn't normal or natural. If the priest saw them, perhaps it would help him decide what was wrong with their house, because after all, until now it had just been her word and that of the Morgans. Now hundreds of flies that had come from nowhere were amassing on her windowpane. She looked at the upper window. They were on there too. With a small scream, she wound up her car window. It was now 9.30. Half an hour until Father Tim arrived.

She stayed in the car where it was safe and watched the flies crawl over the windowpanes. What would the priest do when he arrived? she wondered. Tell her to call a pest-control firm? Perhaps she should call one now, but by the time she'd found a number and had booked an appointment, Father Tim would be here. She continued to sit in the car and watch the windows. They were covered with a thick black blanket of moving flies. It was hypnotic and at the same time repulsive.

At five minutes to ten, a car pulled up behind hers outside their house. She turned in her seat and saw two men get out, Father Tim from the driver's door and another man from the passenger seat. She flung open her car door and rushed to greet them.

'There are flies all over the windows. I haven't been inside yet,' she cried. 'Can you tell me what we should do? I don't know.'

Father Tim put his hand on her arm.

'Of course, we'll help you. Come and show me where they are,' he said calmly, glancing at the house.

She turned towards their home and looked at the windows. They were completely clear and still, no black writhing movement.

'But they've gone!' she exclaimed. 'All of them. They must be swarming inside the house.'

'We'll find them and let them out,' Father Tim reassured her. 'This is my colleague, Father Andrew Peters.'

She managed a small hello and took out her front-door key.

'Can you two go in while I wait outside?' she asked them.

'Of course,' Father Tim said in his polite, self-effacing way.

She went to the door, put her key into the lock and tentatively turned it. She stood back to allow the two priests entry while she remained outside. She half expected an enormous swarm of flies to zoom out past her head. Fathers Tim and Andrew disappeared into the living room, then the study and the kitchen. They reappeared in the hallway.

'There's nothing down here,' Father Tim said. 'Shall we go upstairs and check the bedrooms?'

'Yes, that's where they must be hiding.'

Jasmine continued to wait just outside the front door. She heard the men walk upstairs, then go in and out of the bedrooms and the bathroom. The beds were all unmade, she remembered, the rooms a mess. Pretty soon they came downstairs again.

'It's all clear,' Father Tim said gently. 'There's no sign of any flies.'

'But that can't be true,' she said. 'There were hundreds of them just before you came. I'm not making it up. They must be hiding somewhere.'

'We're positive,' Father Andrew said. 'Come into your house and see for yourself.'

'I don't understand it,' Jasmine said anxiously, as she took a step inside.

She went first to the kitchen and looked around – nothing. Then she went slowly into the living room and the study, examining the walls and ceiling. There were no flies in there either.

'Will you come upstairs with me?' she asked them. 'They must be hiding there.'

The two men followed her upstairs as she went cautiously, one step at a time, up the stairs. At the top she paused and listened for any noise that could be a fly, then she went in and out of all the bedrooms, and the bathroom, while the men waited on the landing.

'I don't understand it,' she said, coming out of Isabel's

room. 'There are no windows open for them to escape through. I shut them before we left for school.' She stared at the men, bewildered. 'I don't know what happened.'

'There's nowhere else they could have gone,' Father Andrew said in a conciliatory manner. 'It's not as though it's an old house with a big disused chimney and lots of crevices. I've seen flies swarm up there. Let's go downstairs and I'll make you a cup of tea.'

She didn't want to leave, but with a final glance around she silently followed them downstairs, wondering where the hell all the flies had gone. She was exhausted and it was only a little after 10 a.m. It was as though the very life blood had been drained out of her and all she wanted to do was lie down.

'Do you mind making the tea?' she asked the priests. 'I'm going to sit in the living room.'

They nodded and went into the kitchen while she flopped into one of the easy chairs in the living room. She couldn't go on like this, day after day, not sure what would happen next. Was she now seeing things in her own home? Mark had seen some things too, but he wasn't here to back her up now and would probably have denied it anyway. For a moment she thought she might be losing her mind.

Father Tim came into the living room, leaving Father Andrew to find the mugs and finish making the tea. He sat down in the other easy chair close to hers.

'Are you all right?' he asked her kindly.

She shook her head. 'I doubt you'll believe me about anything now, but there were hundreds of flies here before you arrived. I'm not disturbed like some of your other clients.'

'Of course not,' Father Tim said quietly.

'Nothing like this ever happened to us before, when we used to live in our flat. Nothing. I promise you. You can ask my husband.'

'There's no need for me to ask him, I believe you,' Father Tim replied.

They sat in silence for a moment, then Father Andrew brought in the mugs of tea on a tray and put it down on the coffee table.

'I didn't know if you took sugar,' he said to her.

She could have laughed at the banality of his mundane comment in a situation that was anything but mundane.

'No, I don't,' she said, pulling herself upright.

She gratefully accepted the mug of tea and took a sip. It tasted very good. She couldn't remember the last time Mark had made her a cup of tea.

'What am I going to do?' she asked them, drained. 'There's nothing for you to see now. Nothing at all.'

'Father Andrew would like to ask you a few questions, if that's all right,' Father Tim said.

She nodded, put down the mug and looked at him. He carefully took out an old notepad and pen from his jacket pocket and smiled at her before he began.

'I would like you to tell me what you've experienced while you've been living here, please. Father Ashridge has told me the broad outline, of course, but I would like to hear it from you.'

'Sure,' she said and began. She told him about the sofa moving, the temperature dropping, the sightings of the woman in Isabel's bedroom, the crows in the loft and the wasps in the flowers. And now the flies.

He nodded and made some notes.

'What about the garden?' he asked. 'Are there any dry patches of land where nothing will grow?'

She was startled as she thought of Mark's vegetable patch. 'Yes, my husband's vegetable patch. He's planted it twice this year but after a few days everything died. We watered the plants regularly. Why? Is that something we should be concerned about?'

'It might be,' Father Andrew said as he wrote. He looked up. 'Apart from the plants and what you have told me about past sightings, has anyone in the house – including the children – experienced anything else?'

Jasmine shook her head.

'What about a sore or a cut that wouldn't heal?'

It was as though he'd dealt with this before.

'My children and I haven't, but my husband has a nasty gash on his hand that won't heal. Last night I dreamt about it. Blood was coming from the cut and running all over the bed. My husband had to wake me. It seemed very real at the time.' She shuddered at the recollection.

'What about the television turning on spontaneously?' Father Andrew asked.

'No,' she said, glancing at it as though it might switch on then and there.

'Anything else you can think of?' he asked.

'I don't think so.'

'Thank you. Father Tim and I will need to discuss this.'

They sat there for a few moments in thoughtful silence. Once they'd drunk their tea, Father Tim said, 'We'll end with a short prayer to Saint Michael and then we'll leave you to your day for now.'

The men bowed their heads and Jasmine looked down as Father Tim began to pray.

'Saint Michael the Archangel, defend us in battle. Be our protection against the wickedness and snares of the devil . . . May God rebuke him, we humbly pray . . .'

Once the prayer was finished, the men got up to leave. As they left the room, they confirmed that they were going to discuss everything she'd told them and then Father Tim would phone her in a day or so. They both advised her to put a cross in each room – it would help, they said. Father Andrew thanked her for her hospitality and tried to make a joke about the flies.

She smiled politely and closed the front door. She walked into the living room and flopped down on the sofa, putting her legs up, and thought about what had just happened. She guessed that when Father Tim contacted her again he wouldn't have a simple solution. There would be nothing new. Just more prayers and advice to put a crucifix in each room. They listened – they were good listeners; it was their job – but beyond that there was no actual advice they could realistically give her. Eventually, her eyes closed and she dropped off into a deep, dreamless sleep.

It was nearly 2 p.m. when she woke – an hour before

she had to collect the girls. She pulled herself off the sofa, had a wash and worked solidly for an hour. She was so far behind. Then, at 3 p.m., she left and drove to the girls' school. They came out very excited and weighed down with books and work from the year.

'Six weeks off!' Leah shouted.

Isabel, though, said, 'I like my school. It's safe there. Nothing strange happens.'

'Nothing strange will happen at home,' Jasmine said positively, and hoped she would be proved right.

TWENTY-FIVE

Jasmine spent some time talking to Isabel in the car, reassuring her that there was nothing to worry about at home. She didn't tell her or Leah, or later Mark, about the flies or the priests' visit. It was the start of the long summer holiday and Jasmine wanted the girls to relax and have fun. She would be at home to keep an eye on everything and had taken the first and last weeks off. After waking up from her nap that afternoon she'd also decided what she would do next. The priests couldn't do anything but listen to her, so she'd decided she needed to speak to Freya Morgan again and ask her about the house. She knew more than she was letting on, for sure, and Jasmine needed to find out what it was.

That Friday night and the weekend passed without incident, much to everyone's relief, although no one admitted that they were worried. When Isabel said, 'I've had a good weekend, Mummy,' Jasmine knew what she meant.

On Monday morning, all the family kissed Mark goodbye

and the girls waved him off at the window. This was a novelty and hadn't happened since they'd moved in, because he always left for work before them in the mornings. They waved until he was out of sight. At 9.30, Jasmine went into the study and pushed the door to. The girls were watching television in the living room. Jasmine had said that if they were good, she'd take them out soon to an activity centre. She sat at her desk and opened what she and Mark called their 'house file'. It contained all the paperwork from the move. She took out the selling agent's blurb and looked at the picture of their house on the front, then she dialled them. A young man answered.

'It's Jasmine Simmons, here. We bought 13 Ravens Lane from you,' she said, and paused.

'Yes, I remember you,' the young man said. 'Have you settled in?"

Jasmine hesitated, but decided he didn't need to know. 'Yes, thank you. The reason I'm calling is that I'd like the address of where Freya and James Morgan are staying now. They lived here before us, and I've got quite a bit of mail here to readdress to them.'

'Yes, of course. Just a minute,' he said and disappeared.

Jasmine allowed herself to breathe again. Strictly speaking, he could have said they weren't allowed to divulge their clients' details, but he was very young and clearly didn't quite know the rules yet. He returned a few minutes later.

'They're at 6 Crescent Road, in a block of flats. We found it for them. They've taken a six-month lease. The postcode is . . .'

Six months, Jasmine thought as she wrote, so they should definitely still be there. Good. As soon as he'd finished, she thanked him and then googled the address. It was about a ten-minute drive away. No wonder she'd seen Freya at their local supermarket. It was surprising she hadn't seen her around more, really. She'd leave her visit until this evening, when Mark would be home to look after the girls. She would tell them all she was going to meet a friend for a drink.

Phone call finished, Jasmine and the girls got into their car to go to the outdoor activity centre, which was about five miles away. The girls were very excited and talked non-stop about what they were going to do. Jasmine had taken them there during the last summer holidays as well.

It was already packed when they arrived. Jasmine found a shady spot and sat there with her thoughts, keeping an eye on the girls while they played. What would Freya Morgan say when she just turned up tonight? she wondered. There would be no prevaricating or making excuses. Jasmine would tell her straight away why she was there and hope for a positive response. Freya was unlikely to close the door in her face, was she?

Jasmine bought the girls lunch from the café, and they stayed at the centre until four o'clock. She drove home growing more nervous with each mile, then she paused outside and looked for flies. All seemed quiet. She told the girls to go straight upstairs for a shower and to change out of their dirty shorts and into their nightwear while she made their dinner. Mark came in at around six o'clock and they all ate together.

'I'm going to see my friend Ellie tonight,' she said casually. Ellie was an old friend of hers whom she met up with every three to four months.

'Good for you,' Mark said. 'That'll be the first time you've been out since we moved.'

'Yes, it will be,' she agreed. 'There's been a lot to do.'

She left Mark to put the children to bed. The girls were allowed to stay up later during the holidays. At 7.30 p.m. she kissed them all goodbye and came out of the living room, leaving them watching a film. She was very nervous about just turning up at Freya's flat and kept running through what she was going to say. She followed the sat nav to Crescent Road. Number six was in a two-storey block of flats immediately to her left. She parked the car and sat with the window down for a few minutes, nervously rehearsing how she would broach the subject, then she got out. She walked to the front of the building and checked the buzzer for number six. She hesitated again before pressing it. It was some time before it was answered, the voice distorted by the intercom.

'Hello?' It was a female voice.

'Is that Freya Morgan?' Jasmine asked, her voice unsteady.

'Yes. Who's speaking?'

'It's Jasmine Simmons.' She paused. There was no response. 'I'd like to talk to you if that's possible.'

There was another long silence and the intercom went muffled before Freya finally said, 'Yes, you can come up.'

The lock released, the front door opened, and Jasmine

stepped in. Her stomach was churning, and she wondered again if she was doing the right thing in coming here. Number six was on the first floor. She trod heavily upstairs. The door was still closed so she pressed the bell. After some time the door opened and Freya Morgan stood there.

'How are you?' Freya asked with a forced sense of brightness.

'I'm good, thank you,' Jasmine said. She waited to be invited in.

'It's a bit of a surprise seeing you here,' Freya said.

'It must be. I'm sorry I didn't call. I'd like to talk to you about our house – 13 Ravens Lane. Ask you some questions, if that's all right?'

Freya's face changed. 'I can guess what it's about,' she said bluntly. 'James said this might happen. You'd better come in. James is out with his mates, but Madison is in.'

'Thank you,' Jasmine said, and went into their flat. That was the biggest hurdle overcome.

She followed Freya through the small hall and into the living room.

'Hi,' Jasmine said to Madison, who was sitting on the sofa.

'Hi. I'm going to my room,' she replied, and disappeared.

'I'm sorry. I've upset your evening,' Jasmine said to Freya.

'Don't worry about it. Sit down. Do you want a drink?'

'No, thank you.' She sat on the sofa.

'What have you done with your husband and kids?' Freya asked.

'They're at home. I lied about coming here tonight.

I said I was meeting an old friend. Mark wouldn't have understood.'

Freya nodded. There was silence. Jasmine didn't know how to begin, despite rehearsing what she wanted to say enough times.

'I can guess why you're here,' Freya said again. 'It's about the supernatural goings-on in the house?'

Jasmine felt a frisson of fear at the mention of the supernatural. 'Yes. That's right. I know you experienced it too.'

'But it wasn't our fault, I promise you,' Freya blurted out. 'It was like that when we arrived. Almost immediately it started and it continued till the day we moved out. Eighteen months of sheer hell. When we bought the place, it was supposed to be our forever home. We were planning on staying there forever. We couldn't. We could never be sure what was going to happen next. Madison would only ever sit in the living room when we had a viewing, then she went straight back to her bedroom.'

Jasmine nodded. 'What sorts of things happened to you and your family while you were there?'

'Where to start?' Freya let out a long sigh. 'The temperature used to drop significantly in the living room for no obvious reason. It never happened anywhere else. Even when the sun was up outside it would still go very cold sometimes. The sofa used to move. That's when we saw her. The woman in a grey jersey and green trousers. Goodness knows who she was. No one we ever knew. Have you seen her?'

'Yes, but not in the living room.'

'Then there was the garden,' Freya continued. 'We were

going to do so much with it, but every time we planted anything it died within a few days. We gave up in the end. One day we had a loft full of dead crows. They'd got in through a hole in the roof, which we got repaired. And flies around the windows. Hundreds of them that kept coming back, time after time. It was disgusting. I thought they must be living in the house somewhere, but we could never find out where. I guess worst of all were the accidents we kept having. James cut his leg and it wouldn't heal. It was awful. I kept taking him to A&E and they dressed it for him. It was fine for a few days, then the cut would reopen. It didn't heal properly until we left the house. Madison kept cutting her fingers, constantly. They've all healed now too. I fell downstairs and knocked myself out. I could have died there. There were hundreds of accidents, which have stopped now. I don't know what else to tell you.'

'And everything is definitely back to normal for you now?' Jasmine checked.

'Yes, we're just a normal family living a normal life. That house is a bad memory for us, but I realize you're still living it. That's why I didn't hang around in the supermarket, in case you wanted to talk. I'm sorry, I really am, but I don't know what else we could have done. All our savings were tied up in that house. We had to sell.'

'What about the people who lived in the house before you?' Jasmine asked. 'Did they experience anything?'

'I honestly don't know. The woman who owned it before us moved some distance away. I never thought to contact her like you have me.'

'Would you still have her address?' Jasmine asked.

'I might have it somewhere, or James might. I'll have a look after you've gone. What's your mobile number? I'll give you a ring if I find it.' She picked up her phone and Jasmine gave her the number.

'Thank you,' she said.

'I don't know what else I can tell you,' Freya said. 'Other than that, I contacted a priest. Father Tim Ashridge. He used to come and visit me. It helped. I'm a Catholic.'

'I've met him,' Jasmine said, without elaborating. 'I'm pleased you're settled now, truly.'

'We're trying to find somewhere to live permanently but it's not easy. We don't want to make the same mistake again. You read about this sort of thing in magazines, but you don't ever think it will happen to you.'

'It won't happen again,' Jasmine said. 'I'm sure of it. It's that house. I'll leave you to it then. Thank you.'

As she walked from the flat, she felt relieved she'd gone there. What should she do now, though? As far as Freya and her family were concerned, the goings-on in the house weren't their fault. They'd simply moved in, inherited the problems, and moved out again. Had the people who'd been living there before them experienced anything strange? she wondered. Hopefully Freya would do as she'd promised and phone her with their contact details.

TWENTY-SIX

Freya sent a text message the following day. It contained the name of the seller – Selina Preston – her address and telephone number. She'd lived at 13 Ravens Lane for fourteen years. It was therefore very unlikely she'd been haunted, Jasmine thought. *I wouldn't just turn up there,* Freya had texted. *Phone ahead of you first.*

She wouldn't just turn up. The address was over a hundred miles away, so there was no way she would drive there. But she needed to speak to Selina Preston in confidence. She'd have to phone her. There was no other way.

She replied to the text, thanking Freya and saying she'd phone Selina. Then she waited until after lunch when the girls were engrossed in a game in the garden before dialling the number from her study. She was as nervous as she'd been when visiting Freya as she listened to the phone ringing. A woman eventually answered with a brisk, 'Hello?'

'Is that Selina Preston?' Jasmine asked.

'Speaking.'

'You don't know me. I'm Jasmine Simmons. My husband and I bought 13 Ravens Lane from the Morgans. We moved in about six weeks ago. Can I talk to you about the property?'

'Is this a wind-up? I thought the Morgans said that house was their forever home?'

'No. It's not a wind-up. They were going to stay, but they only lasted eighteen months, then my husband and I bought the property.'

'Why did they go so quickly?' she asked, clearly puzzled.

There was no easy way to say this. 'They believe, as we do, that the house is haunted.'

Jasmine heard her laugh. 'Rubbish. That's ridiculous. Where did they get that idea from? And what's it got to do with me?'

Where do I begin? Jasmine thought. She cleared her throat and began to tell Selina about the supernatural happenings at 13 Ravens Lane, many of which Freya had experienced too. Selina listened quietly. When Jasmine stopped, Selina said, 'I'm not sure if the two of you are deranged, but my sister and I lived in that house for fourteen years without any problem at all. After my sister died, I sold the house straight away, as I'd decided to move here to be closer to my brother. I know the property has a slightly eerie address, but we never experienced anything remotely weird while we were there. Certainly nothing like you have described. The two of us were very happy there.'

'How did you find the garden?' Jasmine asked, taking all this in.

'Very good. We grew some of our own vegetables and plenty of flowers. Why do you ask?'

'My husband and I can't get anything to grow in it, neither could Freya and her husband.'

'I'm sorry, but that's no fault of mine. I need to be going now.'

'One last question,' Jasmine said quickly. The woman was running out of patience. Jasmine was aware how deluded she sounded. 'You mentioned your sister. Did she die in this house?'

'Yes, she did,' Selina replied indignantly. 'I brought her home to die. It was her wish. Is that all?'

'Can I ask you what she used to wear?'

'What's that got to do with anything?' she replied sharply.

'I'm sorry. It's just that we and the previous occupants have seen a woman wearing a grey top and green trousers, which is rather unusual.'

Selina went very quiet. 'I don't know how you found out about that, but they were my sister's favourite clothes, the ones she wanted to be buried in.'

Suddenly Jasmine felt very cold. 'Where was she buried?' she asked.

'Coleshaw Cemetery. I think that's everything. I'll go now. Goodbye.' She put down the phone.

Jasmine sat at her desk trying to control her breathing. She felt uncomfortable, as though someone had just walked over her grave. The woman in the grey top and green trousers wasn't fictional. She was Selina's sister. She wondered what she looked like and, taking a deep breath, turned to her laptop. She didn't know Selina's sister's first name so she googled, *The funeral of Miss Preston, Coleshaw Cemetery,* and the year she thought the woman must have died. Up came a piece the relatives must have put in the local press with a small photograph. Jasmine stared in disbelief, then enlarged it. Without a doubt, it was the image of the woman they thought they'd seen in Isabel's bedroom, dressed in a grey top and green trousers. Miss Angela Preston.

Jasmine was still looking at it, trying to decide what to do, when she heard Isabel shout from the garden.

'Mum! She's here again.'

Jasmine rushed from the study and out into the garden.

'Up there!' she shouted, pointing to her and Mark's bedroom window.

Jasmine looked up at the woman dressed in a grey top and green trousers as she slowly faded from view.

'It's all right,' she said, comforting her daughters. 'It's going to be OK, I promise you.'

'I saw her too,' Leah said in a panic. 'She was in your bedroom.'

'I know, love. I know.'

It took some time to calm the girls down, and then they wanted Jasmine to stay in the garden while they played. Once they'd been persuaded to resume their game, they kept looking up at the bedroom window, but there was no sign of the woman again. What was she going to do? Jasmine wondered all afternoon. She sat in the garden with the girls and occasionally glanced up at her bedroom window, just as the children kept doing, but none of them saw anything else. She could call Father Tim Ashridge, she supposed, but she doubted he'd have much to offer beyond more prayers and advice to put a cross in each room.

She stayed in the garden with the girls playing for most of the afternoon. Then she made them tea, which they ate indoors. When Mark arrived home the girls were still talking about the woman they'd both seen at their parents' bedroom window. It was the first thing they said to Mark. He was tired and hungry from a long day at work. 'Don't be so silly,' he snapped. 'There's no such thing as ghosts.'

'They're not being silly,' Jasmine said, having run out of patience. She'd had to deal with this all afternoon, and it was only the second day of the summer holiday. 'I saw her too. But I know who she is now. She used to live here. I'll tell you about it later.'

'What Mummy, what?' Isabel and Leah shouted.

Jasmine looked away doubtfully. She was trying to protect them. They waited impatiently and eventually she sat down in the kitchen where they were.

'I spoke to the woman who used to live here before the Morgans,' she said to them all. 'Her name is Selina Preston. She lived here with her sister, Angela, for fourteen years and had a lovely time. But then Angela died and Selina moved away.'

'So why is Selina's sister still living here?' Leah interrupted.

'I don't know,' Jasmine replied.

Selina's sister had died here and for some reason her

spirit hadn't gone to wherever it was they usually went but had remained here. Was it because Selina had moved out soon after her passing? Jasmine wondered. She wouldn't tell the girls anything more if she could avoid it. Just enough to stop their questions.

'Ghost or no ghost, I'm going to get changed in my bedroom,' Mark said, and disappeared upstairs.

'He's brave,' Leah commented.

'It's nothing to worry about,' Jasmine said. She hoped she was right. How long did it take for a spirit to move on after death?

When Mark reappeared, the girls wanted a snack so they could eat with him. He kissed them both.

'She was real,' Leah said. 'I saw her, Isabel saw her, and so did Mummy.'

Jasmine motioned to Mark that they would talk more later, after the girls were in bed. She served dinner and they all ate, the girls having their snack. They'd had enough of playing in the garden for one day and didn't want to go out there again without Jasmine. After they'd finished eating, they watched television for a while, then it was time for them to go to bed.

'Can Daddy take us up? He's not scared of that woman,' Leah said, glancing at their mother.

'I want Mummy to take us,' Isabel cried.

'I'll take you up and then Daddy can come and kiss you both goodnight,' Jasmine said stoically.

There was some argument, but very quickly Jasmine had them on their way upstairs. They wanted to look in their parents' bedroom to make sure *she* was no longer in there and it was safe.

'But she comes in my bedroom too,' Isabel said, quietly poking her head around the door.

'Are you scared?' Jasmine asked her.

'Not really. She doesn't hurt me. She just gives me a fright.'

'I think that's enough talk about it for now. Neither of you will sleep tonight if you keep talking about her.' Although Jasmine knew the truth of what Isabel said.

Isabel had been visited by her more times than anyone else had. She wondered which room Selina's sister had died in. Could it have been Isabel's bedroom?

Once the girls were ready for bed, she called down to Mark to come up and kiss them goodnight, then she went downstairs. He was up there for about a quarter of an hour, talking to them, then he came down. Jasmine straightened in her chair.

'Well?' he asked as he came into the living room and sat down. 'What's new?'

Jasmine began to tell him everything she'd learnt. All the incidents she hadn't told him about before and also the priests' visits. She told him everything she could remember, finishing with that afternoon and seeing the woman at their bedroom window.

'I think she's Selina's dead sister,' Jasmine concluded. 'There's no other explanation.'

She was expecting Mark to pooh-pooh everything and criticize her for adding to the children's paranoia, but he didn't. He turned to her and showed her his hand.

‘There’s something wrong in this house,’ he said slowly. ‘Look at my hand. It’s cleared up.’

She looked. The wound that had been oozing all week, including last night, was now suddenly healed, just like before. There wasn’t even a scratch to show where it had been.

‘It was weeping badly when I went to bed,’ he said. ‘And now there’s nothing.’

‘I’m sure it’s Selina’s sister who is doing this,’ she said. It has to be. She’s playing with us.’

Mark gave a half-hearted nod and checked his phone.

‘I wonder if Selina’s sister died in Isabel’s bedroom, and that’s why she is in there most of all,’ Jasmine said, thinking aloud.

Mark looked up. ‘So why was she in our bedroom this afternoon? And where is she now?’ He glanced around the room.

‘Don’t do that. I’m just about holding it together after this afternoon,’ Jasmine said.

‘Look, Jasmine, I know some odd things have been happening lately, but I’m sure there’s a rational explanation for all of this. I doubt it has anything to do with Selina’s dead sister. I simply don’t believe in ghosts.’

‘So what did you and I see in Isabel’s room?’ Jasmine demanded, her voice rising. ‘And what about all the other strange things that have happened here, not only to us but to the Morgans as well?’ It was impossible to discuss this with Mark. He accepted there was a problem but blanked out the rest with logic. It didn’t add up or work for Jasmine, who was desperate to discuss it and try to get some answers.

'I don't know,' he said quietly. 'Hopefully it will all end soon and we can continue to live here happily.'

'The Morgans were here for eighteen months, and it didn't end well at all for them. They finally had to move out and are now living in a rented flat trying to get their lives back together.'

'So what do you suggest we do?' Mark asked.

She could tell he'd had enough of this conversation and wanted to relax after work.

'I honestly don't know,' she said. 'But we need to do something and fast.'

'Move?' he asked her, narrowing his eyes.

'I said I don't know, but I've got six weeks of this, trying to calm down the girls. Although Isabel doesn't seem as upset as Leah or me.'

Mark looked at her. 'Let me sleep on it,' he said, applying the same logic to this as he did to most other matters in his life. 'Perhaps I can come up with a solution.'

Jasmine was going to repeat, 'Perhaps,' but stopped herself and let it go. This was Mark she was talking to, and she knew him too well. He'd didn't want to talk about it further and he'd leave it, probably to her to sort out. He had his job and went to work for nearly twelve hours each day. As soon as he left the house in the morning his thoughts went to work. She knew how it was and assumed it must be the same for most people with a job with lots of responsibilities. She'd have to sort this mess out at home alone. It was down to her. After all, she'd found the house in the first place. If only she hadn't ignored that drop in temperature when they'd first visited.

'Yes, you sleep on it and let me know what you decide,' she said, and went into the kitchen to tidy up.

The following morning Mark went to work, having apparently forgotten all about the strange happenings in their house, but Jasmine hadn't. They wouldn't move; she'd decided that as she lay awake thinking for most of the night. Tomorrow she would take the girls for a walk through Coleshaw Cemetery and see what, if anything, they could discover about Miss Angela Preston.

TWENTY-SEVEN

Coleshaw Cemetery was where Jasmine's parents lay buried. It was a small cemetery for those who lived in Coleshaw and the surrounding villages. Jasmine and her daughters had visited it in the Christmas holidays, but not since. She told them where they were going in the car.

'What are we going to do there?' Leah remarked sulkily. Jasmine recognized that she was on the edge of puberty.

'I like going to the cemetery,' Isabel said.

'So do I,' Jasmine agreed. 'It will be lovely in summer.'

Jasmine went to visit her parents' grave about every four to six months. Her father had died when she was a child and her mother five years ago. Leah had some memory of her maternal grandmother, but Isabel didn't. They hadn't been to visit since moving into their new home. As she pulled into the cemetery, Jasmine wondered what her mother would have made of what was happening at 13 Ravens Lane. Jasmine would have confided in her, for sure, but now there was no one she could talk to honestly. With a pang of regret, she parked the car and they all got out.

'Do I have to come?' Leah bemoaned.

'Yes, I can't leave you in the car. It's out of view.'

It was a humid day with the possibility of a storm later, so Jasmine took an umbrella with them. They always kept one in the car for days like this, and she reached under the seat for it. She took the flowers she'd brought with them from the passenger seat, got out and locked the car. The girls walked calmly along the path by her side. They tended to walk in an adult manner when they came to the cemetery. There was something peaceful and tranquil about it there, with no shouting or running. Jasmine was pleased they'd come. There were a couple of other children there with a parent or grandparent, but not that many.

They walked along the path to the area beside a small tree where her parents were buried. They knew it well. It was a grave on their right. She bent down and removed some dead leaves and then put the fresh flowers into the vase. She spent a few minutes tidying it before she stood and looked at the writing. *Always in our hearts.* She was unsure of what she was supposed to do now. She'd never known how to behave here, even in the early days when her grief at losing her mother was very raw. Some elderly people sat on benches and just whiled away the day. She'd seen them here in all weathers. Jasmine had done this herself on her first few visits, spent an hour just sitting there watching, but then life had resumed and she'd got into the habit of bringing flowers and then leaving. She felt it was a pity her mother hadn't lived longer so she was able to spend more time with her grandchildren. Mark's parents were both still alive but lived over 150 miles away in the North of England. They'd have to invite them to stay soon, once they'd sorted out whatever was happening in the house. She shook herself back to the present.

'What are we going to do now?' Leah asked, disgruntled at not being allowed to wait in the car.

'Let's go for a walk,' Jasmine said, putting the dead foliage in the bin.

They walked slowly around the perimeter path. If Selina's sister had been cremated, it would have been virtually impossible to find her, but Selina had said on the phone that she'd been buried in Coleshaw Cemetery. They continued around the perimeter path until they came to the newly dug area. It had been just over eighteen months since Selina's sister had died, Jasmine had learnt from her Google search, so she began to check the dates on the graves.

'What are you doing?' Leah asked her.

'I'm looking for a more recent grave.'

'Why?'

'Just to have a look.'

Thankfully, there weren't that many burials and Jasmine was soon up to a couple of years ago, then she spotted it. It was a plain grave that still looked new and shining white, with the name Angela Preston engraved on it.

Jasmine stood beside it and wondered if Selina ever came to visit; she hadn't said. A small weed was growing up through the white pebbles and Jasmine pulled it up. So this was it. Now she was here, she wasn't sure why she'd come. She read the wording on the grave, still fresh and untarnished by the weather.

In loving memory of our beloved sister,
Angela Preston.
Rest in peace.

Then there was the date, eighteen months before. She'd been just fifty-one when she'd died. That was young, Jasmine thought, and wondered what she'd died of. There was nothing further to be gleaned from the grave, other than that Selina had told her the truth.

'Why are we here?' Leah asked petulantly.

'I just wanted to visit this grave,' Jasmine said. 'She was Selina's sister, Angela.' She turned to go.

'Do we know her?' Isabel asked, following her mother.

'Not really,' Jasmine said, and continued to walk away.

The girls fell into a leisurely step beside her. As they began around the perimeter path again, she thought of her own dear mother. A tear came to her eye, which she quickly wiped away. What am I going to do about Selina's sister? she silently asked her mother, and waited for a reply. None came; unlike at other times when her mother had seemed to provide a solution from beyond the grave, or at least point her in the right direction, now there was nothing at all.

They'd seen Angela Preston's grave, but how did that throw any light on what was going on in their house? She honestly had no idea. She'd discovered nothing; it was just another grave. She was grateful that she hadn't told the girls why they'd come.

'Where shall we go now?' she asked them, looking up at the storm clouds.

'The leisure centre,' Leah said.

'Good suggestion,' Jasmine said with a smile, and she kissed both her daughters. They hurried to their car.

'Just in time,' she said as a large raindrop landed on the roof, and they got in.

They closed their car doors and Jasmine pressed to start the ignition. Nothing happened; the engine didn't turn on. She tried again. Still nothing. And again. She sighed. The rain beat heavily on the roof.

'I'm going to have to call out the breakdown service,' she said to the girls, trying the engine one more time.

Leah sighed, while Isabel looked worried. Jasmine took out her phone and called the number. It connected to the call handler straight away, and she explained that her car wouldn't start, while trying to start it again. Still nothing. The call handler asked her where she was and promised to have someone there in about an hour.

'It's going to be an hour,' she told the girls, and pulled a face as she hung up.

It soon got hot in the car with the windows up to keep out the rain, so Jasmine suggested that the girls wind theirs down a little. She did the same. Every so often a few large raindrops bounced in and the girls squealed. It became something of a game.

She phoned Mark and left a message saying only that she'd broken down. After an hour had passed, during which time she and the girls played 'I spy' games, still no one had come to see them. She tried the engine again and then called the breakdown service and asked where they were.

'It's going to be about another half an hour,' the woman said. 'We're very busy today.'

Jasmine couldn't do anything other than accept this and tried the engine one more time, without any real hope. It wasn't working; it was completely dead.

The rain eventually stopped, and they wound their windows down fully. The air felt fresh and cool as it drifted in. Jasmine suggested the girls might like to stand outside, but neither of them wanted to in a wet cemetery. The mechanic phoned to say he was on his way. Jasmine thanked him and tried the engine again. It still wasn't working.

He arrived within about ten minutes and asked her to try the ignition. To her utter amazement, the car started straight away.

'I don't believe it!' she exclaimed. 'I've been trying to turn it on for over an hour.'

'Turn it off and on again,' he told her.

She did and it worked fine. She switched it off and back on a few times to make sure. It was all working.

'I'll just check under the bonnet to be certain,' he said. 'Switch off the engine.'

She did as he asked and then he released the bonnet using the switch on the driver's side. She got out and joined him, looking under the bonnet. There was nothing to see.

'Sod's law,' he said, and closed the bonnet. 'Start the car again.'

She did, and it was no surprise to either of them that the

engine started first time. She looked at him, embarrassed, then signed the document he presented on his phone. He waited while she started the car and watched them drive away.

'Is the car fixed now?' Isabel asked.

'It was never broken,' Leah said disparagingly, and glanced at her mother.

Jasmine then drove them to the leisure centre where they had lunch straight away. The girls spent the entire afternoon playing before they went home. The car started first time.

It was nearly 5 p.m. when they arrived indoors. Mark wasn't home yet, but the first thing Jasmine noticed was that the answerphone on the small table in the hall was bleeping with a number of alerts, which was unusual these days. People usually called her mobile. She scrolled down the list and saw it was the same number that had phoned several times, but they'd only left two messages. She pressed to listen to the messages.

'It's Selina Preston. Can you give me a ring when you're home? Thank you.'

The second message said similar: 'I guess you're still out. Please call when you return,' Selina said.

The other alerts were Selina phoning again, but no message was left. Puzzled, Jasmine settled the girls in the living room and went into the study to call Selina.

'You're back,' she said, sounding relieved. 'I haven't been able to settle to anything. I need to talk to you. I wasn't completely honest when you called yesterday. There's so much more to the story than I told you. It's true that nothing supernatural happened while we were at 13 Ravens Lane, but my sister, Angela, had a dreadful death. I was just wondering . . .' She stopped, and Jasmine assumed it was to compose herself. 'She had a particularly vicious form of skin cancer.'

'I'm so sorry,' Jasmine said.

'Thank you. She wanted to stay at home and for me to look after her. I took a lot of time off work. Her bedroom was at the front of the house, but she kept coming into my room, the double one at the back. She didn't like being left alone. I couldn't have her sleep with me. She had lesions all over her body by then. It was shocking to see and they oozed and wept for days. Then they'd heal and another would open up. I didn't think I'd be able to cope alone, but somehow I did. When she finally died, in all honesty it was a release. Your phone call came as a complete shock. It brought it all back.' She stopped and Jasmine thought she might be crying. She waited before asking her next question.

'So, Angela had the small bedroom at the front of the house?'

'Yes, that's where I put her, but she kept coming into my room. I didn't know how she could walk by then, she was so thin, but she did. It was all so traumatic for both of us.'

Jasmine thought about this, then said, 'I've just come from Angela's grave.'

'You have?' Selina asked, surprised.

'Yes. My parents are buried in the same cemetery and after I'd been to their grave, I went to Angela's. Then my car wouldn't start. I had to call out the breakdown service and when the mechanic arrived it started first time. It was so strange.'

There was silence on the phone before Selina said, 'My car was always playing up in the cemetery, not starting at all. Angela loved that car. It was only three years old, but I got another one after she died. I park outside the cemetery now and I haven't had any problems since. Thanks for going to my sister's grave. I try to drive down once a month but what with work, it isn't easy.'

'I'm sure it's not,' Jasmine empathized.

'I don't know what else I can tell you, although from what you've said it seems that some of my sister's anguish has stayed in that house. She always wanted to wear that grey top and green trousers when she got dressed. In the end, they lay on the chair in her room when she could no longer get out of her nightclothes. The whole thing was a nightmare. I had some help towards the end, but it was nowhere near enough.'

'Thank you for sharing this with me,' Jasmine said. 'I wonder why the neighbours haven't said anything. We've seen Poppy and Harry a few times.'

'I'm afraid I fell out with Poppy, and we never got on with the Sullivans, especially Bert, but Sandra on the other side was good to us. She and Angela were very close.'

'I don't really know her,' Jasmine admitted. 'One final thing. Out of interest, which room did your sister die in?'

'She didn't. For some reason she went into the garden and died there. Sandra saw her and rang my bell. It was the final episode in a very tragic saga.'

TWENTY-EIGHT

Jasmine put the phone down and sat at the desk, deep in thought. She could imagine Angela covered in weeping lesions, staggering into Selina's bedroom to be with her. Jasmine hadn't mentioned that Mark had developed an angry cut that wouldn't heal, and that the Morgans had experienced unusual injuries too. Was that relevant? She wasn't sure. How much of this was connected with what the Morgans and her family had been experiencing? She didn't know. Two months ago, she would have said there could be no connection, but now she honestly had no idea. This had all begun after Angela's death – first with the Morgans and now them.

She thought back to Sandra and realized she wasn't the weird old lady Jasmine had thought; she probably just didn't want or know how to share her grief at losing her friend. All those times Jasmine caught her staring at them, she must have been reliving that awful moment when she saw Angela dead in the garden. Should she visit her? Invite her to dinner as she had once thought of doing? It would give Jasmine the opportunity to say that she knew what she'd been through and to try to forge a friendship, or just be neighbourly with each other, if nothing else. She'd think about it.

While it had been decent of Selina to phone, it didn't really add much or resolve anything, Jasmine decided. True, it seemed that Angela's death was connected to what was happening now – the lesions, the car not starting, the sighting of the ghost, but she still had the dilemma of what to do to make it all go away and allow her family to get back to a normal life.

Still thinking about this, she stood from her desk and crossed the living room where the girls were watching television, then made her way through to the kitchen to make dinner. Perhaps she should talk to the priests again and see what Father Tim had to offer beyond more prayers. He and Father Andrew seemed to be the only people who were fully aware of what was happening and who could talk freely and calmly about it, having dealt with it before. Sometimes she felt she was thinking herself round in circles. Sometimes she thought she was going mad.

She came back to the present and began to peel the potatoes slowly, still deep in thought, when she heard Leah shout at Isabel.

'Stop it, will you? I'm watching that. Put it back on.'

'I'm not doing anything,' Isabel retaliated.

'Yes, you are.'

'Whatever it is you're doing, stop it now!' Jasmine shouted back. She knew that Isabel sometimes wound Leah up by fiddling with the remote control and turning the television off.

It went quiet for a few minutes, then she heard Isabel say, 'It's not me.'

'Yes, it is,' Leah replied.

Jasmine put down the peeler – enough was enough. She was tired and frazzled. She went into the living room.

'What is it you're doing?' She glared at them. 'You've had a good day out. If you don't want to watch television, then find something else to do.'

'It isn't me,' Isabel insisted. She was holding the remote and pressed it to turn the television on. As soon as it was on, it immediately switched off again. She did it again with the same result.

'Here, let me see,' Jasmine said, and took the remote.

Jasmine pressed for it to come on and the television programme reappeared.

'There!' she said, and put the remote on the coffee table. 'Now leave it alone, both of you.' She began to walk away.

As she did, the television switched off. She turned and saw that the remote control was where she'd left it on the coffee table.

She returned and picked it up. 'It could be an electrical fault,' she said, looking at it. 'Leave it until Daddy gets home.' She replaced it on the coffee table.

'But I want my programme on,' Leah moaned.

'So do I,' Isabel said.

'You'll have to do something else until dinner is ready. Get a board game out or play in your bedrooms.'

She returned to the kitchen and continued with dinner as the girls went upstairs. A few minutes later, the television switched itself on again. That was odd. She went into the living room and pulled out the plug. Something was wrong. She'd ask Mark to look at it as soon as he got home. She returned to the kitchen and was just about to put the dish into the oven when the television turned itself back on again. But that was impossible. Leaving what she was doing, she went into the living room. The girls were nowhere to be seen. The remote control was still on the table where she'd left it. She went to the back of the television and saw the plug lying on the floor. She must have taken out the wrong plug, she supposed, so she picked it up and traced it back to the television, then stood, trying to work out what had just happened. It was the right plug, yet it wasn't plugged in. So how did the television come on again? How could that happen? Then she remembered that the priest had asked her if the television had switched itself on and off.

At that moment the front door opened and Mark came in from work. Jasmine went to him.

'Hi, darling,' he said. Then he saw the look on her face. 'What's up? I thought you were taking the girls out today?'

'We did go out,' she said. 'But something strange has been happening since we got back. The television is unplugged but keeps switching itself on.'

She saw the smallest smile pass across his lips, then he kissed her.

'Don't be silly,' he said. 'Of course it's not.'

'I'm not being silly. Come and see.'

'Daddy, Daddy,' Leah and Isabel shouted as they came thundering downstairs, pleased to see him again.

'Can you fix the television?' Leah asked him.

'I'll try,' Mark said, and he picked them both up and kissed them.

He set them down again to take off his shoes and then went into the living room where the television was off. He pushed the plug into its socket, then switched it on.

'What's the problem?' he asked them.

'It kept switching off and I got blamed for it,' Isabel said.

'Even when it wasn't plugged in,' Jasmine said. 'Is that possible?'

'Not on this television,' Mark said. 'But it seems to be working now. Leave it on.'

Mark found the channel the girls had been watching and left the two of them sitting in the living room, side by side on the sofa. He went upstairs while Jasmine went into the kitchen to finish making dinner. She could hear the television as she worked. It seemed to be fine now and didn't keep switching off. Mark came downstairs and went into the living room to check on his repair work.

'Everything all right?' he asked the girls.

'Yes, thanks, Dad,' Leah replied.

'It's fine now,' Isabel said.

Presently they sat down for dinner and talked of their day. 'We saw another lady's grave,' Isabel said, but Mark wasn't listening. He was scratching his left hand.

'How's your hand?' Jasmine asked him.

'I think it's OK,' he said, and showed her. There was a fine pink line where the gash had been, but that was all.

'Leave it alone,' Jasmine told him as if she were talking to a child, 'or you'll make it worse.'

When the children had gone up to bed, Jasmine sat on the sofa ready to talk to Mark about her day, but he was looking very odd. He had put a plaster on his hand and was holding it, a grave expression on his face.

'What's the matter?' she asked him.

'It's my hand again, that's all.'

'What's the matter with your hand?' she asked. 'It was fine an hour ago.'

'I guess I must have caught it on something sharp.'

She looked at him carefully.

'Caught it on what?'

'I don't know,' he said, and rose from the sofa.

Jasmine watched him go out through the patio doors and down the garden, where he wandered around for a while. The vegetables were no longer there but the flowers were doing all right. He walked up and down the path as though he had something on his mind, then he returned indoors. He went upstairs to the bathroom before coming down again. Jasmine looked at him as he came into the room, then returned her gaze to the television. He sat beside her on the sofa and peeled back the edge of the bandage to show her. There was a fresh, bloody cut. Jasmine gave a small gasp.

'How did you do that?' she exclaimed.

'I didn't. It just appeared,' Mark said, staring at her, upset and confused.

Jasmine was quiet as she looked at the cut, then she said, 'Selina's sister, Angela, had cuts all over her body, lesions, before she died.'

'Don't be ridiculous!' Mark snapped. 'As if that has anything to do with my hand.' He stood up and left the room.

Was she being ridiculous? She didn't know any more, but something clearly wasn't right with his hand. Cuts shouldn't keep suddenly opening up, then just as quickly disappearing. At that moment she made the decision to call Father Tim Ashridge again. He'd said he'd contact her but he hadn't, so she'd phone him first thing in the morning and see what he suggested.

Mark didn't return to the living room that evening. She heard him moving around in the bedroom, then the bathroom, then he went to bed. She didn't go up herself for another hour, only to find Mark still wide awake.

'My hand hurts,' he said, holding the one with the plaster on.

'Take some paracetamol,' she replied. 'Do you want me to get them?'

He nodded.

She went downstairs, brought up the paracetamol and a glass of water, and waited while he took the tablets. She got into bed and they lay there without talking for some time, each lost in their own thoughts. Mark went to sleep before she did. Jasmine lay awake, wondering how all this would end and whether they would move house. At some point after midnight, she dropped off and slept through until morning, by which time Mark was already up. She could hear him moving around on the landing and wondered how his hand was. When he came into their room, she noticed he'd taken off the plaster.

'Is your hand all right?' she asked.

'For now,' he said despondently. 'But what it will be like this evening is anyone's guess.'

'Perhaps there's something in the cut that means it keeps getting infected?'

'Perhaps,' he said, and left.

At 10 a.m. that day, Jasmine phoned Father Tim Ashridge.

'I'm sorry,' he said. 'It's been on my mind to call you.'

'I was wondering when you would be able to visit us again,' Jasmine asked.

'Why? Has something else happened? I'm away on church business until Sunday.'

'Can you visit us on Monday? I'll have the girls with me, though. They're on holiday from school.'

'Of course. There's nothing you want to tell me now?'

'No, it can wait. I'll tell you on Monday.'

That day was fine and sunny again, and the girls played outside for most of it. Jasmine looked at them every so often from the sofa in the living room. She was off work for the week but still felt exhausted, too tired to go and tend to the garden. She'd water the flowers later when the mood took her, but for now she'd stay there watching the girls play. What they all needed, she thought, was a family meeting like they used to have at their flat, when they were thinking of moving. Instead of them discussing the houses they'd viewed, they could talk about what was happening to them all in the house, the sightings they'd each had. The girls were old enough and would probably appreciate the chance to speak up and be listened to by both parents. Mark had said he'd be home at 6 p.m. that evening. They could do it then. Once they'd talked about their feelings, she and Mark would be in a better position to find a way forward. If the girls really wanted to move, then it was something they needed to consider seriously.

TWENTY-NINE

Mark arrived home at 6.15 that evening and Jasmine told him of her plan to have a family meeting to give Isabel and Leah the chance to talk. He didn't reply but looked very down.

'What's the matter?' she asked.

He showed her his hand. It was the same cut as before, only longer.

'It was all right at lunchtime,' he said dejectedly. 'I knew this would happen.'

'We'll show the girls and ask them what they think,' Jasmine said brightly.

Mark raised his eyes and, without speaking, went upstairs to change. He was clearly annoyed by her response. When he came down, Jasmine was plating up their dinner.

'Leah told me not to go into her room,' he said, and sat down.

'Why not?' Jasmine asked, frowning.

'I've no idea.' He shrugged.

With a silent sigh, Jasmine went upstairs to check on the girls as Mark began his meal. It seemed that during the school holidays the childcare was her responsibility. Isabel and Leah had had their dinner earlier. She knocked on Leah's door and then went in. Both girls had changed out of what they had been wearing during the day and into smart dresses.

'For the house meeting,' Leah said with a smile. 'Have you forgotten?'

'No,' Jasmine said. 'I haven't forgotten. Give Daddy and me fifteen minutes to eat our dinner, then come down. We'll be ready for you. Have you made some notes on what you want to say?'

'We'll write a list,' Leah said excitedly, and picked up a pencil, then handed one to Isabel.

'Good girls,' Jasmine said, and she came out, leaving them to it.

Once Mark and Jasmine had finished eating, the girls came into the dining area, looking very solemn and studious. Leah was carrying a clipboard that she used at school sometimes and was holding a pencil. Isabel was carrying a pencil and a sheet of paper.

'Are you ready?' Leah asked.

'Yes, we are,' Jasmine said, and she quickly cleared away the plates. 'Are we going to use this table?'

Isabel looked at Leah, who said, 'Yes.'

Mark, who obviously couldn't see how a family meeting was going to help them at all, stayed silent. He'd probably only agreed to go along with it for the sake of the girls.

They all sat at the table. The girls looked earnestly at their parents.

'Shall I start?' Leah asked.

'Yes, please,' Jasmine said with equal seriousness.

Leah studied her clipboard.

'Number one,' she began. 'We want to be able to stay up later now it's the summer holidays.'

Mark was going to say something, but Jasmine nodded to him not to. They needed to hear what Leah was going to say. She was still looking at her, waiting for a reply.

'Yes, that seems reasonable,' Jasmine said. 'You already are staying up later than normal, but we can push that back a bit more, I suppose. Just for the summer holidays.'

'Good.' Leah ticked it off her list. 'Number two. We would like an ice cream every day during the holidays. The ones we bought from the supermarket that are in the freezer will do.'

'Yes,' Isabel agreed.

'OK,' Jasmine said. 'That's acceptable. One a day, but no more.' Isabel smiled as Leah looked at her notes again.

'We want to go out of the house on an activity at least twice a week during the holidays,' she said. 'It's boring staying in all the time.'

'That might be a bit difficult on the weeks I'm working,' Jasmine pointed out.

'On the weeks you're not working,' Leah clarified.

'Yes. OK. That's doable. Twice a week. It doesn't have to be anywhere very expensive,' Jasmine said.

Leah nodded and made another tick.

'And lastly,' she said, looking up, 'Isabel and I think I should be allowed to stay up later at night as I am the eldest.'

'I see,' Jasmine said. 'And what do you think about that?' she now asked Isabel.

'I don't mind. We are both staying up later anyway.'

'Fifteen minutes. Is that all right?'

'Half an hour. It's not worth it for fifteen.'

'OK. We'll see how it goes.'

Leah made another tick, then sat back and smiled, relieved.

'Is that everything you wanted to raise?' Jasmine asked.

Both girls nodded. 'Apart from the house stuff,' Leah said.

Jasmine took a breath. 'What do you two think about the house stuff?' she asked. 'This is the first chance we've had to discuss it all together.'

She looked at them and waited.

'I don't like it here,' Leah admitted. 'It's very creepy.'

'This meeting was supposed to be you telling us your feelings, and then your mother and I were going to decide what to do about them,' Mark said.

'Isabel and I talked about it in my room, and we don't know what else to say,' Leah said. 'We want to live in our flat again, but we know we can't do that. Is there somewhere else we can go?'

'I was happy at our flat,' Isabel added.

Jasmine reached for her daughter's hand. 'I know you were, love. We all were. But perhaps we can be happy here too?'

'I don't see what this meeting has achieved,' Mark said. 'Apart from the girls getting their own way.'

'It was worth a try,' Jasmine said. 'Perhaps it's time to show them your hand?' He'd been fiddling with the plaster throughout the meeting.

'No, thank you,' Mark said churlishly, refusing to take off the plaster.

'I think we should ask the other lady to come here and see what she says,' Isabel said.

'What other lady?' Jasmine asked.

'The one who you were speaking to on the phone yesterday, before the television started breaking.'

'Selina?' Jasmine checked, taken aback that Isabel was aware of that conversation.

'Yes,' Isabel said. 'She's Angela's sister, so she should know what the matter is here.'

'I see,' Jasmine said. 'The problem is, there weren't any issues when she lived here. The strange things only started happening after she'd gone. But I could check with her, I suppose.'

Could Isabel be right? Jasmine wondered. The two sisters had obviously been very close when Angela was alive. Could Selina maybe pick up on something that had stayed in the house after Angela had died? She'd told her on the phone that she'd sold the house very quickly after Angela's death. But she lived over a hundred miles away now. Would she make the journey down to see them all?

'I think that's something to consider,' Jasmine said. 'I'll phone her.'

Isabel smiled, pleased that she had contributed something.

'Is the TV working now?' Mark asked.

'Yes, it's been fine,' Jasmine said.

'Good. Is that everything then?'

They looked at the girls.

'Yes,' Leah said, and Isabel nodded.

'Thank you for attending this meeting,' Jasmine said with a smile.

'Can we have another meeting soon?' Leah asked. 'I like them.'

'If we have something to discuss, absolutely,' Jasmine said.

'Maybe after Selina has been?' Isabel suggested.

'If she will come,' Jasmine said. 'I'll phone her.'

Once the girls were in bed, Jasmine called Selina from the study. Mark was in the living room, looking through some papers for work. Selina recognized Jasmine's voice straight away and said she'd been thinking about her. She asked how things were, and Jasmine said, 'All right,' without going into details. Jasmine asked when she was planning on visiting her sister's grave next. As luck would have it, it had been over a month since Selina's last visit and she said she was planning to come the following week, on Tuesday. Although she worked on Tuesdays, she preferred driving down during the week rather than the weekend. She said she would call in to see Jasmine after she'd been to the cemetery. It would be around lunchtime. 'What was it exactly you wanted?' she finished by asking.

'To see if you pick up on anything odd in the house. My youngest daughter suggested it.' Selina was quite hesitant and said she doubted she would, but that she would come anyway.

'The girls will be here,' Jasmine added. 'I hope that's all right.'

'Yes, of course,' Selina said. 'Isabel sounds very sensible. I'd love to meet her and her sister. See you on Tuesday.'

The weekend passed without any supernatural activity and Jasmine dared to think the hauntings had passed and that she should cancel Father Tim Ashridge on Monday. Mark's hand had healed, there hadn't been any sightings of any ghosts and nothing else strange had happened. It was the longest period yet since they'd moved in without something happening.

It rained for most of the weekend, and Jasmine wondered if that had anything to do with the lack of activity, then she dismissed the idea as preposterous. The children stayed indoors playing games and arguing, while Mark did the odd jobs around the house he had been putting off since they'd moved in. But then on Sunday night, Isabel was absolutely dreadful. From the moment she went to bed she kept crying out that the woman was in her room. They went in, but it was empty and so they tried to resettle her. Eventually they took her into their own bed and closed her bedroom door. She didn't go to sleep until after 2 a.m. By Monday morning, Jasmine was looking forward to seeing Father Tim Ashridge, whatever he offered. She'd have to make up the time she took off work since she was supposed to be working this week.

The girls were late getting up, and when they came

downstairs they looked exhausted, even Leah, who'd been woken by her sister's crying. Jasmine, Mark and Isabel had slept three in the bed, which wasn't really big enough, so they'd all had very little sleep that night. They began the week tired and snappy, with very little patience. Then the accidents started to happen. Isabel knocked over her glass of juice, which immediately ran all over the floor. Jasmine fetched a cloth and Leah accidentally trod in it. There were footprints of sticky juice everywhere. Then Leah burnt her mouth on her bowl of Ready Brek, which shouldn't have been that hot. And so it continued: a cut to Isabel's leg, a bruise on Leah's arm. It was a myriad of small accidents that had to be cleared up. It all took time. The girls then refused to play in the garden even though the sun was shining by now. So by the time the doorbell rang shortly before midday, Jasmine, who hadn't done any work at all, answered it in a bad mood.

'Oh, it's you,' she said. 'Come in.'

Father Tim Ashridge was alone and smiled, embarrassed, as he stepped into the hall.

'We made an appointment, but I wasn't sure of the time,' he said.

'It's all right.' She showed him into the living room, which was a mess. She began to tidy up.

'Don't do that on my account,' he said, so she left it.

'My colleague Father Andrew won't be coming today, but we talked about everything that's been happening here, and he passed on his thoughts to me.'

Jasmine nodded, offered him a drink, which he refused,

and they both sat down. The girls, hearing someone in the living room, rushed in and looked timidly at Father Tim. Jasmine had told them that a priest was coming today and that he was going to talk to them about some of the strange happenings in the house.

'This is Leah and Isabel,' Jasmine said.

He smiled and said hello.

There was then silence before he asked, 'Do you know why I'm here?' He looked at each of them in turn.

Leah shook her head, while Isabel replied, 'To get rid of the ghost.'

'I suppose you're right,' he said thoughtfully. 'Tell me what you know about the ghost.'

Jasmine wasn't sure she wanted Isabel to be reminded of it all, after the night they'd had.

'I saw her last night in my bedroom,' Isabel began matter-of-factly, pleased to have an audience. 'She kept trying to talk to me and she kept me awake. I slept with Mummy and Daddy in the end, but she followed me in there and kept talking.'

This was the first Isabel had said about the ghost being in their bedroom. Father Tim looked slightly taken aback, while Jasmine gave a small shiver.

'What did she talk to you about?' he asked her, his voice steady and reassuring.

Isabel looked at him. 'If you want to, you can ask her yourself. She's listening on the landing. Come on up and I'll show you.'

THIRTY

The room fell silent as they all turned to look towards the stairs and listened. Jasmine wanted to tell Isabel not to be so silly, but she'd heard something too. A faint noise as though someone far away was talking to themselves. It was impossible to understand what they were saying. It was more of a continuous whisper.

'Have you left something on upstairs?' Jasmine asked Isabel quietly.

'No, Mummy. I've told you, it's her. She's up there now.'

Leah had gone deathly pale, while Father Tim sat there, unsure of what to do.

'Aren't you going to go up to say hello?' Isabel asked him. 'She's in a good mood right now.'

Father Tim looked at Jasmine.

'I think we should go up and investigate,' she said. 'I'm sure the radio or something has been left on.'

'I'll stay down here,' Leah said.

Jasmine slowly stood. Father Tim bent down and took

a bible and a wooden cross from his briefcase and blessed them all. They walked slowly to the foot of the stairs. Father Tim held the cross up in front of him as the whispering continued and grew louder. Jasmine clutched Isabel's hand, although Isabel appeared to be the only one who was not petrified. The whispering continued as they went up, a step at a time. It was impossible to understand any of the words.

On the landing, it became obvious the whispering was coming from Isabel's bedroom. Jasmine stopped and felt her heart racing. Father Tim paused outside Isabel's bedroom door and, holding the cross and bible in front of him, began to mutter something in Latin. He went ahead into Isabel's bedroom. Jasmine and Isabel followed slowly. The whispering grew louder. Father Tim held the cross up higher and continued chanting, his voice rising up and over the whispering. Suddenly the whispering stopped. Jasmine and Isabel stayed where they were, just inside the bedroom door. It was all quiet now. There was nothing to be seen or heard. Father Tim stopped chanting and looked around, then he said another short prayer in English. He stayed where he was, then turned and began to come out. As he did so, something unseen hurled itself at his back and struck him between the shoulder blades, sending him flying forwards.

Jasmine and Isabel screamed. He righted himself before he hit the floor.

'I'm all right,' he said, flustered. 'She's very angry with me.'

He turned and faced the empty room, then made the

sign of the cross and said something in Latin again. Then he came out.

'Are you hurt?' Isabel asked him.

'No,' he said, clearly still unnerved.

'Did you get her?' she then asked. 'Did you tell her to go?'

'I did. I think she's gone for now,' he said shakily. Jasmine didn't like the way he'd said 'for now'. 'Can I use your toilet?' Father Tim asked.

'It's through there,' Jasmine said, pointing to the bathroom.

Father Tim went into the bathroom and locked the door, while Jasmine and Isabel returned downstairs in silence, still holding hands. Jasmine was shocked by what she'd just witnessed. She couldn't put her feelings into words. She and Isabel walked into the living room where Leah was waiting for them. She looked petrified. Jasmine went to her daughter and put her arms tightly around her, then hugged both girls. She couldn't say anything for some time. There were no words to explain what had just happened.

'Are you OK, Mummy?' Leah asked her after a moment.

'Yes, I think so.'

They heard the bathroom door open as Father Tim came out. He went briefly into Isabel's room, then he came downstairs and went into the living room. He still looked very shaken. He sat down and they waited for him to speak. He kept his cross and bible on his lap.

'I wish Father Andrew had been here to witness that,' he said at last.

'But you heard it,' Jasmine said. 'We've never experienced the whispering before. Each time she comes, it seems to be something different.'

He gave a slow nod.

'What else has happened since my last visit?' he asked.

Jasmine thought back and told him everything, ending with, 'We've got Selina visiting us tomorrow.'

'Why?'

'It was Isabel's idea. She thought Selina might pick up on a presence. She never experienced anything in the house herself, but then she left soon after her sister, Angela, died.'

'So you think that voice is Angela?' the priest asked. 'Selina's dead sister?'

'Yes. Don't you?'

He thought for a moment. 'I wouldn't like to say.'

'Could it possibly be someone else?' Jasmine asked, horrified.

'I don't know who or what it is,' Father Tim said.

He put away his cross and bible and made a point of looking at his watch.

'If there's nothing else you want to discuss? I have another parishioner to see shortly.' He still looked agitated.

'You go,' Jasmine said. 'We'll be OK here.'

'I'll discuss all of this with Father Andrew and then I'll give you a ring,' he said. 'Before I go, let us say another prayer together.'

He lowered his head and the girls did the same. He stood, said a short prayer in English, then crossed himself.

Jasmine went with him to the front door.

'He was scared of her,' Isabel said as Jasmine returned to the living room.

She gave a small nod but didn't say anything. She had to agree that Father Tim clearly had been scared of the whispering. Thankfully, it had stopped now, and the house was silent again. It was 1 p.m.

'Let's go out for lunch,' Jasmine suggested.

Both girls agreed and quickly put on their sandals, wanting to leave the house as soon as possible. It felt safer that way, even though Jasmine knew she would have a lot of work to catch up on later. She'd have to do it this evening. They climbed into the car. As Jasmine waited for the girls to fasten the buckles on their seat belts, she looked out of her window, up at Isabel's bedroom, and jumped. There she was, as blatant as anything – the woman in a grey top and green trousers – framed in the window. Just standing there, looking at them. Jasmine quickly started the car and pulled away. What the hell were they going to do to get rid of her once and for all?

They took longer than they should have eating their burgers and fries. Jasmine sat there deep in thought, not saying much. The girls seemed quieter than usual too.

'Are we going to tell Daddy?' Leah asked at length.

'I guess so,' Jasmine replied. 'Isabel won't want to sleep in that room tonight, will you?'

'I don't know,' Isabel said with a shrug and finished her burger.

Typical child, Jasmine thought; sometimes she was very upset by the ghost and at other times it washed over her.

Eventually they had to return home, although Jasmine could happily have spent the afternoon wandering around the shops. What awaited them in the house? She switched on the radio and drove home thinking about what had happened. She braced herself as they pulled into their road and approached the house. Isabel's window was now empty. She let out a small sigh of relief. As they went inside, she was grateful the house was quiet and everything seemed normal.

'Why don't you play in the garden while I do some work?' she suggested to the girls.

It was 3.30 and she really needed to get on. She opened the patio doors and reluctantly the girls wandered outside. Jasmine went down the garden and unlocked the shed so they could get their bikes and other toys out. As she returned to the house, she automatically glanced up at the bedroom windows. They were clear. Thank goodness. Her life seemed to be determined by whether or not she caught a glimpse of that woman.

She left the patio doors open so the girls could come in whenever they wanted to, and went through to the study. She needed to get going. With a final glance down the garden, she turned on her computer and waited. Nothing happened. Shit. Not now. Then suddenly the screen sprang to life. Instead of the start-up screen, though, it was a still photograph of Isabel's bedroom window. What was going on? There was nothing there but the window. Then the image of the woman suddenly appeared. Jasmine gave a cry of alarm and moved her chair back.

'What the hell!'

The woman stood there on her screen looking directly at her, dressed in the grey top and green trousers. Then, as quickly as it had appeared, the image vanished and the start-up screen returned. There was nothing left to see, and Jasmine wondered if she'd imagined it. It seemed like the better option, as there was no sign of the photograph now. She tentatively opened the folder she needed to work on and got on with it. Every so often she looked down the garden to check the girls were all right. The house remained silent.

She answered some emails and then turned again to look down the garden. She could see Leah sitting on the grass, but where was her sister? She stood and looked through the glass. She still couldn't see her. She went out through the patio doors.

'Where's Isabel?' she called to Leah.

'Behind the shed.'

'What's she doing there?'

Leah shrugged and carried on picking at the grass.

Jasmine walked to the bottom of the garden. The girls knew they weren't supposed to squeeze down there behind the shed. She peered down the narrow strip of land between the shed and the neighbour's fence. Isabel had her back to her and was in conversation, telling someone that she needed to go now.

'Isabel, who are you talking to?' Jasmine asked her evenly.

'Angela,' she said.

'Selina's sister?' Jasmine checked.

'Yes.'

THIRTY-ONE

Jasmine told Isabel to play in the garden, not behind the shed, and then waited while she said goodbye to Angela, matter-of-factly, as though it was very normal to be talking to a dead woman. Jasmine hadn't the stamina or time to ask her what she'd been talking about. She needed to finish her work. Having said goodbye, Isabel slid out from behind the shed.

'I like her,' she said, and returned to her sister on the lawn.

'Do you both want a drink?' Jasmine asked them.

They nodded and she fetched them a drink each.

'I've just got another half an hour of work to do,' she said. 'What are you going to do?' They were both sitting on the lawn, fiddling with the grass.

'I'm going to play on my bike,' Leah said, and getting up crossed to her bike.

'Me too,' Isabel said, and she picked up her own bike.

Jasmine waited until they were both riding around the

lawn and then returned indoors to the study. She sat at her desk and tried to concentrate. It was now gone 4 p.m. She'd stop before long and continue this evening, when Mark could look after the girls. A few minutes later, the phone rang and she answered it.

'Jasmine, it's Mark,' he said anxiously. 'I'm at the hospital. It's my hand. It won't stop bleeding. It's dripping everywhere.'

'Oh, no. What have they said?' she asked.

'I've just seen a nurse so far. They're going to stitch it. I have to wait for now. They've put a lot of bandages over it for the moment.'

'Did you catch your hand on something at work?' she asked, already knowing the answer.

'No. The cut just opened up again at lunchtime and began to bleed. They're going to do some blood tests to make sure there's no underlying issue. It seems there are some diseases like haemophilia that can cause your blood not to clot. I told them it kept opening up like this.'

A disease? Like haemophilia? Jasmine thought, and clung to that hope. Right now, it seemed the better option.

'Do you want us to come to the hospital?' she asked.

'There's no need. I might be here for some time. I've phoned work and said I doubt I'll be back today.'

Jasmine put down the phone and, worried, looked down the garden at the girls. They were playing nicely. She thought about Mark and how he loathed being in pain. If she was honest, she didn't think it was anything to do with an underlying illness that Mark might have – it was their house. His hand had first been cut when he'd touched the box of broken photographs when they'd first unpacked. It had healed and then reopened many times.

She texted him half an hour later and he said he was still waiting to be seen but that the cut had stopped bleeding.

She and the girls ate at 5.30, when she texted Mark again. He didn't reply. She plated up his dinner, ready for the microwave, and he texted back saying he should be going in for his stitches shortly.

By 7.30, when she took the girls up to bed, having not heard from Mark again, she was worried. Leah didn't want extra time downstairs without him being there, and Jasmine knew she was scared. As they washed in the bathroom, they heard Mark let himself in the front door. They instantly stopped what they were doing and rushed downstairs. His left hand was heavily bandaged from the fingers to the wrist.

'I've had stiches,' he said and held his hand out.

'How do you feel now?' Jasmine asked.

'They've given me these painkillers,' he said, and showed her a small box of tablets. 'I have to take two now.'

The girls were all over him as he took the tablets with water, but Jasmine could see he wasn't in the mood. He was in pain and didn't want to be bothered with them right now.

'Come on,' she said to them. 'Say goodnight. You'll see Daddy in the morning.'

Jasmine took the girls upstairs and tucked Leah into her bed and Isabel into their bed. She couldn't bear the thought of leaving her alone in her room tonight, not after all that whispering earlier. On her return downstairs, Mark was sitting in the living room looking very pale. He'd taken off his shoes and jacket and had poured himself a whisky.

'Do you want your dinner now?' she asked him.

'Later,' he said. 'They've put in six stitches. They should dissolve on their own in a few days.'

'Something is clearly stopping it from healing,' Jasmine said.

'When I told them at the hospital it had been happening for nearly eight weeks, that the cut kept reopening, I'm sure they didn't believe me. The nurse said the cut looked fresh, as though I'd just done it recently and had maybe forgotten.'

'What did you say?' Jasmine asked him.

'I didn't say anything. How could I explain what's been going on here?' He ran his hand across his forehead and took another sip of whisky. 'If it doesn't heal, I'll have to go back to the hospital. If I go back there, they'll think I've done it on purpose.'

'No, they won't,' Jasmine said. 'Perhaps the blood tests will show there is something wrong with you.'

He shrugged. 'Maybe.'

She could tell he didn't believe that any more than she did. She let the matter go and changed the subject.

'Father Tim visited us this morning,' she said. Mark gave a small nod and held his hand as if it was hurting him. 'There was a strange whispering coming from Isabel's bedroom while he was here. I've put her to bed in our room tonight.'

'What sort of whispering?' Mark asked, taking another sip of whisky. 'I expect something had just been left on.'

'No, it hadn't. As he turned to leave the room, something hard hit him between the shoulder blades. He nearly fell over and was clearly very shaken by it.'

'And you're sure nothing was left on in that room?' Mark checked. 'Not one of Isabel's toys? You know how some of them talk.'

'No. I'm sure of it. I took them out for lunch. I thought we needed a change of scene. But as I was driving away from the house, I saw her at Isabel's bedroom window. The woman in the grey top and green trousers was standing there, just staring at me and the girls. They didn't see her. Then, when we returned, I found Isabel behind the shed talking to someone – she said it was Angela, Selina's dead sister. I brought her out and took her to play with Leah.'

Jasmine stopped. Going through all this was utterly exhausting. She felt nearly as tired as Mark looked. The painkillers must have taken effect, for he'd rested his head back on the sofa and closed his eyes. She lay her head back too. They were silent for some time, then Mark began to doze. She tapped him gently on the shoulder and he came round.

'Do you want your dinner now?' she asked.

'No, thanks, love. I'll get some sleep instead.'

He pushed himself up from the sofa and went upstairs. It was nearly 9 p.m. Jasmine went through to the study and switched off the computer. She'd get up early to catch up. She had a lot to do. She returned to the living room and stood by the patio window, looking at the garden as the light slowly faded. It should have been wonderful – the house they'd always dreamed of where they would raise their children. Their forever home. But if the priest couldn't help them, then who could? She was at her wits' end. Selina was coming tomorrow. What would she find when she came into their house? She had no idea.

Jasmine finally locked up and went to bed, squeezing in beside Isabel. Mark was on the other side of her. They were both flat on their backs with their arms spread out and fast asleep, like a pair of guardian angels, she thought.

Surprisingly, they all slept well with Isabel sandwiched between them, much better than Jasmine would have expected. They were all exhausted.

In the morning, she woke before the alarm, and when she opened her eyes she found Isabel staring at her.

'Are you all right?' she asked her.

Isabel nodded and rubbed her eyes.

'When will Daddy wake up?'

'Soon, sweetheart.'

'Can I get out and go and see Leah?' Isabel asked.

'Yes, if she's awake.'

'I heard her.'

Jasmine helped Isabel clamber out of the bed, then she heard her pitter-patter into Leah's bedroom. The girls were always awake early during the school holidays – which was the opposite of term time, when she struggled to wake them and get them up on time.

She wondered how Mark's hand was healing. He'd slept well – probably as a result of the painkillers. His hand was concealed beneath the duvet at present. She lay in bed with the early-morning light coming through their curtains, thinking about their home again. Everything was quiet now, like anybody's home – silent, pleasant and welcoming. But what would today bring? Selina was visiting them. And just for a second, for reasons she couldn't say, Jasmine felt a sudden pang of dread. Maybe it wasn't a good idea for her to visit. Maybe she should cancel it.

The alarm clock sounded, vibrant and brusque, making Jasmine start. Mark automatically reached out his right hand and switched it off. He yawned and stretched. It was the same routine every morning. Then his left hand came up over the duvet. Jasmine looked at it. There was no blood seeping through the bandage.

'How is it?' she asked him.

'OK, I guess,' he said, looking at it. 'It's not hurting now, at least.'

'Good.'

'Where's Isabel?' he asked.

'In with Leah.'

He rose and went into Leah's room, where he said a few words to the girls. Then he went into the bathroom to shower and dress. Jasmine lay in bed. She knew she should really get up, but she could have stayed there all day. In that moment, everything that was wrong with them and their house felt far off and removed. Would the strange things that had been happening stop? She doubted it. She lay there thinking while Mark got dressed – it was so easy for him; he went to work every day and escaped the house.

After about a quarter of an hour, the girls came in, still in their nightwear.

'Can we go downstairs and watch some television?' Leah asked.

'Yes, of course. It's the school holidays.'

Jasmine listened to their footsteps as they ran downstairs. Then Mark appeared and, after saying goodbye, left for work.

She really needed to get up and make up for the work she hadn't done last night. She stretched and moved her right leg slowly to the edge of the bed, ready to get out. She stopped. It wouldn't go any further. She tried to move it again, pushing her foot against the edge, but with the same result. Her heart began to race. What was the matter with her? Thinking there must be something wrong with her leg, she pulled back the duvet and looked at it. It seemed normal, and she didn't have pins and needles suggesting she'd slept on it. She pulled herself up in bed and tried to move the left leg out. Exactly the same thing happened. It went to the edge of the bed but no further. Panic set in. Was she having a bad dream? A nightmare in which she couldn't get up?

She looked around the bedroom. It all seemed as it should. She tried again to get her legs off the bed, but again they went to the edge and that was it. It was like hitting a brick wall. She tried the other side of the bed, Mark's side, and pushed her legs to the very edge. They stopped dead and wouldn't go any further. She tried the bottom of the bed, pushing hard. They wouldn't go beyond the end. It was as though there was an invisible barrier preventing her from leaving the bed. She felt the side of the bed with her hand, and it seemed normal. What the hell was going on? What was she going to do? She thrashed around, trying to find a way out, but there wasn't one. She was trapped in her bed.

She began to feel very hot and started sweating. She needed to get up, out of this bed. Whatever was the matter with her? Had some strange paralysis set in during the night? But no, she could move her legs. It wasn't that. She flopped back on the pillows and tried again. The result was the same. She was trapped in her bed with no way out. She'd have to call for help from the girls. Ask them to call an ambulance. Mark had gone to work. She tried to get out one last time and then shouted for them.

'Leah! Isabel! Come now, please. I need your help.'

She heard their feet run upstairs. They came into her bedroom and stopped by the bed.

'What is it, Mummy?' Leah asked, very worried by her mother's shouts.

But as they'd come in, Jasmine had felt a sudden release and knew the moment had passed and she could now get up. She slowly swung her legs out of the bed and onto the floor. They were working again.

'What's the matter?' Leah asked again.

'Nothing. Thanks for coming so quickly. I was just feeling strange but I'm fine now. You go downstairs. I'll be down shortly.'

They looked at each other and, giving a shrug, left the room.

Shaken, Jasmine picked up her clothes, then took them into the bathroom, where she sat on the closed toilet seat and wept. She was going mad in this house. She was sure of it, and there was nothing she could do about it.

THIRTY-TWO

Jasmine slowly recovered, got dressed and went downstairs. She felt a bit better after a good cry. She made breakfast for the girls, which they ate in front of the television, and took a coffee through to the study. It was now 8.30 a.m., and she switched on the computer and found the document she'd been working on yesterday. She continued typing in the figures while thinking about what had just happened that morning. Did she have a medical condition that had made her legs seize up and stopped them from working? If so, it had come on very quickly, overnight. After some time, she saved what she was working on and did some research online.

Legs that won't work, she read, *can be as a result of autoimmune diseases, spinal conditions and injuries, or a stroke . . . Leg weakness will in some cases resolve over time, but it can be a medical emergency, especially if the weakness comes on suddenly.*

Hers had come on very suddenly and disappeared as

quickly. She read on: . . . *it can be caused by many different conditions, including amyotrophic lateral sclerosis, slipped disc, Guillain–Barré syndrome, autoimmune diseases, multiple sclerosis, Parkinson's disease, peripheral neuropathy, pinched* . . . and so it continued.

She didn't have any other symptoms as far as she knew, so, partly assured it was a temporary aberration, she went back to work. She wondered if it would happen again. If it did, she'd seek medical help straight away, but for now she needed to get on with her work.

At 9.45 Leah came in.

'Are you going to tell us to get dressed?' she asked her mother.

'Get dressed, please,' Jasmine said, concentrating on the computer screen. 'We've got Selina coming this afternoon.'

'Who's Selina?' Leah asked.

She stopped what she was doing and glanced at her daughter.

'She lived in this house before Freya and James did, remember?' she said. 'Some time ago.'

'Why is she coming here today?' Leah asked.

'Just to see us,' she said. 'Now, go and get dressed, please.'

Leah ran from the study and Jasmine heard the girls go upstairs to wash and dress. After about half an hour she went up and found them in her bedroom. They had taken out most of her clothes and were trying them on.

'What on earth are you two doing?' Jasmine cried, annoyed. Her clothes were everywhere and getting ruined. She began picking them up.

'We wanted to see what we would look like when we're grown up,' Isabel said.

Jasmine instantly felt bad for telling them off.

'All right. Put them away again, please, and come downstairs. What are you going to do this morning? Go in the garden?'

'We'll play in Leah's bedroom,' Isabel said. 'We can't use mine.'

'But no more dressing up in my clothes, please.'

She helped tidy some of the clothes away, then saw them settled in Leah's bedroom. She went downstairs, where she made herself another coffee before taking it into the study. She worked uninterrupted for the next hour as the girls played in Leah's bedroom. At midday she stopped and made lunch. This morning had gone well.

She called the girls downstairs for lunch. Then she tidied up the living room and waited for the doorbell to ring. She was nervous about meeting Selina for the first time. What would she say?

She was looking through the kitchen window shortly after 1 p.m. when she saw a blue car draw up outside. It parked and a middle-aged woman got out. She was alone. She began to walk up their front path, glancing at the top windows as she came. She was smartly dressed in navy trousers with a matching short-sleeved top. Jasmine waited until she'd pressed the bell before she answered it.

'Selina?'

'Yes.'

'Come in. I'm Jasmine.'

Selina smiled and stepped into their hall. She took it all in.

'Can I get you a tea or a coffee?' Jasmine asked her nervously.

'A coffee would be lovely, thank you. I've come straight from the cemetery.'

Jasmine led Selina into the kitchen. She looked around.

'You've made some changes,' Selina said. 'Well, either you or your predecessors.'

'We haven't done much, really. I believe it was Freya and James.'

As the kettle boiled, Jasmine heard the girls come downstairs. They came into the kitchen.

'This is Leah and Isabel, my daughters,' she said.

'Hi, lovelies. How are you? Enjoying your school holidays, I bet.'

They were both suddenly rendered shy and said a small hello. Isabel stared at her.

'You look just like Angela,' she said.

Jasmine saw the look on Selina's face, one of shock and consternation. She'd seen a likeness when she'd first come in too. It was a moment before Selina could reply.

'Lots of people comment on the likeness,' she said. 'How do you know we look alike, though?'

'Angela is often in my bedroom,' Isabel replied. 'I used to be scared of her, but I'm not any more. I see her in other places too, like the garden.'

Selina studied the child, then said, 'Angela loved gardening. It was her favourite pastime when she was well enough.'

'I know,' Isabel replied. 'Are you here to see her?'

The poor woman didn't know what to say.

'Let's have a drink and a chat,' Jasmine suggested, and poured the drinks.

'Do you want me to stay?' Isabel asked her mother.

'Not right now. What are you two going to do while we talk?'

'We'll play in Leah's bedroom. Angela says hi,' Isabel said to Selina. 'She's in my bedroom when you're ready to see her.'

Selina looked at Jasmine and didn't know how to reply.

'Off you go,' Jasmine said, and put the cups and a plate of biscuits on a tray. She carried it into the living room as the girls disappeared upstairs. Selina was clearly struggling, trying to come to terms with what Isabel had said and with whatever was going on in their house.

'Does your daughter always speak so directly?' she asked Jasmine as they sat down.

'I guess so. We're used to it. But she doesn't make things up. She usually speaks the truth.'

Selina picked up her cup, took a sip and placed it on the table again. There was silence as neither of the women knew where to begin. Then Selina said, 'I expected to feel something when I came in here, but I don't, nothing at all. Your daughter seems to be more acquainted with my sister than I am, now.'

'How about if you start by telling me what Angela was like?' Jasmine suggested to her.

'Yes, that's a good idea.'

Selina paused for a moment to collect her thoughts, then she began.

'Angela was one of the kindest people you could ever wish to meet. She was three years younger than me. She was forty-eight when she died. She was a teacher in a local primary school, and she loved her job – invested everything in it. She made the children she taught very happy indeed. Many of those who had been in her class over the years came to her funeral, and the staff were there too. It was a very sad time indeed.' She paused a moment for reflection.

'Neither of us had ever been married,' she continued. 'Nor were we likely to, so we decided to buy this house together many years ago. It made sense, rather than having us both keep paying rent. Our parents had died some years before and left us a bit of money. We did this place up and lived here for fourteen years. It was beautiful. We had such a lovely time. I had the double bedroom at the back of the house – where I assume you and your husband are now. Angela had the bedroom at the front.'

'Isabel's room,' Jasmine said.

'That's right. It was close to my bedroom, and later on I could hear Angela when she wanted something and called out. I took a lot of time off work after she got sick. They were very good to me. Angela always wore those green trousers and the grey top when she felt like getting up. I washed them in between. She used to love gardening. She grew vegetables and flowers. I was useless but she had the knack. Towards the end of her life, I couldn't keep the garden going by myself and I'm afraid I let the plants die.

It was sad really, but what could I have done?' She paused and looked away.

'Angela slept in Isabel's bedroom but towards the end she kept coming into my room, then she'd wonder where she was. By that time, she was covered in lesions – all over her body except for her face. It was weird the way the cancer left her face alone. The lesions used to weep and open up. It's a dreadful form of cancer. I had to look after her. There was no one else. When she couldn't talk any more she began to whisper, which was fine when I was upstairs or in her room, but if I was downstairs I couldn't hear her. She used to become very distressed with me not being able to hear her, so one day I had the idea of buying her a baby monitor, which we installed, and it did the trick. I could sit down here and wait for her to whisper something, then I would go up.'

'We've heard it, that whispering,' Jasmine said. 'Recently.'

'You have?' Selina asked. 'Where?'

'It began yesterday when we had a priest come to visit. We heard whispering coming from Isabel's bedroom. It was the first time we'd heard it. We went up and into the bedroom. There was no one there but as the priest left, he was hit between his shoulder blades quite forcefully, as if someone was angry and had thumped him.'

'Angela was very angry at having to die,' Selina said thoughtfully. 'She wanted to stay with me. She had no time for religion.' A tear appeared at the corner of her eye, and she quickly wiped it away.

'I guess when the whispering started, she was coming to the end of her life,' Jasmine said.

Selina nodded. 'She died a couple of weeks later.'

They sat for a moment, then Jasmine said, 'My husband has a cut on his hand that won't completely heal. He's had it for eight weeks. He cut it when we first moved in here. It heals very quickly, then dramatically reopens. He went to the hospital yesterday and they put six stitches in it. I doubt that's the end of it, though. They're doing some blood tests to see if he has an underlying health condition, but I don't think they'll find anything.'

'But that can't have anything to do with Angela, can it?' Selina asked.

'I've no idea,' Jasmine replied. 'Lots of strange things have happened since we moved in, and we spoke to Freya and James, who experienced a lot of the same things when they were living here.'

Selina held her gaze. 'I don't know what to tell you. You seem like a very sensible family to me.'

She picked up her drink and finished it. Jasmine did likewise. The biscuits remained untouched on the plate.

'I honestly don't know what to tell you,' Selina said again as she set down her cup. 'As I said, I expected to feel something when I walked into this house, but there's nothing. It could belong to anyone now.'

'I see. Well, it was nice of you to come and visit us in any case. Thank you.'

At that moment, Jasmine heard it. A faint whispering in the distance, just like when Father Tim had been there yesterday, indistinct and almost inaudible at first. Selina didn't appear to notice it, or perhaps she thought it was the children playing upstairs. But Leah's bedroom door was shut. Jasmine had heard it close earlier.

Jasmine straightened in her chair and looked towards the hall as the whispering continued. Parts of sentences, said in a voice that wasn't really there – distant and far off. She knew what it was now. Then Selina heard it too and looked at her, puzzled.

'What's that?' she asked. 'It sounds familiar.'

'It's the whispering,' Jasmine said. 'It's your sister. She's upstairs in Isabel's room. I think she's waiting for you.'

THIRTY-THREE

Selina stayed sitting where she was on the sofa, very still and pale, listening to the whispering. It was growing louder now, floating downstairs and into the living room.

'Angela?' Selina asked Jasmine, unsure.

'She's upstairs,' Jasmine said again, still hardly believing she was having this conversation. 'I think she wants to speak to you.'

Selina slowly stood. Jasmine stood too and then led the way out of the living room and upstairs. Neither of the women spoke. The whispers were growing louder now. Leah opened her bedroom door and looked out.

'You two can carry on,' Jasmine said. 'There's nothing for you to worry about.'

Leah closed her door again, obviously aware that something was taking place in the house but with no wish to know what. Selina and Jasmine continued past Leah's bedroom to Isabel's door. It was closed right to. The whispering continued on the other side, although it was still impossible to understand what was being said.

'I'm coming,' Selina said, and slowly opened the door.

She went inside and stopped. Jasmine saw the look on her face and warily followed her. Standing in the centre of the room was the ghostly image of Angela.

'Angela?' Selina said. 'You're here!'

'You've come. I knew you would, but why did you take so long?'

Tears sprang from Selina's eyes as she looked at her sister. 'I didn't know you needed me.'

'Why did you leave me?' Angela asked.

Selina wiped her eyes. 'Because it seemed the right thing to do. I was very distressed when you died. You've no idea. I needed to make a clean start and this house was ours. It was too big for just me, so I moved closer to our brother.'

'But I lost you,' Angela said. 'I didn't know where you were. I've been trying to find you ever since, by attracting the attention of those who live here. I've done bad things. But you're back now, and I won't do bad things any more.'

'I can't stay here, Angela. It's not my house any more. It belongs to Jasmine and her family now. You shouldn't be here.'

'Where am I going to go?' she asked.

'I don't know. But you can't stay here, Angela. It's not fair on them.'

Selina looked at her sister and more tears formed in her eyes.

'Don't be upset,' Angela said. 'I'll leave if you want me to, for now at least.'

'Yes, but you need to go for good.'

At that point Angela gave a small cry and disappeared. Jasmine and Selina saw her go. Not a trace of her was left. Nothing. They stayed where they were and looked around, unable to believe what had just happened.

'Has she gone?' Jasmine asked tentatively, after a moment.

'I think so. I don't feel her presence any more.'

They stayed in the room for some minutes, waiting to see if anything else would happen.

'Angela?' Selina asked a few times. There was no reply.

They left in silence, heading past Leah's bedroom door and then downstairs. They returned to the living room, both astounded and reeling from what had just happened.

'Can I get you another coffee?' Jasmine asked.

'Yes, please.'

Selina handed over her empty cup and Jasmine went into the kitchen and made another round of drinks. She returned to the living room, hardly daring to think that Angela could have gone at last. The house remained quiet and still. They sipped their drinks and Selina talked more about her life with Angela. It was a happy and sad life – like most people's are. Jasmine wondered what Selina would make of their lives here if she told her everything that had happened since they'd moved in. After a while the girls appeared and Jasmine fixed them a snack and a drink, then they went upstairs again to Leah's bedroom.

'They know they can come down here if they wish?' Selina asked Jasmine.

'They're fine,' Jasmine replied. 'I have work to do most days, so they're used to playing alone.'

They continued talking until, shortly after 4 p.m., Selina said she needed to be going.

'I'll just pop up to Isabel's bedroom once more and make sure it's all clear,' Selina said. She went upstairs as Jasmine remained in the hallway and waited for her return.

'There's no sign of Angela,' she said. 'Thank goodness for that. I hope you and your poor family can enjoy your home now.' She called goodbye to the girls upstairs. They came out of the room to wave at her.

Jasmine hugged her at the door, then watched her go to her car. Before Selina got in, she looked up at Isabel's bedroom and shook her head.

'She's gone for good,' Selina said, and Jasmine nodded in agreement.

Jasmine watched her drive away, then returned indoors. She really hoped that was the end of it now. The house was quiet. Mark would be home before too long. She wondered how his hand was as she went upstairs to Leah's bedroom. The girls had been very good, amusing themselves all afternoon. She knocked on their door and went in.

'You did well today,' she said, then stopped in her tracks. She stared at the dolls on the bed.

'We found them,' Leah said. 'Are they yours?'

Jasmine slowly shook her head. The bed was littered with china-headed dolls. They were sitting, lying and pretending to eat. There must have been twenty, all in excellent condition and dressed in the costume of their era. So this was what had occupied the girls all afternoon.

'They're not mine,' Jasmine said. 'Where did you find them?

'They were in a box under my bed,' Leah said. 'I haven't seen it before.'

Jasmine went closer and looked at the dolls. Leah and Isabel had sat six of them in a circle. They were eating from small china plates, having a tea party.

'They're very nice, but I don't understand where they've come from,' Jasmine said. 'What about the china plates?'

'I don't know,' Leah said with a shrug.

'Do you know?' she asked Isabel.

'No, but we like playing with them.'

Jasmine took a closer look. The dolls were all immaculate. She picked one up and turned it over, and began undoing the tiny fasteners on its satin dress. Beneath the handstitched dress was a satin camisole with lacy knickers over a body stuffed with horsehair or sawdust. They were perfect.

'They look very old,' Jasmine said, turning the doll back over. 'Much older than us or this house. Early nineteenth century, I would say.'

'Can we still play with them?' Leah asked. 'We've been playing with them all afternoon.'

'I don't see why not. But be careful with them.' She was about to ask if Selina had brought them with her, but then she remembered that she'd seen her arrive and she hadn't been carrying a very large box. In fact, she'd hardly been out of her sight all afternoon.

'Yes, you can play with them, but be careful,' she said again. 'We don't know whose they are.'

She picked up another doll and examined it. Then she set it on the bed again.

'Are you all right for an hour? I need to do some work,' she asked the girls.

They nodded and returned to the dolls. Jasmine went downstairs, thinking about where the dolls could have come from. It was very strange indeed. Perhaps they had come from Mark's mother, and he hadn't thought to mention them. She continued to the study where she answered some emails from work. She'd have to make up the work that evening or get up early in the morning. She was even further behind now.

At 5 p.m. she stopped what she was doing and made dinner, then called the girls down to eat. They gobbled down their food and as soon as they'd finished they returned upstairs to play with the dolls some more. Jasmine returned to her desk. She was still working when Mark came home at 6.30. He seemed in a reasonably good mood. His hand was no longer hurting him, although the bandage was still on. The girls were still upstairs in Leah's bedroom. Jasmine assumed they were playing with the dolls.

'I've had a very interesting day,' Jasmine said as she served her and Mark's food.

They sat at the table and she told him about not being able to get out of bed that morning, about Selina's visit and finally about the dolls in Leah's bedroom.

Mark didn't comment. Jasmine hadn't really expected him to. What Mark didn't see for himself, he didn't believe.

'The dolls aren't your mother's, then?' Jasmine asked him.

'No. Why would I have a box of dolls from my mother?'

'I'll show you one,' she said.

She pushed back her chair and went upstairs to fetch a doll. This part she could prove easily. She went into Leah's bedroom and stopped dead. There were no period dolls to be seen, just a heap of Barbies littering the bed. Jasmine assumed the girls had got fed up with playing with the china dolls, which had to be played with carefully, and had moved on to their Barbies, which they could do what they liked with.

'Where are all those china-headed dolls?' she asked. 'Have you put them away?'

Leah and Isabel looked at her, baffled.

'The very old ones,' she prompted. 'The ones you had spread out on your bed. You've been playing with them all afternoon.'

'We've been playing with the Barbie dolls,' Leah said. 'Honestly, Mum.'

Jasmine looked under the bed, but there were just the plastic carrier bags that had held their collection of Barbies under there.

'I don't understand. Where's the box the other dolls came in?' She looked around their room.

'It's the first time we've played with the Barbies since we moved here. They were in carrier bags.'

Jasmine stared at them. 'You're lying to me,' she said sharply.

'No, we're not,' Isabel cried, close to tears. 'We've been playing with the Barbies all afternoon. You came in and saw us.'

Jasmine stared at the plastic dolls that were arranged on the bed just as the others had been. They were in virtually the same position, either eating or lying down, just like the dolls they'd been playing with earlier. There was also a small china plate the dolls were pretending to eat off. It was all exactly the same except it was a different set of dolls. These were nothing like the original ones, nothing at all.

'Here's the one you took the dress off,' Isabel said. She picked up a blonde doll and handed it to her mother.

Jasmine examined the doll, turning it over in her hand. There were no fasteners on the back of the dress to take it off, nor any camisole or fancy knickers beneath. It was just another plain Barbie doll that she'd never liked anyway.

She looked around again and then handed back the doll. She left the room in a hurry. What on earth was going on? Was she going mad? She was sure she'd seen the girls playing with a set of china-headed dolls. But where had they gone now?

Mark looked up as she entered the kitchen, expecting her to have brought down a doll.

'It seems I made a mistake,' she said, and sat down.

She needed time to think, to understand what had actually happened. It was impossible at present. It defied logic and belief, like much of what had happened in their house.

There were no china-headed dolls. Had any of them been there at all? She thought back. She was the only person to have seen them apart from Leah and Isabel, who now denied their existence. Selina hadn't visited the girls in their bedroom. Had Selina even been here at all? She looked at the two cups on the side and decided she had. The biscuit tin was still out, which was a relief. She wasn't going completely crazy.

Mark wanted to talk about work, and she made a pretence of listening, all the while wondering what had happened for her to imagine the dolls. Each one had been in its own unique dress. She was sure of it. Twenty dolls arranged on Leah's bed – only now it seemed like they hadn't been there at all.

Mark offered to put the girls to bed, as he thought she must be tired. She went and sat in the living room, and as she did the landline rang. She answered it. It was Selina, thanking her for a pleasant, if rather shocking, afternoon.

'You're welcome,' Jasmine said, spent.

'I wanted to ask you,' said Selina, 'I've got a collection of dolls here that were Angela's. I was wondering if your girls might like them. There's twenty of them. They're very old, with china heads. I don't have any use for them, but I wondered if your girls might like playing with them.'

Jasmine stood still in the living room, with the phone in her hand, not knowing what to say.

'Dolls,' she said at last.

'Perhaps you think they're too old?'

'No. Thank you. That's very kind of you. They'll love them. Are you sure you don't want to keep them?'

'I'm sure. I'll drop them off when I visit the cemetery next month.'

'That would be lovely.'

'No more noises coming from that bedroom then?' she asked.

'No more noise,' Jasmine confirmed.

'Good. See you next month.'

She slowly cut the call and wondered how on earth she'd seen the dolls that afternoon. It was impossible for her to have imagined them all.

Mark came down, having said goodnight to the girls. He said he had work he needed to do. Would she tell him about the dolls? She wasn't sure, because really, what could she say? The twenty dolls had materialized and then just as quickly disappeared. She'd need to think about it.

THIRTY-FOUR

The day after the dolls appeared, Jasmine was up early to catch up on her work. She took a coffee through to the study at 7 a.m. and worked non-stop. Mark called goodbye as he left for work at 8 a.m., leaving the girls to get up when they were ready. Jasmine worked until 9.30 and then stopped to make them breakfast, which they ate watching television in the living room. Jasmine worried they were watching too much television, but it kept them amused while she worked.

At 10.30, their front doorbell rang. Saving the file she was working on, Jasmine went to answer it. The girls were still watching television but at least they were dressed now.

It was Poppy.

'Hi,' Poppy said, with her bright, enticing smile. 'Long time no see.'

'Indeed,' Jasmine replied, wondering what she wanted.

'Sorry I haven't been in touch. We've all been busy with

the end of term. Hudson is going to secondary school in September. How are you all? I do see Mark coming and going from work sometimes.'

'Yes, we're fine,' Jasmine said. 'How are you?'

'OK. I'm guessing your two girls are at home while the schools are off?'

'Yes. For six weeks.'

'Same here. I was wondering if they'd like to come and play with Hudson and Liam this morning? Then you could have my two this afternoon? We both have work to do, and it would certainly help me out.'

Jasmine thought about it. She could get a lot done during that time. The downside was that she would have to entertain Hudson and Liam that afternoon. She wasn't sure.

'Let me ask the girls,' she said. 'Come in.'

Poppy stepped into their hall as Jasmine went to the girls in the living room. They were both still engrossed in their programme.

'Poppy wants to know if you'd like to go and play at her house for a couple of hours this morning? We'd then have Hudson and Liam to play here this afternoon.'

'Yes!' they cried, delighted, their eyes lighting up. 'We'd love to.'

Jasmine smiled and turned to Poppy.

'Thank you. That would be great.'

'They can come with me now, if they're ready. I'll return them in a few hours for some lunch.'

'Yes, please, Mummy,' Leah shouted and rushed into the front hall. Isabel followed, equally excited.

‘Good. I’ll bring my boys round at two if that’s all right with you,’ Poppy said.

‘That’s fine.’ If Jasmine thought it sounded a little too pre-planned, she dismissed the idea as Poppy simply being neighbourly.

‘Thank you,’ Jasmine called after her as the girls disappeared down the path. ‘I can catch up with my work now. See you in a couple of hours for lunch,’ she added to the girls.

Poppy threw Jasmine a wave as they turned into her garden. The girls were too excited to remember to give her a kiss goodbye. They were happy, though, and therefore so was she. Jasmine closed her front door and went straight to her computer. Two or three whole hours of no interruptions. Plus, if it worked today, then they could do it again another day, she thought.

At 12.30, the doorbell rang and it was the girls.

‘Poppy said she’ll send the boys over at two,’ Leah said, coming in.

‘Did you have a nice time?’

‘It was terrific.’

Jasmine made a sandwich lunch and listened to tales of what they’d done that morning. The girls were very excited and couldn’t wait until Hudson and Liam returned that afternoon.

The time flew by and at exactly 2 p.m. Poppy sent her two sons round to Jasmine’s house.

‘We’ve to go back at four,’ Hudson said, striding in. He was the elder of the two and now a big lad.

'What do you want to play with?' Jasmine asked awkwardly. She was used to what her two girls played with.

'We'll go in the garden,' he replied, and strolled towards the patio doors.

The others followed him.

'I'll bring out some drinks shortly,' she called after them.

She stood on the patio and waited while they settled in the garden. The girls took their toys out of the shed, then Jasmine returned indoors, telling them to call her if they needed anything. She sat at her computer, every so often glancing down the garden to check on them. They were sitting in a small circle on the grass and kept looking towards Poppy's house, then giggling conspiratorially.

Half an hour passed and Jasmine stood, went into the kitchen, made lemonade and arranged biscuits on a plate. She carried the tray out into the garden. They were still sitting on the grass, giggling and looking over at Poppy's house.

'What's funny?' she asked them, setting down the tray.

'Nothing,' Leah said, a little too quickly.

Hudson helped himself to a drink and a biscuit while Jasmine followed her daughters' line of vision to what she assumed was Poppy and Harry's bedroom window at the back. The big window was open; it was a hot day, after all. She thought she saw Hudson nudge Leah, who looked away.

'Is everything all right out here?' she asked them.

'Yes, Mum,' Leah said.

'Thank you for the drink and the biscuits,' Hudson added.

She was about to go into the house and get on with her work again – two hours wasn't long – when she heard a noise, a squeal of delight floating down from the bedroom window. She instinctively looked over again and heard Poppy's voice.

'You naughty boy,' Poppy cried, followed by a high squeal.

The children broke into laughter again.

'It's nothing,' Hudson said, while Isabel giggled uncontrollably.

It took Jasmine a moment to realize what the noise was. It was Poppy, having sex. She looked up at the window and a noise came again, this time a high-pitched moaning.

'I think you should all come indoors for a while,' Jasmine said, embarrassed.

'No, we're fine here,' Hudson said with a smirk.

She looked at her daughters, hoping they would follow her direction. Normally they would, but Leah said, 'We're fine here, Mummy.'

The noises grew in volume. Surely Poppy must be aware that the children could hear her in the garden? Apparently not. What should she do? If she made a fuss and demanded that they all went indoors, it could do more harm than good, especially if Hudson refused point blank, which seemed very likely.

She stayed where she was, watching and waiting.

'Thanks for the drinks,' Hudson said again, clearly meaning she should go. He took another biscuit and began eating it. The show next door continued.

Jasmine would have been mortified to know her daughters

were listening to her and Mark making love – not that they seemed to do that very often now. She looked at her children and said again, 'I think you should come inside. We'll find something for you to play with indoors.'

At that moment Poppy climaxed, and the children exploded into laughter. Jasmine looked away, embarrassed. She'd have to talk to Leah and Isabel later, when the boys had gone home, and explain what it was all about.

It went quiet in the bedroom. Jasmine stayed where she was for a few moments, checking that the noises had definitely stopped, then she went indoors. She needed to say something to Poppy – now or later? She decided later, when she returned to collect Hudson and Liam.

She sat back down at her computer but couldn't concentrate. She looked down the garden. The children had stopped listening to what was going on next door and were playing again. She assumed the show had finished. At 4 p.m., she went into the garden and rounded up the children, telling the lads it was time for them to go.

They came obediently.

'We can go home by ourselves,' Hudson said as they went through the house. 'There's no need for you to come.'

Jasmine hesitated. She supposed she could speak to Poppy later, after Mark came home.

'All right,' she said, and saw them to the front door. She waited with Leah and Isabel and watched the boys go.

'Bye!' Leah shouted as they disappeared around the hedge.

'Bye,' Hudson returned.

After a few moments their door opened and they went inside.

Jasmine knew she needed to talk to Leah and Isabel – get it out of the way. She took them into the living room and asked them to sit down.

'We want to play in the garden,' Leah said provocatively.

'Please sit for a moment,' Jasmine replied firmly.

Leah pulled a face. This confrontational behaviour came from playing with Hudson, she thought. Jasmine had never really liked that child.

'Do we have to?' Leah moaned.

'Yes. You do.'

They reluctantly sat on the edge of the sofa, their arms crossed defiantly. Isabel always copied Leah when it came to confrontation with their mother.

'This afternoon you heard some strange noises coming from Poppy and Harry's bedroom. Do you know what they were?'

Leah flushed, while Isabel nodded.

'What do you think was happening?' Jasmine asked them.

'Poppy was having sex,' Isabel said bluntly. 'Hudson told us. But not with Harry. It was with someone else. That's why they had to come here to play – to get them out of the way.'

Jasmine was shocked. 'What do you mean, it was with someone else? Who was it with?' she asked. She looked from one of the girls to the other. There was plenty they weren't telling her.

'I don't know,' Leah said, shrugging her shoulders.

'Hudson wouldn't tell us. Just that his mother was seeing someone from work.'

'Has Harry gone now then?' Jasmine asked.

'I don't know,' Isabel said, shrugging in an imitation of Leah.

'Well, that's not good, is it?' Jasmine said, annoyed. 'I thought Harry was the boys' stepfather.'

The girls stared at her, unknowing.

'So, do you know what they were doing?' she asked them.

'Making babies,' Isabel said. 'Only they weren't. Hudson said his mother used a condom to stop the babies from coming.'

Jasmine felt herself blush. 'Clearly Hudson has told you plenty,' she said. She was very upset now, annoyed that she'd left them in the garden to play together for so long. 'Is there anything you want to ask me?' She looked at them. This wasn't turning out the way she'd imagined, not at all. Clearly, they knew a lot about reproduction – far more than she did at their age.

Both girls shook their heads.

'Are you sure?'

They nodded.

'OK. You can go and play now.'

They ran off into the garden, laughing and giggling. Jasmine was furious and decided that would be the last time they played with Hudson and Liam. She was annoyed at being taken advantage of. Poppy had said she was going to work, although now Jasmine came to think of it, Poppy had told her she worked part-time in a dress shop in town. How could she have been so easily manipulated into looking after her boys so Poppy could spend the afternoon in bed? She was also furious with herself that she had allowed her daughters to be exposed to this type of behaviour. It just showed how easily it could happen.

She couldn't settle again and kept blaming herself. She was still struggling when Mark returned home at 6 p.m. Although Jasmine had calmed down enough to see that there was nothing to be gained by knocking on Poppy's door and having it out with her that evening, she remained in a bad mood. She'd refuse to see Poppy again if she was asked. The moment Mark walked through the door, she told him what had happened. The girls were upstairs, having eaten, and were now playing in Leah's bedroom.

'I guess that's up to Poppy,' Mark said dismissively.

'Don't you care that your daughters had to listen to that all afternoon?'

'I'm sure they've heard worse,' he said in the same tone.

'Not in this house they haven't. I thought it would be a good idea to let them play together because I was trying to work, but clearly I was wrong.'

He was about to say something, then abruptly stopped.

'Have you talked to the girls?' he asked her.

'Yes.' She put his plate in the microwave. 'But it wasn't very productive.'

'I guess that's the end of it then. You haven't asked me about my hand,' he said.

'How is it?' she asked, still thinking about what had happened.

'It's healed up and the blood test was clear. So I'm all right.'

'Good,' she said without conviction, and put the plates of food on the table. It was going to be a bad evening. She could feel it.

THIRTY-FIVE

Jasmine stood at the patio window and looked down the garden. It was Friday and the weekend began soon. The house had been quiet since Tuesday, when Selina had visited. It was as if something had lifted from their lives. She couldn't quite believe it, but she had taken the girls up to bed on Wednesday and Thursday and nothing had happened at all. Isabel must have felt the change in energy too, for on Thursday she had wanted to sleep in her own bedroom.

'I'm sure she's gone,' she said quietly, going in.

'How do you know?' Jasmine asked, looking around. She didn't want to say anything, to acknowledge the presence, but she had felt it too.

'I can just feel there's something missing. She's not here any longer.'

Nevertheless, Jasmine tried to persuade Isabel to stay with them for another night, but she was adamant she wanted to sleep in her own bedroom. Jasmine stayed with her for some time, sitting on the edge of her bed, stroking her forehead. Eventually she drifted off to sleep and so, with another look around, Jasmine came out, leaving the bedroom door wide open. She checked on her every half an hour during the evening and then when she came up to bed. She was still sleeping more peacefully than she had ever done since moving in, and the room seemed quiet too.

On Friday, Jasmine woke feeling very refreshed. She couldn't explain it. Perhaps they were finally feeling settled in their home. She certainly knew it hadn't felt so comfortable since they'd moved in. She set about her work straight away. She usually worked four days a week, and Friday was due to be her day off this week, but as she'd got very behind, she spent most of the day catching up. The girls played nicely and quietly, which was unusual. They were like different children, she thought; like they had been before the move. Jasmine felt happy they were all feeling more settled and gratefully got on with her work. By the end of the afternoon, she'd caught up. She was relieved. They could all do something together tomorrow, if the girls wished.

It was a little after 5 p.m. when she switched off her computer for the weekend and made the girls their tea. They were still playing happily together. It made such a difference. Mark wouldn't want much to eat tonight, if anything at all. He was going to a leaving do at work where there was a buffet and drinks. He wasn't expected home until much later – after nine, he'd said. So she ate with the girls, having quiche and salad.

Partway through the meal, Isabel suddenly said, 'You know she's gone for good, Mummy?'

'Who has?' Jasmine asked.

'Angela.'

'Let's talk about something else, shall we?' Jasmine replied.

'Why do you think she's gone?' Leah asked her.

'It's just a feeling I have.'

'In that case I'm glad,' Jasmine said. 'We can be a normal family again, living in a house that we love. Let's wait and see, though, shall we? It's only been a few days.'

'I want to paint my bedroom, like you promised,' Isabel said.

Jasmine was pleased. 'Sure. What colour would you like it to be?'

'Peach.'

'We could go shopping tomorrow and buy the paint.'

'What about my room?' Leah asked. 'I want blue.'

'That's fine with me. We'll buy paint and decorate both bedrooms.'

It was after 10 p.m. when Mark arrived home from his work party, and the girls were asleep in their beds. Jasmine hadn't felt so bad about leaving Isabel in her own room tonight. The whole house felt more peaceful. She was finally admitting to feelings she'd put aside to protect the children. Feelings of fear, dread and stress.

She made a point of asking Mark if he'd had a nice time and how his hand was. He showed her. It was fully healed. There wasn't a mark on it at all and the stitches had dissolved.

'Hopefully that will be the end of it now,' Jasmine said.

Mark glanced at her but didn't say anything. He began talking about the leaving do as he went into the kitchen to make himself a snack. Jasmine followed, eager to hear the snippets of gossip from his new role. They returned to the living room and Mark sat next to Jasmine, put down his snack and wrapped his arm around her shoulders. She leant her head against his for some moments.

'I've told the girls we'll take them shopping tomorrow to buy paint for their bedrooms,' she said lazily.

'We promised them we'd paint their rooms if we moved, so of course that's fine,' Mark said. 'You seem happier now?' he added.

'Yes, I am. I feel as if something has gone from this house. Something not nice that was doing us a lot of damage.'

'Good,' Mark said positively. But Jasmine doubted he'd ever truly believed her stories, even though he'd had some strange experiences himself. That was Mark. He believed what he wanted and dismissed the rest.

He left his snack uneaten and kissed Jasmine's lips passionately. A little while later, without speaking, he took her upstairs to bed where he made love to her. She couldn't remember the last time they'd made love like this – so impulsively and feverishly – not since they'd moved, she thought. When they'd finished, she lay by his side for some time, savouring the moment. Everything was as it should be: marvellous.

* * *

On Saturday morning, they were up early and went shopping for paint for the girls' bedrooms. Pale blue for Leah and peach for Isabel. Once home, they cleared Isabel's room of furniture and Mark washed the walls and gave them a first coat of paint. Isabel slept with them that night, and then on Sunday, he gave the room a second coat of paint and then that evening they moved all the furniture back in. Isabel was absolutely delighted.

'Next weekend we'll do yours,' Mark told Leah.

It was a good weekend, and on Monday, Mark was up at his usual time to go to work. He was full of life. He kissed Jasmine passionately and left her in bed. Jasmine rose with the girls at 7.45 and flung open the curtains. She couldn't believe her eyes. They'd had rain overnight and the garden was green again. Very green. The soil, which had lain barren since they'd tried to plant vegetables, now had a lot of green shoots growing all over it. She rubbed her eyes, thinking she must be dreaming. She wasn't. She opened them again. The garden was still there, green and alive. She hurried downstairs and went outside. The air was very fresh and the grass still damp from the rain. She walked along the path at the edge of the garden and looked at the flowerbeds. Shoots of green were pushing up from all the seedlings they'd planted when they'd first moved in. Some were almost two inches high. It was incredible. Perhaps they hadn't waited long enough, and now these dozens and dozens of tiny plants had come up overnight, all in the rows they'd planted. It was August and Jasmine had no idea when they were supposed to bloom. She couldn't even remember what the plants were. They'd pushed labels into the soil to mark the end of each line when they'd first put them in, but they'd long gone now, blown away by the wind.

As she walked up and down, she thought that it looked like a proper garden with all these green shoots covering the soil. Even the grass looked greener today. She assumed that was from the rain. Mark would be delighted when he returned home from work. She couldn't wait to show him.

The girls were downstairs now and watching her through the living-room window. She returned to the house, smiling.

'All our plants are growing. Look at them.'

The girls stared down the garden.

'What made them grow?' Leah asked her.

'The rain we had last night, I guess. We just had to be patient.'

The girls soon lost interest in the garden, so Jasmine made their breakfast, and once they'd eaten they got dressed. She kept checking on the garden, half expecting the plants to disappear again. But they didn't. They had a proper garden now, with lots of plants growing in it. It was fantastic.

The girls wanted to play outside and Jasmine told them to keep off the flowerbeds. Every so often, as she worked at her computer, she turned and checked on them. They were doing as they'd been told. She made them lunch and then at 3 p.m. she saved her work and went into the garden. It was a very hot day and the ground had dried out, so, unwinding the hose, she gave the plants a good watering.

Later, when Mark came home, she drew him to the patio doors.

'There. I knew they'd grow eventually,' he said, pleased.

He hadn't known that, she thought. Like her, he'd believed all the plants had died. It was typical of him to feign knowledge, but Jasmine decided not to say anything. She was as pleased as he was.

After dinner, they went into the garden, where he watered the plants again and peered at the rows of shoots.

'If I didn't know better, I could swear there are a lot more now than when we planted them,' he said. 'We'll have our own vegetables growing soon. I seem to remember planting carrots, sweetcorn and lettuce.'

It was exciting to think about growing and eating their own food after living in a flat for so long. And the flowers she'd planted would come up year after year, if they took care of them properly.

Mark checked on the garden again before he went to bed and then got up early in the morning to water the plants. They were all still doing well.

Jasmine worked until 1 p.m., then took the afternoon off work. She went out with the girls to a park. She felt very happy. Happier than she had done in a long time. They were now settled in their new home with everything they could possibly wish for, and despite what had happened previously, she knew they would all be fine. She hadn't seen Poppy since she'd looked after her boys, which suited her. If she asked her again to look after them, she'd have to say no. She didn't want the girls to spend any more time with Hudson, and she wasn't going to be used to facilitate Poppy's goings-on. What Poppy chose to do with her life was up to her, but Jasmine wanted no part of it.

The week passed. Every morning, Jasmine got up, opened her bedroom curtains and admired their garden. It was still doing very well. They watered the plants twice a day because it was still hot, and by Friday the shoots were six inches high. Not only was the garden doing well, but the house had remained quiet and still. She embraced it afresh and couldn't quite believe it. Each day she rose half expecting the worst but then enjoyed another normal day. Life was good.

THIRTY-SIX

A loud knock sounded on the front door. It was Monday morning and Jasmine was working while the girls played upstairs in Leah's freshly painted bedroom. Jasmine clicked save on her computer, but before she got to the front door, the knock sounded again, this time more loudly and insistently.

She opened the door and was surprised to find Hudson standing there, looking very worried.

'Can you come? Mum's not well. She told me to come to get you.'

'Have you called a doctor?' Jasmine asked, pushing her feet into her shoes.

'No. She said she wants you. Please come. I don't know what to do.'

Jasmine called upstairs to the girls to stay inside, that she was going next door to Poppy and wouldn't be long.

She left the door on the latch and followed Hudson into their house. Poppy was on the sofa next to Liam.

'What's the matter?' Jasmine asked her, going in.

Poppy turned to face her. Jasmine let out a cry of alarm.

'It came up last night,' she said. 'It looks like one of those things Angela had, I'm sure of it.'

Jasmine swallowed her revulsion and went closer. Poppy had a huge scab covering most of her forehead. It was raised and dark brown.

'It couldn't just have come up last night,' Jasmine said.

'I felt my forehead itching all day yesterday, then it came up like this overnight. Honestly, didn't it, Hudson?'

'Yes,' he said, staring in dread at his mother. 'I don't know what it is.'

'You feel all right? I mean, you're not ill?' Jasmine asked her.

'I feel OK. Apart from the shock of this. What am I going to do?' The poor woman looked close to tears.

'Go to the doctor. Or perhaps the hospital would be better.'

'Can you look after the kids?' Poppy asked her.

'Isn't there anyone else you know who can look after them?'

'Not at such short notice. And I don't want anyone else to see me like this,' she said, touching her forehead.

'All right then. I'll look after Hudson and Liam until you get back. I'm sure the hospital will be able to give you something for it.'

Poppy stood and, pulling her fringe over her forehead, picked up her handbag and walked hurriedly from the house. She was beside herself, Jasmine thought, quite understandably. What the hell was it? She watched Poppy get silently into her car, start the engine and pull away.

Checking the boys didn't need anything from their house, she closed their front door and came away.

'I'm sure a doctor at the hospital will know what to do,' Jasmine said to the boys.

'So am I,' Hudson agreed, while Liam slipped his hand into hers.

'It's going to be all right, Liam,' Jasmine said, feeling sorry for him.

Leah and Isabel were waiting in the hall, looking very anxious.

'There's nothing for you two to worry about. Poppy is just going to the hospital.'

'What's the matter with her?' Leah asked.

'She's got a massive thing on her forehead,' Hudson said. 'It's like a big scab, just like Angela had.'

'OK, that's enough about Angela,' Jasmine said. They'd only just stopped talking about her. She certainly didn't want her name resurrected now.

The children were looking very worried. Jasmine tried to reassure them. 'Mummy will be back soon. What would you like to play with?'

'Let's go in the garden,' Hudson suggested.

'All right, but keep off the flowerbeds, please,' Jasmine said, which sounded churlish, given what Poppy was going through.

Jasmine went into the garden and opened up the shed to get the girls' play things, but Liam was still very worried about his mother.

'I wish I'd gone with her,' he said.

'That wouldn't have been possible,' Jasmine said as kindly as she could. 'I'm sure your mother will be fine.'

Jasmine suddenly realized she should have asked for Poppy's mobile number, and at that moment a bleep sounded from Hudson's trouser pocket.

'Do you have a phone?' she asked him.

He nodded and slid a small phone from his pocket, then read the screen.

'Mum says she's just arrived and she'll be in touch.'

'Give me her mobile number, please,' Jasmine said, and she entered it into her phone.

From then on, she was in direct contact with Poppy. She settled the children in the garden, making sure Liam was all right, and went inside to try to work. Poppy texted to say she'd been seen by a triage nurse and was now waiting to be seen by a doctor.

Everyone keeps staring at me, she texted.

Poppy was still waiting to be seen by a doctor an hour later. By then it was after twelve o'clock, so Jasmine made them all a sandwich lunch. She and Poppy texted on and off for the next two hours. It was 2.30 when Poppy arrived back, a large crepe bandage on her forehead.

'Come in,' Jasmine said. Poppy looked upset.

Liam threw himself into his mother's arms and hugged her.

'They don't know what it is,' she said, still obviously very worried. 'I have to go back for more tests. They've given me some cream to apply and put me on antibiotics. But I can't go out like this in the meantime.'

Jasmine made her a cup of tea and listened to what she had to tell them, about the hospital with all its comings and goings. Eventually Poppy said she needed to go, and stood.

'Thanks for looking after the boys,' she said.

It crossed Jasmine's mind to mention that the children had been laughing at her in the garden when she'd had someone in her bedroom, but she decided against it. Now wasn't the time. She called for Hudson and Liam to come, as they were going home now. The girls stood with her at the door and they all saw them off.

'What's wrong with Poppy's head?' Leah asked her as the door closed.

'The doctors aren't sure. She's been given some cream and needs to go back. Don't worry, they'll find out in time.'

'Hudson is convinced it's like whatever Angela had.'

'I know, but forget that, please,' Jasmine said. 'What has just happened to Poppy can't be connected to Angela. It's impossible.'

It was 3.30 and Jasmine had hardly done any work, neither had she watered the garden. The plants were still doing well and she now went outside and unwound the hose and began watering, thinking of Poppy. She shouldn't be alone in the house; she'd dwell on her condition. Every so often she stood on tiptoes and tried to peer over the garden fence, but Poppy's children weren't there and the house was quiet. When Mark came home from work she'd tell him the whole story.

'I expect she picked a spot,' he said, which showed he

hadn't been listening properly. Jasmine swallowed her anger.

'No, she didn't,' she said forcefully. 'It covers most of her forehead. It's huge and pretty disgusting, if I'm honest.'

She waited for Mark to reply, and when he didn't she said, 'I think I'll check on her later. Pop round there. Just for a few minutes.'

'Can't you just text her?' Mark asked, finally looking up from his phone.

'I can, but it might be nice for her to see someone if she's alone, which I think she is.'

Jasmine heard Mark sigh and ignored it.

At 8 p.m., when the girls were in bed, Jasmine went next door. She rang the bell and waited. If Poppy had company, then she'd come away.

After a few moments, Hudson came to the door and opened it slightly.

'Is your mother there?' Jasmine asked.

'Mum! It's Jasmine from next door,' he yelled over his shoulder.

'Let her in,' came Poppy's reply.

Jasmine stepped into their house. Poppy was in the living room, the crepe bandage still over her head. She had her feet up on a small stool and was staring into space. There was no one else there.

'I thought I'd call in to see how you are,' Jasmine said.

'About the same,' Poppy replied, turning her head to look at her.

'Are you alone?'

'Just me and the boys. Harry left three weeks ago. It wasn't working out.'

Jasmine gave a small nod. 'I just wanted to make sure you're all right.'

'That's kind of you.'

'Have you got everything you need?'

'Yes.'

'I'll text you tomorrow morning and see how you are,' Jasmine said.

'Thank you.'

Poppy rested her head back on the sofa. She seemed utterly exhausted, probably from the medication. Jasmine let herself out the front door. Her heart went out to Poppy. That poor, wretched woman. She looked a shadow of her former self. Poppy cared a lot about her appearance. This was one of the worst things that could have happened to her. Whatever 'this' was.

On Tuesday morning, as soon as she was up, Jasmine sent Poppy a short text message. *How are you?*

The same, came Poppy's reply.

Let me know if there's anything I can do.

Thank you.

Poppy messaged Jasmine again at lunchtime to say she'd just had a call from the hospital asking her to go there that afternoon, and could Jasmine look after Hudson and Liam from 1.30? Jasmine replied that she would.

I think I've got another one coming up on my hand, Poppy texted an hour later.

Oh, no, Jasmine thought, but she texted back, *I'm sure it'll be fine. See you later.*

Poppy dropped off the boys at 1.30 and showed Jasmine the new mark on her hand. It was much smaller than the one on her forehead. Poppy agreed not to panic before she had shown it to the doctor, and left.

Jasmine got the children organized with activities in the house, as it had started to rain. She didn't hear from Poppy all afternoon, other than a text saying that she was waiting to see a specialist. Then, at around 5 p.m., she got a message saying they were going to keep her in isolation until they had figured out what was wrong, and could Jasmine let her sister, Lily, into her house? She'd already messaged Hudson, who had the key. The boys were going to stay with Lily while she was in hospital. Lily would come and collect them when she finished work.

Hudson was already aware of the arrangements through the texts from his mother and didn't want to stay with Aunty Lily, who lived five miles away.

'I want to stay at home,' he said, disgruntled.

'It won't be for long,' Jasmine reassured him quietly, pleased that Poppy hadn't asked her to look after them.

He pulled a face and sulked for the rest of the afternoon. Liam needed a lot of attention, though, which meant Jasmine didn't do any work at all.

A little after 6.30, when Jasmine had fed everyone chicken nuggets, chips and peas, Mark came home. She'd already texted him a warning to expect her to be looking after Hudson and Liam – for reasons she would explain later.

How long are they staying for? he'd texted back.

Until Poppy's sister collects them.

Lily arrived shortly after Mark.

'Hi, I'm Lily, Poppy's sister,' she said. 'I think you have Hudson and Liam?'

'Yes. Come in,' Jasmine said. She looked very much like her sister, with her long blonde hair. 'They're through here. Have you heard from Poppy?'

'Only that she has been put into isolation. She's seeing another doctor tomorrow.'

Jasmine nodded. 'Yes, I got that message too. Let me know if there's anything I can do.'

'I will. Hopefully she won't be in for long. Have you seen the mark on her forehead?' she asked. 'It's dreadful. She sent me a picture of it from the hospital.'

'Yes. It's very big,' Jasmine agreed, as she led the way into the living room.

All the children were in there watching television. The boys were engrossed.

'Come on, lads, we need to be going,' Lily said, rattling her keys.

They stood and came to her, Hudson still in a sulk and Liam needing a hug.

Mark had disappeared upstairs to change out of his suit, having said a quick hello to Lily. Jasmine could hear him moving around.

'See you soon,' Jasmine said to the lads. 'Let me know if you want me to check on the house,' she told Lily.

They left without looking back. Jasmine felt sorry for the boys. She closed the door and sank into a chair. It had been a long day. At least Poppy was in the best place to receive the treatment she needed, though. Jasmine was sure of it.

THIRTY-SEVEN

The following day, Jasmine received a number of text messages from Poppy telling her she was waiting to see a specialist and that it was boring being in isolation. Jasmine thought she sounded a bit brighter and texted her back, asking how her forehead was. She replied, *The same really*. The rest of the day continued as planned, with Jasmine doing some work and the girls playing. She had booked the following week off work. Then there was just one more week to go until the schools returned.

On Thursday morning, Jasmine received an unexpected phone call from Selina. She said she was having to go into her head office and asked if she could call in with the dolls when she'd finished. They were in the car with her. She'd be there around 4 p.m. This immediately sent Jasmine's thoughts crashing back to those days of uncertainty, when Angela's whispering could be heard through the house. That time already seemed so long ago, and even though it hadn't been long in terms of days, they'd forgotten all about it and no longer mentioned it. Jasmine felt sure she knew what the dolls looked like, though – she'd seen them in Leah's bedroom, sitting there having a tea party. She was tempted to tell Selina they'd planned to go out, but that would only postpone the inevitable, when Selina visited the cemetery again.

'Yes, OK. See you later then.'

The call threw her into a mood and she couldn't settle, so she tidied the house, made lunch and told the girls that Selina was coming later with the dolls she'd promised them. They were delighted and looked forward to her arrival.

She fiddled with work during the afternoon and when the doorbell sounded at 4.05 p.m. they all knew who it was. Jasmine answered it to see Selina standing there in a light-grey trouser suit.

'It's for work,' she said, and came in smiling brightly, carrying a large bag. 'How are you all?' she asked.

'Good, thank you.' Jasmine said. 'Tea?'

'Yes, please. Here are the dolls.'

Selina took the bag into the living room. The girls followed her as Jasmine went into the kitchen and filled the kettle. She then joined them in the living room and stared at the bag as she braced herself for what was to come. Selina began carefully taking the dolls out and sat them on the sofa, a big smile on her face.

'Aren't they lovely?' she said as she continued removing them.

'Yes,' the girls chimed.

'Are you going to leave them here?' Isabel asked.

'Yes, of course, they're yours to keep. I hope you're going to look after them just as Angela and I did.'

'We will,' they said.

Jasmine looked at the dolls and felt faint with relief. She'd convinced herself they would be the dolls she'd already seen on Leah's bed. But while these dolls were pretty, they were nothing like the ones she'd seen, which were different shapes and sizes and came from different eras. These were ordinary dolls.

'They're beautiful,' Jasmine enthused, relieved. 'Thank you so much for bringing them. I know the girls will have a great time playing with them.'

Selina smiled, pleased. 'Angela in particular loved playing with them. I hope you two will get the same enjoyment.'

'We will,' the girls squealed.

It never crossed Jasmine's mind that she was bringing something of Angela's into their house. She made tea and Selina drank it as the girls dressed and undressed the dolls. They were immaculate, well made, but nowhere near the calibre of dolls Jasmine had seen before. She was happy and drank her tea, feeling very relieved. They were a normal family now and it would stay that way.

Selina stayed for about an hour and then said she'd better be going. Jasmine had noticed that every so often since she'd been there, she'd rubbed her leg through her trousers, as if itching it.

'It's very sore,' she said as she stood, noticing Jasmine looking. 'I don't know why. I must have been bitten by something.'

'Do you want some cream for bites?' Jasmine offered. It was the time of year for midge bites.

'No, I'm sure it'll be OK. Can I use your bathroom before I go?'

'Yes, of course.'

Selina headed upstairs and Jasmine went into the kitchen, leaving the girls playing with the dolls in the living room. She came out into the hall when she heard the bathroom door open.

'I think I'll have to try to see a doctor when I get home,' Selina said, slowly coming downstairs. 'My leg really is very sore. A large scab has formed. It must have come up during the last hour or so.'

She was at the foot of the stairs now and raised her trouser leg to show Jasmine the mark. Jasmine stared at it, unable to believe what she was seeing. It was an exact replica of the mark Poppy had on her forehead, only smaller. It's a coincidence, she told herself. Nothing more. A coincidence.

'Yes, call your doctor when you get home,' she said. 'Shall I get you that cream after all?'

'No, I'll wait until I've spoken to the doctor.'

Selina lowered her trouser leg and hobbled into the living room, where she said goodbye to the girls. They thanked her again for the dolls, and then she went into the hall. She looked very worried.

'I know this sounds paranoid, but the scab looks exactly the same as the ones Angela had,' she said quietly.

'Get it checked as soon as you're back. I'm sure it's nothing.'

Selina managed a small smile and left.

Despite her reassurances, Jasmine wasn't sure at all. As she closed the door, she thought again how similar it was to the mark on Poppy's forehead. It was raised, uneven and dark brown. What the hell was it? She looked at the clock. She had time. She checked that the girls were all right – they were still playing with the dolls – and went into the study. She sat at the laptop and googled, *Marks on skin that suddenly appear – images*. There were some pretty gruesome photos but nothing like what she'd seen, even when bite marks had been scratched and had turned septic.

If it was a midge bite, then the insect had surely come into their living room? She got out the vacuum cleaner and thoroughly hoovered the whole of the downstairs, getting into the crevices and corners. She checked around the windows for any sign of a fly trying to get out and found only a large, half-dead bluebottle, which she let go. She then put away the hoover and started making dinner, all the while thinking about Selina and Poppy. It's a coincidence, nothing more, she told herself, and got on with preparing the food.

When Mark arrived home the girls were eager so show him their dolls.

'Where did they come from?' he asked.

'Selina brought them,' Leah said.

He frowned, puzzled.

'She lived here with her sister, Angela, remember?' Jasmine reminded him. 'Selina had to drive down today for work and brought them for the girls. She thought they might like them, which they do, very much.'

He nodded and checked his phone.

As he was home at a reasonable time and dinner was later than usual, they all ate together and talked about their day. The girls were full of excitement about their new dolls.

'Any news on Poppy?' Mark asked after a while.

'Not really,' Jasmine replied. 'About the same, as far as I know.'

She hadn't told him about Selina's leg. She'd wait and see what the doctor said first. It might be nothing to worry about.

The girls played with their dolls again after dinner and then put them to bed, which basically involved putting them back into the bags they'd arrived in. Mark took the girls up to bed and Jasmine went up to kiss them goodnight, then came down again. It was now 8.30 p.m. and Jasmine texted Selina.

Did you speak to your doctor? she asked.

It was a quarter of an hour before Selina replied. *I'm at casualty. I came straight here as my leg really came up on the drive home. They're not sure what it is and are running some tests. Thanks for asking.*

Jasmine decided not to say anything to Mark until Selina had a diagnosis. Just before she went to bed she texted again, and Selina's reply was instant.

They're keeping me in. My brother is going to bring some of my things tomorrow. Night night x

Night. Take care x, Jasmine replied, and worried even more.

Before she got into the shower that night, she stripped off all her clothes and checked her body for any bite marks, looking at her back in the mirror. She couldn't find anything. It was a coincidence, she told herself again, that was all. Selina would be home soon, very soon indeed.

On Friday morning, Jasmine checked her phone as soon as she woke for any updates, but there was nothing. Then, a little after 9 a.m., Father Tim called her. The last time he had been there was when he'd got pushed out of Isabel's room by Angela.

'Hello,' he said. 'How are you all doing?'

'We're doing very well, thank you.'

'That's good. I've had a chat with Father Andrew and we both think we should visit you again this week.'

'No,' Jasmine said, more forcefully than she intended. 'It's not necessary. We're fine, honestly. Everything is back to normal now.'

'What about the whispering in the bedroom?' he asked.

'It's stopped. We've heard nothing for ages.'

He was silent for a moment, then he asked, 'Have the other unexplained happenings stopped too?'

'Yes, they've all stopped, and the garden is growing wonderfully, like it should.'

'I see. Well, that is good news. I'll leave you to it then. Phone me if you need me.'

'I will. Thank you for all your help. Please thank Father Andrew too.'

They said goodbye and Jasmine felt relieved. That was the end of the priests' visits. She began her work while the girls and their twenty new dolls watched television in the living room. Just before lunchtime, she remembered to water the garden. All the plants were still growing healthily. By the time she returned indoors both Poppy and Selina had texted her.

Poppy: *Still wired up in isolation. They're waiting for the test results.*

Selina: *They're sending me home later with cream and antibiotics. Leg no better but not thought to be contagious.*

That's good news, Jasmine replied to Selina.

Good luck, she said to Poppy.

The messages proved to Jasmine that this was nothing more than a coincidence, just as she had thought.

She made herself and the girls some lunch and then worked until late afternoon when she switched off her computer with some satisfaction. She'd booked the following week off work and was really looking forward to it. Occasionally she'd thought about Poppy, but no more than one would a friend who was in hospital. She concentrated on the girls, as usual feeling guilty for having to do so much work. She went into the living room and sat with them.

'What would you like to do next week?' she asked. 'We could make a list of places we can go.'

She fetched a pen and paper. The girls were very excited. They'd stopped playing with the dolls and concentrated on the list, which eventually included the zoo, the castle, an activity centre and lots of parks.

'We'll have a full day out and then a day at home to recover,' Jasmine said, smiling. 'That's what we did last holiday.'

'Yes!' they cried, delighted.

She cuddled them and felt more guilty than ever. They were good girls, but she would have to work again the week after – the last week of the summer holidays.

On Saturday, Mark announced he had to work, so she took the girls shopping to buy their school uniforms for the new term. It was a hot day, so on their return she watered the garden. While she was out there, she saw a movement in Poppy's house. She hadn't heard from her that day, so she switched off the hose and hurried next door, telling the girls to stay put. It turned out to be Lily with the boys. She said they were collecting some more clothes and their school uniforms. Poppy was still the same, she said.

'Oh dear,' Jasmine said. 'Do they know what it is yet?'

'If they do, they're not telling us,' Lily said. 'She's still in isolation. They won't let her out until the marks respond to treatment.'

'Marks?' Jasmine repeated. 'How many has she got?'

'About eight, I think. Some are covered up.'

And before Jasmine could stop her, she'd pushed her phone under Jasmine's nose and showed her a picture of a woman she would never have recognized – not in a million years. Propped up on a pillow in a hospital bed, with a drip going into her arm, Poppy had her head bandaged. There were other crepe bandages stretching up both arms.

'She has marks on both her legs,' Lily said. 'And on her back.'

'How awful. Give her my love,' Jasmine said.

Later that night, as Jasmine was supervising Isabel in the bathroom, she noticed that she was very quiet and seemed worried about something. Eventually, after a lot of persuading, she admitted what was wrong.

'I think I might have hurt one of my dollies,' she said, her face looking sad.

Isabel was about to brush her teeth. She stopped and looked at her mother in the mirror above the sink.

'No, I'm sure you haven't,' Jasmine reassured her. 'Maybe it just got broken when you played with her. What's the matter with her?'

Isabel looked at her mother's reflection.

'Shall I show you?' she asked.

'If you can't tell me, then yes,' she replied.

Isabel put down her toothbrush and ran downstairs into the living room. They left the dolls downstairs at night to stop arguments over whose room they would sleep in. Mark was there listening to Leah read and looked up. He asked her what she was doing but she said she needed something. She rummaged for the doll and ran back upstairs. Leah continued reading.

'Here,' Isabel said. She pulled up the doll's dress and thrust it towards her mother.

Jasmine felt her heart stop and her breath start to come fast and shallow. She couldn't believe it. On the body of the doll was a mark the same texture and colour as the marks Poppy had. She stared at it and then wetted her finger and tried to rub it off. It wouldn't budge, no matter how hard she rubbed.

'It came up earlier,' Isabel said sadly. 'I didn't want to show you. I don't think I did it, but Leah said I must have done, because she didn't.'

Jasmine rubbed at the mark some more. Nothing happened. She rubbed again. It was like a large birthmark – on a doll? It stretched over most of the doll's torso. The mark remained as vivid as ever. 'Accidents happen,' Jasmine said, rubbing as hard as she could. The mark still didn't fade.

'Have any of your other dolls got these marks?' she asked.

'I don't think so, not yet.'

'What do you mean, "not yet"?' she said, rounding on her daughter.

Isabel looked startled, as though she was about to burst into tears.

'I meant, I don't think so,' she stammered.

'It's all right,' Jasmine said, and hugged her daughter. 'We'll put this doll to one side. You don't want to play with it when it's like that.'

She took the doll out of the bathroom and put it on her and Mark's bed, then she returned to where Isabel was finally brushing her teeth.

'It feels strange it happening to a doll,' Isabel said, voicing Jasmine's thoughts. 'Do you think she'll get better?'

Jasmine looked at her daughter. They were discussing a doll as if it were a living entity. 'I honestly don't know,' she said.

She thought that anything was possible in this house, and perhaps a doll that had developed a strange mark on its torso could fully recover, just as the plants now grew in the garden. But she didn't say anything more to Isabel.

Jasmine saw Isabel into bed and called for Leah to come up. She came straight away.

'Did Isabel show you the doll?' Jasmine asked her.

'Yes.'

'What do you know about it?'

'Nothing. Honestly. The mark just appeared, as if by magic.'

Jasmine waited while Leah brushed her teeth, thinking of the words *as if by magic*. She helped Leah into bed and kissed her goodnight.

'What's the matter with the doll?' Leah asked.

'I don't know, love.'

'I think Angela has something to do with it,' she said.

'Like what?'

She shrugged. 'I don't know, but I think it's the same kind of mark that she used to have, and that Poppy has now.'

Jasmine didn't reply but said, 'You get off to sleep now.'

She tucked Leah in and waited until she'd settled, then, leaving the doll in her and Mark's bedroom, she went downstairs into the living room. She tipped out the bag of dolls that was in one corner of the room. She began going through them, removing their clothes and checking them for any newly developed marks. She'd never removed their clothes before, but the girls had and hadn't mentioned anything unusual. She couldn't find anything wrong.

Mark asked her what she was doing, and she explained as she worked.

'You're kidding me!' he exclaimed. 'A doll can't develop a mark the same as its previous owner. It's impossible.'

'Can't it?' Jasmine said, and she ran up to their bedroom.

She brought down the damaged doll and pulled its dress up and showed him.

'What?' Mark said.

He took hold of the doll and tried to rub off the mark. Nothing happened.

'My guess is it's been there all along,' he said. 'You just didn't notice it.'

THIRTY-EIGHT

The mark on the doll was no different the following morning, and after Mark's reaction the night before, Jasmine began to wonder if it had been there all along, without Selina or the girls realizing. Leah must have been wondering something similar too, because she said over breakfast, 'I wonder if that mark has always been there.'

'It wasn't there when the dolls first arrived,' Isabel insisted. 'I took off that doll's dress, I know I did.'

However, just to err on the side of caution, Jasmine kept that doll apart from the others, just in case it was contagious, as if it were in isolation. Then she realized what she was doing. Of course a doll couldn't possibly pass on a condition to another doll or a human. Mark was right. She was being ridiculous, and Jasmine quietly laughed to herself.

They were going to the zoo that day, and Jasmine got the girls ready and into the car for 9.15. She drove the three-quarters of an hour to the zoo and they enjoyed a marvellous day out. The dolls and everything at home were forgotten. Except that Jasmine checked her phone quite regularly, and on one occasion there was a text from Selina. It said she'd been discharged from hospital, but her leg was no better. Jasmine didn't know what to say so she texted back: *Take care. I'll be in touch.*

It was true, she felt some responsibility for Selina. They'd become friends of sorts. There was a link between them, and Jasmine felt it, just as she was sure Selina did. It wasn't like the relationship she had with Poppy – even though she lived next door and Jasmine felt compassion for what she was going through, they would never truly be friends.

They arrived home at 6.30 p.m. and Mark was already inside. The girls were exhausted but exhilarated from their day out and wanted to tell him all about the zoo before having something to eat and going to bed.

'It sounds like you had a good day,' Mark said to Jasmine, pleased.

'Yes, we did,' Jasmine agreed. 'It was more for the girls than anything. They've been really good.'

'Is everything all right?' he asked her after a moment.

'Yes,' she said, and smiled.

Nevertheless, she checked the doll with the mark before she went to bed and saw that it was the same, no bigger or smaller.

'What do you want in your sandwiches?' she asked the girls the following day. They were in the supermarket, wheeling the trolley slowly up and down the aisles.

'Cheese,' Isabel said.

'Ham,' Leah said after some thought.

Jasmine took down the packets and placed them in her trolley. She also put in a packet of white rolls, cherry tomatoes, salad, crisps and some other things they needed, as they were going on a picnic today. Then they headed for the checkout.

'Jasmine!' A half-familiar voice called her name.

She turned and saw Freya Morgan standing a little way from her.

'How are you?' Jasmine asked, going to her. 'It's been a while.'

Freya looked absolutely dreadful. In fact, Jasmine would have struggled to recognize her.

'Worried,' Freya admitted straight away.

'What about?' Jasmine asked her.

'Madison. She came home from hospital yesterday and is in a foul mood.'

'I'm sorry,' Jasmine said. 'I hope she feels better soon.'

'So do I, but the doctors don't know what the problem is. She's had a number of large marks come up, including one on her cheek. You know what teenage girls are like about their appearance. The doctors thought it might be contagious, so they put her into isolation. Now they say it's not contagious and they sent her home with creams and antibiotics. She's in a right state.'

Jasmine held the trolley handle tightly as the supermarket spun out of control. Marks, she thought. Including one on her face.

'Are you all right?' Freya asked her, seeing her distress.

'Yes. It was just a shock.'

Leah and Isabel were staring at her uneasily, while Freya was looking at her oddly, waiting for an explanation.

'It's just that Poppy and Selina – the woman who used to live in your house – are both suffering from large marks on their bodies. Poppy has one on her face and several others. Are they raised, uneven marks?' she asked.

'Yes. But I don't understand.'

'Neither do I,' Jasmine said. 'Poppy is still in hospital. Selina has been discharged.'

There was silence between them as the noise of the supermarket went on around them, then Freya asked: 'If all three of them have the same condition, what does that mean?'

'I honestly don't know, but the house has settled down now for us. Well, apart from the doll.'

'The doll?' Freya queried.

'Selina gave us a bag of dolls, twenty of them, and one of them has a mark on it just like Selina and Poppy have.'

'I'd get rid of that doll if I were you,' Freya said determinedly. 'There's something not right in that house, for sure. You don't want your girls catching whatever it is, do you?'

'No, definitely not.'

On arriving home, Jasmine unloaded the food shopping and then went straight to collect the doll. She picked it up and examined the mark. It looked the same as it had done yesterday. She went out the back door and threw it into the bin. Then she returned indoors and checked the other dolls. None of them had any marks.

Two days later, Jasmine received a text from Poppy saying she was out of isolation and that the marks had improved. She was getting a little better each day. Jasmine was delighted and texted her back.

I'm so pleased. When will you be discharged?

By the end of the week, I hope.

Jasmine said nothing about the doll, or what had happened to Selina.

Later that night, she texted Selina and asked her how she was.

I'm doing OK, thank you. The marks are fading so I guess the cream and antibiotics are doing their job. I'm back at work next week.

That's good news! replied Jasmine.

Again, Jasmine didn't mention anything about the doll. She wondered how Madison was getting on, so the following day she sent a message to Freya.

She seems a bit better, Freya replied. *The marks are slowly improving. Did you get rid of that doll?*

Yes, I did, Jasmine admitted.

The week continued as planned, with days out interspersed with days at home. Poppy was discharged from hospital on Friday and came home. Jasmine heard her boys in the garden and picked a few flowers from the garden, which she took round to her.

'So pleased you're back,' Jasmine said, smiling brightly. Poppy had a small sticking plaster on her forehead but that was all.

'So am I,' she said with feeling, and told Jasmine all about her stay in hospital.

The last week of the school holidays passed and all was well. It was the new school term for the children. The girls were going on the bus, and they were very excited about it. Jasmine saw them off at the door. They were looking smart in their new school uniforms. She waved until they were out of sight, then closed the front door. She was secretly pleased they were no longer on holiday – although she'd enjoyed spending quality time with them, it had been quite a strain at times.

Nothing else untoward happened in the house; it remained quiet and still, and Jasmine assumed a confidence she hadn't felt before. One evening she was sitting on the sofa and thought back to everything that had happened. She decided she could probably justify most of the odd occurrences that had taken place since they'd moved in. All those crows had flown into the loft through a hole caused by Poppy's kids, and had died trying to find a way out. She knew that similar things had happened in other people's homes – a large number of birds effectively committing mass suicide. It was sad, but it happened. Mark was always irritating his hands one way or another, and the cut had healed completely now. The morning she'd been unable to get out of bed was purely psychological – a deep-seated wish to stay in bed. The wasps and the flies – well, she may have misremembered the exact number. It seemed a lot at the time, but perhaps she'd misjudged what she saw.

And the ghost they'd all seen . . . Mark had already decided it was an optical illusion created by the position of the mirror in Isabel's bedroom. Of course there wasn't a ghost – ghosts didn't exist. The time when Selina had talked to it was a little harder to explain, but maybe they had all been suffering from a group hallucination? The garden. She stood and looked out onto it. It was perfect now, and they'd soon be eating their own vegetables and picking flowers, which they put in a large vase on the table in the dining room. Everything was as it should be – they were a normal family doing normal things, living a normal routine in their nearly new home.

THIRTY-NINE

It was late September, and the air was just beginning to chill towards autumn. Jasmine sat at her computer in the study, dressed in joggers and a jumper, getting on with her work. She felt perfectly content in her home now. Just as she should do. Every so often she stopped work to give her arm a scratch, but she didn't think anything of it. After a while, when the itching persisted, she pulled up her sleeve to see what was causing the irritation. There was a red mark there. She gave it another scratch, then pulled the sleeve down and got on with her work. The midges always loved her.

A few minutes later, she bent under the desk and absently scratched her right leg, then her arm again, but she continued working. After a while she stopped typing and pulled up her jumper sleeve again. Was that blood from her scratching? She wetted her finger and tried to rub it off. It seemed to diminish, and she got on with her work.

She continued to type. Her concentration was on the

document. She typed some more, then stopped to scratch her arm through her jersey. It was really itching now, unbearably so. She pulled up her sleeve to examine the mark. It must be her imagination, but it seemed to have grown bigger since she last looked. She gave it a rub, pulled down the sleeve and tried to concentrate on her work again.

She couldn't. The itch was too much. She needed to put some antihistamine cream on. She had a tube in the bathroom. She clicked save on the document and went upstairs. On the way up she began scratching something on her chest.

She ran the last few steps into the bathroom and, with her heart beating loudly, went in. She stood in front of the mirror and pulled off her jumper, then stepped out of her trousers. She stood there in her bra and pants gazing at her body in the mirror. She couldn't believe what she was seeing. She counted six marks on her body – the ones on her wrist and leg were the largest. They hadn't been there that morning when she'd showered and dressed. She'd have seen them. She was sure of it.

As she stood there staring, a nagging feeling began to emerge. These marks were identical to those on Poppy, Selina and Madison. They'd grown larger in a very short space of time – in the last half an hour. But what were they and where had they come from? she thought blindly.

'Calm down,' she told herself. 'Try to think rationally what to do.'

The cream. She opened the cabinet door and reached for the antihistamine cream as another mark emerged right before her eyes. She screamed. Then another broke out at the top of her leg. She stood there, petrified, gripping the basin and dreading what would happen next.

Then she heard a voice and looked in the mirror. She was standing immediately behind her. A woman wearing a grey jumper and green trousers, staring at her.

'It's you or your daughters,' she said, and pointed to Jasmine's chest as another mark appeared.

Jasmine threw down the cream and turned from the cabinet. The woman disappeared. Jasmine ran downstairs in her bra and pants to the phone in the living room. She needed to do this now. She dialled the estate agent they'd used when they'd bought the house.

'I want to put our house on the market as soon as possible,' she told the receptionist. 'It's Jasmine Simmons.'

'Just a minute,' the receptionist replied.

She sat there in a hot sweat, and a moment later the agent they had dealt with before came on the line.

'Hello, Jasmine. How can I help you?'

'I know we haven't lived here long, but I want to sell this house now,' she said in a panic.

'Really. Can I ask why?'

'It's because of my husband's work,' she lied.

There was a slight hesitation before he said, 'All right. I can come and see you at two o'clock tomorrow if that suits you, and we'll get the process started.'

'Thank you,' she said gratefully.

'I'm sorry you're not staying,' he added.

'So am I, but these things happen.'

She set down the phone and breathed a sigh of sheer relief, then she put her head in her hands and wept. They'd go into rented while they looked for somewhere else. They just needed to leave here as soon as possible, no matter what. *It's you or your daughters,* Angela had said.

It took Jasmine some time to persuade Mark to leave the house. To begin with, he had refused to move, saying it was all her imagination and it would sort itself out in a few months' time. Then he saw the marks on her and how depressed she was and asked his daughters what they wanted. Without any hesitation, they said they wanted to move. So, two months later, the removal van was parked in their driveway. The house had sold easily for a lot less than the market value. The removal men finished loading all their possessions into the van and were ready to pull away, heading for their rented apartment. A couple with two teenage children were moving in. Jasmine had only seen them once and had made a conscious decision not to think about them or what they might encounter in the house. Besides, nothing untoward had happened since they'd made their decision to move; maybe it was all over. The marks on her body had disappeared as quickly as they had arrived.

'All set,' Mark said as he got into the driving seat of their car, having done a final check of the house.

'Yes,' Jasmine said sombrely, with only the tiniest hint of regret.

'Well, I guess that's it then,' he said and, closing the car door, started the engine.

They both looked at 13 Ravens Lane for one last time. As they did so, a woman dressed in a grey top and green trousers appeared in Isabel's bedroom window. They all saw her, and felt a flood of relief that they were leaving the house for the last time. She would be someone else's problem now.

AUTHOR'S NOTE

People ask me where my stories come from. *The Forever House* began one evening when I was alone at home, sitting on the sofa, and I felt it rumble. The sofa moved. Then it happened again. I don't know why, but it was the start of this story. I hope you've enjoyed it. Thanks for reading.

SUGGESTED TOPICS FOR READING-GROUP DISCUSSION

Jasmine and Mark are very different people. Describe their personalities. How do they each show their different characters when reacting to the haunting?

When Jasmine and Isabel share the same dream Jasmine wonders if it is possible. What do you think?

Juxtaposing normal family life with the weird and extraordinary events of the haunting highlights the tension in the story. Discuss.

Mark's hand, the swarm of wasps, the crows and the garden – how do the family justify these incidents? Are there rational explanations?

Jasmine says the downside of working from home is the interruptions. What other drawbacks are there for her?

Jasmine's heart sinks when Poppy brings her boys to dinner. Why?

The priests don't really offer much beyond prayers, and Jasmine eventually stops them from coming. Discuss.

Jasmine eventually follows up with Freya and Selina about their experiences. Do you think this was a good idea?

Jasmine and her family move out of their home after a short while. What would you have done in their position and why?

ACKNOWLEDGEMENTS

A big thank you to my editors, Kathryn Cheshire and Belinda Toor, my literary agent, Andrew, and all the team at HarperCollins.